The Cryptographer's Dilemma

Center Point
Large Print

Also by Johnnie Alexander and available from
Center Point Large Print:

What Hope Remembers
When Love Arrives
Where She Belongs

**This Large Print Book carries the
Seal of Approval of N.A.V.H.**

HEROINES OF WWII

The Cryptographer's Dilemma

Johnnie Alexander

CENTER POINT LARGE PRINT
THORNDIKE, MAINE

This Center Point Large Print edition
is published in the year 2021 by arrangement with
Barbour Publishing, Inc.

The text of this Large Print edition is unabridged.
In other aspects, this book may vary
from the original edition.
Printed in the United States of America
on permanent paper.
Set in 16-point Times New Roman type.

ISBN: 978-1-63808-043-5

The Library of Congress has cataloged this record
under Library of Congress Control Number: 2021939640

For Tamela Hancock Murray—the
treasured answer to a fervent prayer.

*Can any hide himself in secret places that
I shall not see him? saith the LORD. Do not
I fill heaven and earth? saith the LORD.*
JEREMIAH 23:24

CHAPTER ONE

Washington, DC
July 1942

Green or brown. Brown or green.

Phillip Clayton set the unwrapped crayon upright on the diner's Formica tabletop so it stood like a mocking sentinel. He could stare at it until the war was won or lost, and his 50 percent chance of guessing its color wouldn't change. He flicked the offensive object onto the pile of wrappings he'd torn from each crayon in the box.

The bell over the diner's door jingled. Phillip raised his eyes without lifting his head to assess the newcomer—a suit-wearing, middle-aged man with a misshapen fedora—the furtive maneuver more from habit than a professional interest in who entered the door at the far end of the long diner.

The renovated aluminum travel trailer sported booths beneath a row of windows that were separated from the stool-lined counter by a narrow aisle. Located on an out-of-the-way side street, the greasy spoon mostly attracted working stiffs like Phillip who were stuck on the home front while their buddies fought overseas to avenge the dead and wounded of Pearl Harbor.

Phillip's gut clenched as he plucked a different

crayon from the pile that resembled a stack of jumbled pick-up sticks. The pristine white one. That color he knew.

He couldn't explain what prompted him to stop in the five-and-dime to buy the box or why he'd come in here, dumped the crayons on the table, and removed the wrappings. Maybe he expected the childish impulse to somehow offset the burn of the letter stuffed in the inner pocket of his suit jacket. If so, he'd sadly miscalculated. His thumbnail dug into the crayon's waxy surface. Then, with little effort, he snapped it in two with one hand.

The bell over the door rang again, and Phillip inwardly groaned. His uncle, impeccably dressed as usual in a three-piece gray suit complemented with a slender gray tie, appeared as cool as an icebox cucumber despite the sweltering July heat. Richard Whitmer acknowledged Phillip with a dip of his chin then maneuvered his way along the aisle.

Phillip quickly shoved the crayons back into the box and swept the torn wrappings toward the napkin dispenser situated beneath the window.

Richard settled in the opposite bench and steepled his fingers. "Should I have brought coloring books?"

"How did you know I was here?" Annoyed at the petulant tone in his voice, Phillip deliberately lightened it. "Or is this just a coincidence?"

"I've taught you better."

Phillip let a wry smile stretch his lips. "A coincidence is never a coincidence."

"Exactly. Though perhaps this instance is an exception to the rule. I was on my way to headquarters when, lo and behold, who should I see out the window but my own dear nephew trudging down this street. I suppose that could have been mere chance."

" 'Trudging?' " Phillip didn't *trudge*. He strode. Sprinted. Raced.

Richard tapped the crayon box. "Is this an indication of bad news?"

The waitress, wearing a pale pink uniform and a frilly cap, appeared at the booth carrying a carafe. "Coffee?"

"Thank you, Irene." Richard directed a smile her way. "Have you heard from Michael recently?"

"I received a letter last week." She set a cup onto a saucer then filled it with the strong brew. "I have no idea where he is, but he says he's fine and he got the package I sent him. That's a blessing."

"Especially if your special oatmeal raisin cookies were inside," Richard said. "I don't suppose you have one or two of those hidden away behind the counter?"

Irene flushed at the compliment. "If I'd known you were dropping by, I'd have baked you a dozen."

"Maybe next time then."

9

"How about you, hon?" Irene gestured toward Phillip's untouched cup. "Would you like me to freshen that up for you?"

"I'm fine." Phillip forced a smile. As much as he wanted to lash out at the world, he couldn't blame Irene because her son passed his physical with flying colors. Or that Michael's youthful heroism led him to sign up with the army in the days following the Japanese attack. The kid should have graduated from high school a few weeks ago. Instead, he was only God knew where doing his patriotic duty. Phillip had never met the boy, but Irene had been a fixture at the diner for years. As regulars, Phillip and his uncle had heard numerous stories about her only child.

Her gaze shifted from Phillip to the crayon wrappings and then back again. "I'll leave you alone then. Let me know if you need anything."

After she was out of earshot, Phillip said, "Seems like someone at this table could find out where Michael is stationed. And that someone isn't me."

"A phone call or two would suffice." Richard lifted one shoulder. "But it's not my place."

"I suppose not." His uncle was right, of course. He might set Irene's mind at rest for a time, but she wasn't the only mother concerned about her son's whereabouts and if he was getting enough sleep or enough to eat. Sometimes it seemed every woman Phillip knew carried worry around her shoulders like an iron collar. Most of the men too. Yet here he was, still stateside, because his work was considered essential. And because of this ridiculous issue with his eyes.

Phillip ran the edge of his thumb along his eyebrow, an old and unbreakable habit that somehow eased the saying of difficult words. "My appeal was denied."

As Richard poured cream in his cup, the black coffee lightened to brown. *Not green.* A tidbit of knowledge Phillip had somehow picked up over the years but not a fact he could verify with his own eyes.

"Thus, the great crayon massacre."

Despite his deep disappointment, Phillip couldn't help a clipped laugh at his uncle's quip. At least Richard was too diplomatic to say *I told you so.* He'd warned Phillip of this likely outcome.

Richard blew into the cup then took a slow sip. "I hope this means we get to keep you."

"Flying a P51 Mustang isn't my only option." Just the one he'd dreamed about, imagining himself circling and swooping high above the earth during an aerial combat. "I can't stay out of this fight like a weak-kneed coward."

"I would argue that highly trained agents of the Federal Bureau of Investigation are neither weak nor cowardly. Not all battles occur in Europe and Asia."

"The important ones do. The ones that matter

do." Phillip left unsaid that it wasn't only Irene's teenaged boy who had volunteered to face the enemy. So had Phillip's cousins—Richard's only two sons who had joined the air force and trained to be pilots. So had Phillip's childhood friends, his closest chums. He was the only one still at home. The only one left behind.

"I assume you've considered other options," Richard said.

"You know me. Always a plan B." Flip a coin. Heads, army. Tails, navy. What did it matter when he could never join his cousins to fight the enemy in the clouds?

"I won't insult you by listing reasons this setback may be for the best," Richard said. "Neither will I put undue influence on you to stay the current course."

Phillip's antennae went on full alert at his uncle's tone. "But . . . ?"

A slow smile crossed Richard's face. "Your country needs you." He leaned forward and lowered his voice. "I need you."

Phillip mirrored his uncle's posture then cupped his hands around his mug and stage-whispered, "Did Hoover misplace his secret decoder ring? Did Roosevelt lose the map of the secret tunnel out of the White House?"

"Nothing that drastic. Yet a matter has arisen that may be vital to national security."

"And we're discussing it here?" Phillip waved

12

his hand to encompass the diner's interior. At this time of the day, the customers were few. But his uncle's reputation as a stickler for protocol was well-earned and dogma by even the lowliest staffer at the agency.

Richard straightened, his eyes soft and his voice warm with affection. "Will you leave a tip for Irene? Or should I?"

As Phillip held his uncle's gaze, the resentment that had weighed upon him since he'd opened the denial letter seemed to ease. Not by much but enough to temporarily shove aside his self-pity.

He placed money on the table and followed his uncle out of the diner.

CHAPTER TWO

Even though the random letters were in static blocks—five rows of five each—they danced before Eloise Marshall's eyes in a staccato rhythm. The individual letters advanced, then receded, in a pattern of their own choosing that the cryptographer couldn't explain. Not that she needed to. Her work spoke for itself.

The tempo of the dance changed as repeated letters took precedence over the others. With her focus on the coded message and barely aware of her actions, Eloise tapped the eraser end of a pencil on her desk and whispered the order of frequency for single letters, "E T O A N . . ."

Her voice trailed as the most common letters found in the first grid seemingly transformed before her eyes into possible substitutions.

She switched to the frequency of doubled letters and digraphs, still tapping the beat only she could hear with her pencil. "S S, E E, T T . . . T H, E R, O N, A N, R E . . ."

More of the dancing letters seemed to uncloak themselves enough for Eloise to pencil in the possibilities on a sheet of paper with the alphabet printed across the top. She meticulously wrote possible answers beneath the more common letters used in the grid. An *E* beneath a *J*. A *T* beneath a *Q*.

There was no consistency to the code, but it didn't matter. After surmising several of the substitutions, Eloise switched to a decoding sheet, similar to graph paper but with larger boxes. First, she outlined five-by-five grids and used her preliminary alphabet key to fill in as many individual boxes as she could.

Next, she considered the trigraphs. "The, and, tha, ent, ion . . ." She focused on where these letter combinations appeared together, trying out possible substitutions for the remaining blank boxes and adding more answers to her alphabet key.

Each success boosted her spirits, giving her the same satisfaction as completing a complicated crossword puzzle or mastering a Bach fugue. Deciphering the codes, especially the more complex ones, could be tedious. But the more difficult they were, the more joy she experienced in successfully decoding them.

This one, however, was fairly routine. Caught up in her work, Eloise didn't realize her supervisor hovered nearby until he cleared his throat. She glanced up at the grim, bespectacled man with his pursed lips and prominent Adam's apple, rubbing her aching neck as she did so. Some of the girls called him Mr. Twitchy Twig behind his back. An apt description though not a kind one.

"Good morning, sir." Expecting he wanted an update on her work, she continued, "I'm making progress, but it'll be a bit longer before I'm done."

"No matter." He gathered her papers into a neat pile and placed them in a folder. "Your presence is requested. Upstairs."

Upstairs? She'd never been summoned to that hallowed place before, and she couldn't think of a reason for receiving a summons now.

"Are you sure they asked for me?" Eloise hated the involuntary squeak in her voice. She could control her vocal cords through an entire octave but never when her nerves took over. As they were doing right now.

"Unless there's another Miss Eloise Marshall in this department of whom I am completely unaware." He bent slightly at the waist though he still managed to keep his shoulders and head in perfect alignment. "Go with courage. I assure you there could be no complaints regarding your work here. Or any doubt about your abilities."

A compliment from Mr. Twitchy Twig? Another shock to absorb.

He tucked the folder under his arm. "Now go. They're expecting you."

Eloise smoothed her skirt as she stood. "Who exactly are 'they'?"

"As if any of us know." He gestured toward the door. "An escort is waiting for you in the hall."

At least that answered the question of exactly where to go. Grinning to herself at the mental image of figuratively girding her loins, she marched toward the hallway door as if her insides weren't a mass of lime gelatin and her knees made of rubbery goop.

In the hallway, an older woman wearing a trim jacket over a slender skirt greeted her with a gracious smile. "I'm Lisa Archer, Commander Jessup's secretary. Please come with me."

Eloise rubbed her bare arms. Like most of the other girls in the code-breaking unit, she wore a simple short-sleeved dress and bobby socks. A more professional style wasn't expected of the cryptographers who worked in the lower-level warrens. Thankfully so, since the women didn't earn enough money for a more upscale wardrobe. Besides, the area was almost unbearably hot. The few fans placed around the large rooms were adjusted to avoid blowing papers off the desks. A gal had to stand in front of one to get much comfort.

As she followed Mrs. Archer to the elevator, Eloise admired the quality of her outfit while shoving aside the feelings of inferiority, which, despite her accomplishments, often overpowered her. Not even being recruited to the secretive position of a naval code breaker had bolstered her feelings of inadequacy. Apparently, some wounds never closed.

They stepped into the elevator, and Eloise wrapped her arms around her stomach in preparation for the upward lurch.

"I don't like it either." Mrs. Archer gave a gentle laugh. "But we don't have time to take the stairs."

Her kind demeanor momentarily eased Eloise's nerves. "Do you know why Commander Jessup wants to see me?"

"That's not a question I can answer. But the commander respects skill, aptitude, and a strong work ethic. From what I understand, you excel at all three."

Eloise's cheeks warmed. "I've never met him. That's very kind."

Mrs. Archer merely smiled but said no more during the short upward ride.

The elevator door slid open to a well-lit, carpeted corridor. The walls were a pale yellow, a stark contrast to the institutional green found in the basement. The two women made their way to a large anteroom lined with filing cabinets. Several women sat at typewriters, busily pounding the circular keys.

"This way." Mrs. Archer gestured toward a short hallway. They entered an outer office of paneled wood containing two desks and a seating area. "Wait here. I'll let the commander know you've arrived."

Eloise perched on the edge of a padded chair while Mrs. Archer rapped on the inner door then disappeared inside. Framed prints of Presidents Washington and Lincoln hung side by side on the opposite wall. Men who'd faced their own wartime challenges. Similar and yet so unlike what the United States was facing now. At least this time, the battles were being fought far away in places Eloise hadn't heard of before she joined the code-breaking unit. Places like Guam, Bataan, and the Coral Sea. Plus so many more.

The inner door opened, and Mrs. Archer beckoned. Eloise took a deep breath as she stood. "You'll be fine," Mrs. Archer whispered as Eloise passed by her. "He doesn't bite."

Eloise swallowed a giggle then entered the room. An imposing figure in navy dress whites stood statue-straight in front of his desk.

"Miss Marshall. Welcome."

Eloise didn't know whether to extend her hand or salute. Maybe a curtsy? The vivid image almost brought on another giggle. She opted for keeping her hands at her side. "Sir."

He gestured toward his left, where two men stood in front of a large pull-down map, their expressions impassive.

"I'd like you to meet Richard Whitmer and his nephew, Phillip Clayton," Commander Jessup said. "They are with the Federal Bureau of Investigation. Shall we all take a seat?"

When they were seated across from him, Commander Jessup lifted a folder from a stack on his desk. "We've been reviewing your file, Miss Marshall. You're doing tremendous work."

Eloise folded her hands in her lap. "I appreciate that, sir."

"So tremendous that Mr. Whitmer believes your skills may be of value to the Bureau."

Eloise darted a glance toward Mr. Whitmer. His warm smile seemed meant to reassure her. Despite her doubts she had anything to offer such a mysterious organization, she responded with a smile of her own. "I suppose I could try."

"I am confident you can do much more than that." Mr. Whitmer gave her an appraising look, dispassionate yet piercing, as if he could assess her character with as much ease as he could evaluate her appearance. "Your family. What do they think of the work you're doing for the navy?"

"There's only my mother," Eloise admitted, tamping down thoughts of her father and only brother. "She believes I sharpen pencils and fetch coffee."

"She's unaware of your talent for decoding complicated messages?" Mr. Whitmer asked. "That must be a hard secret to keep."

"I signed a secrecy oath, sir."

"We call that a redirect." The nephew, Phillip, spoke for the first time. Neither his expression nor his tone was as affable as his uncle's.

"A what?"

"We know you signed the oath. But you didn't actually answer the question."

"No." She held Phillip's stony gaze while lifting

her chin. "My mother is not aware of my talent for decoding complicated messages."

Phillip's expression didn't change, but Mr. Whitmer laughed. "She's perfect." He shifted his attention to Commander Jessup. "Will you approve her transfer to my investigative team?"

The commander turned to Eloise. "It's your decision, Miss Marshall."

A transfer? She glanced from the commander to Mr. Whitmer. *To the FBI?* She hadn't known what to expect when she entered the office, but if she'd made a list of possibilities, the FBI would not have been on it. "Will I still be breaking codes?"

"In part," Mr. Whitmer replied. "The assignment involves more than cryptography. I can't provide additional details unless you agree to the transfer."

"Are you a risk-taker?" Phillip asked, a hint of a challenge in his voice.

"Obviously." Eloise matched his tone. "I moved here from Massachusetts all by myself with no idea what I'd be doing once I got here. All I had was an address and the promise of an opportunity to serve my country." She gave him a brief up-and-down look, noting the wrinkles in his pants and the scuff marks on his shoes. "What risks have you taken?"

His eyebrow rose, as if he were taken aback by her assertiveness. Then his expression seemed to relax for the first time since she'd entered the room.

"She reminds me of Debbie," he said to his uncle. "Same spunk."

Eloise bit the inside of her lip to keep herself from asking who Debbie was. Even if they told her, she wouldn't know if the resemblance was a compliment or an insult. Besides, she had the sense Phillip wanted her to ask, and she wasn't in the mood to give him the satisfaction.

"I agree," Mr. Whitmer said, his smile even broader than before. "Are you willing to take another risk, Miss Marshall? Perhaps more than one?"

Eloise hesitated, quickly evaluating the strange situation. If she walked away, she'd never know what she missed. That thought left her empty and lost. Any risk was worth satisfying her curiosity of what the FBI wanted from her.

The same sense of excitement, of independence, that had gripped her when she received the secretive offer to come to Washington gripped her again. Adrenaline boosted her heart rate, and the future seemed to beckon with a promise of breathtaking adventure.

She could only give one answer.

CHAPTER THREE

Taking her cue from Lisa Archer's appearance the day before, Eloise dressed in her nicest suit for her morning appointment with Richard Whitmer and his nephew. She studied her reflection then frowned at a small stain on her lapel. Where had that come from?

She'd last worn the outfit, a blue skirt with matching jacket, when she traveled by bus to DC. A glance at her watch told her that she didn't have time to change. If she were late to this meeting, Mr. Whitmer might lessen his seemingly high opinion of her. At least, he'd seemed impressed yesterday when she met him in Commander Jessup's office. Definitely more impressed than his nephew had been. That young man had a chip on his shoulder just begging to be knocked off. What a coup if she were the one to do exactly that!

Phillip had been polite enough. She couldn't fault him for his manners, but his thoughts often seemed to be at a distance from the conversation. When she accepted the assignment, he tried to hide his lack of enthusiasm behind a too-charming smile.

No doubt he was one of those exhausting men who believed the only suitable job for a woman

23

was as a teacher, nurse, or secretary. But the war that took away the men also prompted the women to step out of their traditional roles.

Phillip's views on such changes didn't matter to Eloise. She would wipe that fake smile from his face by proving her value to Mr. Whitmer's investigative team.

But she couldn't make a good impression if she were late. She frowned again at her reflection then brightened. A brooch would do the trick. She rummaged through her small collection of costume jewelry and found a golden pin that would hide the offensive spot.

She turned one way in front of the mirror then the other, especially satisfied with the jaunty angle of her ivory cloche. Her eyes shone with the excitement of a new experience. Somewhere a grandfather clock boomed the quarter hour. Eloise grabbed her handbag and fled down the stairs of the Francis Scott Key Book Shop, where she and a few other women code breakers rented rooms behind the store, to catch a cab.

She arrived at FBI headquarters with five minutes to spare. She took a deep breath, smoothed her skirt, and assured herself one more time that the brooch hid the stain on her lapel. Perfectly poised with a smile on her face, she started to enter the room where she was to meet Mr. Whitmer. But the sound of her name stopped her near the doorway.

"I can do whatever needs to be done," the voice continued. Phillip Clayton's voice. "Whatever this assignment is, I don't need anyone's help."

"You can't break codes." Richard Whitmer's soothing voice was softer. Eloise leaned closer to the doorframe to hear what he had to say. "Besides, I strongly believe that this specific mission requires a woman's touch."

"Why don't you let me be the judge of that?" Phillip's tone hit a respectful medium between arguing and pleading. "Tell me what I'm supposed to be investigating."

"I'll tell you and Miss Marshall both. As soon as she gets here."

Though Eloise couldn't see either man, she envisioned the frown on Mr. Whitmer's face, his glance at the door. She entered the room, shoulders back, chin lifted high. Phillip might not want her on this mission or investigation or whatever it was, but her role must be important, or she would never have been chosen.

Men!

"I'm here," she announced, managing to keep her voice from wavering. She focused her gaze on Mr. Whitmer. "And ready to get started, sir."

"Good." Mr. Whitmer moved toward her and clasped her hand in his. "I was just telling my nephew that this particular assignment required a woman's touch. I am delighted you agreed to join us."

The tension in Eloise's shoulders eased at the warmth of his greeting. She responded to his gracious smile with one of her own. "I want to do whatever I can for the war effort. Thank you for your faith in my abilities."

Try as she might, she couldn't help throwing a triumphant gleam in Phillip's direction. He was perched on the edge of a table in the small room, his expression impassive and his eyes unreadable. Excellent qualities for an FBI agent, she supposed. But not so wonderful for an investigative partner. Hopefully, his prejudice against her wouldn't hinder their mission.

As she stared at him, he slowly stood and joined his uncle. "You heard what I said." His tone was direct but not accusatory. Nor apologetic. "Didn't you?"

Eloise chose to be similarly straightforward. "I did."

"It's nothing personal." His lips curved in a slight, self-deprecating smile. "I prefer to work alone, that's all."

"Why is that?"

A strange noise emanated from Mr. Whitmer's throat, a combination of a gasp and a chuckle that he quickly turned into a cough. Was he horrified by her audacity? Or amused?

"Excuse me?" Phillip stared at her, the smile fading. Eloise's cheeks burned, but she stiffened her shoulders again. She refused to be intimidated by his glare. "I don't have to explain myself to you."

As much as she wanted him to see her value, she didn't want to get off on the wrong foot. His uncle wanted them to be partners, so whether he liked it or not, they needed to work together.

"Of course you don't," she said. "But I trust you will give me a chance to prove myself. Especially when you know little about my abilities."

"Well said, my dear." Mr. Whitmer propelled her toward the table and pulled out a chair. "Phillip isn't as crotchety as he'd like you to believe. He'd rather be on his way to a different type of service, you understand, but here he is, at my request, ready to investigate a puzzling mystery. I can always count on him, and I believe you will come to count on him too."

As Eloise took her seat, he lowered his voice to a stage whisper. "I confess he's my favorite nephew. And he's grown into a fine agent. Though when he and my sons were boys, they got into their fair share of trouble. The stories I could tell you."

"No stories," Phillip said firmly as he took a seat across from Eloise. "And I didn't get into that much trouble."

"He's not good at taking criticism either." Mr. Whitmer winked at Eloise then took his place at the head of the table.

"Could we please stop talking about my

27

faults?" Phillip tapped the folders stacked in front of his uncle. "We have more important matters to discuss."

"I simply want Miss Marshall to know what to expect from your partnership."

"Okay, then." Phillip shifted his gaze from his uncle to Eloise. "I'd like Miss Marshall to know that I know a great deal about her abilities. That I spent last night reading her dossier, and she may be surprised to learn that I am most impressed with her accomplishments."

"What does that mean, you read my dossier?" Eloise suddenly felt exposed. She folded her arms across her body as if to protect herself from prying eyes. "What's in my dossier?"

"It's what the agency knows about you," Mr. Whitmer replied. "Your biographical information, your college transcripts, the navy's personnel records regarding your cryptology work."

The college transcripts and personnel records didn't concern her. She graduated magna cum laude from Wellesley College with a bachelor's degree in mathematics and a minor in music. Her personnel reviews were exemplary. But what about the biographical information? Did that mean the basic data of her existence? Name, date of birth, gender, daughter of Leonard and Sylvia Marshall? Or did the dossier delve into the deeply personal?

She wanted to ask the questions burning a hole

in her spirit, but she couldn't form the words. Did the FBI know about her brother's death at Pearl Harbor? Of course they did. What about her father? What did the FBI—what did Phillip—know about him?

Anger roiled in the depths of her stomach.

"What about his dossier?" She pointed at Phillip. "When do I get to read about him?"

"You can't," Phillip retorted.

Mr. Whitmer pulled a thin folder from the stack and slid it toward Eloise. "It's heavily redacted, of course. You don't have the security clearance to know about his previous operations."

"Wait a minute." Phillip reached for the folder, but Eloise snatched it out of his reach.

"Turnabout is fair play," Mr. Whitmer said. "But you'll have to read it another time, Miss Marshall. We have work to do."

Eloise placed the folder, along with her handbag, on the empty chair next to her. She couldn't help flashing a triumphant smile at Phillip, who scowled and looked away.

"I'm ready," she said to Mr. Whitmer with a pert smile.

But was she really? Or had it been a mistake to leave the safe, underground world of ciphers and codes? A place where mathematics and transposed letters were priorities and so-called biographical information didn't matter.

She was about to find out.

CHAPTER FOUR

Though his poker face was legendary, Phillip placed his hand over his mouth and bent his head to hide his amusement. Eloise's confident facade was simply that—a facade. Despite her professional demeanor and rapt attention, she was one ticked-off lady. The set of her chin, the tilt of her head, the primness of her folded hands spoke a language he understood. She reminded him so much of Marcy in that moment. Calm on the outside but boiling on the inside.

Not that he could blame her. Even though he didn't want Eloise or anyone else reading the personal information in his dossier, he should have quelled his impulse to grab his folder. But he had to admit Uncle Richard made a good point. He'd read her dossier. Now she could read his.

Her qualifications were superb. Graduating at the top of her class and with honors from both high school and college. Volunteer work as a math tutor at an orphanage. Turning down more prestigious jobs so she could continue living at home to help support her mother. Both musically and mathematically gifted—two attributes that indicated a knack for cryptography. No surprise that the navy recruited her.

The more interesting aspect of her dossier, the sections that had given him pause, concerned her family. The effects of the Great Depression on her social status. The family's tragic loss when the Japanese bombed Pearl Harbor. Who could blame her for feeling her privacy had been invaded? Certainly not him.

A twinge of guilt poked him in the gut, but he swatted it away. His job required him to know his partner. Even a partner he didn't want.

He raised his eyes to his uncle. "Who or what are we investigating?"

Richard opened the top folder. "We have reason to believe that an American traitor is providing information to our enemies. The two of you are tasked with finding this spy and bringing him to justice."

"Why would an American do such an awful thing?" Eloise asked. The shock in her eyes didn't surprise Phillip. Though she'd experienced brutal heartache because of the war, this young woman had no idea how cruel life could be. Violence rocked the country even during peacetime. Less than ten years before, lawmen killed Bonnie Parker and Clyde Barrow in an ambush after they robbed, kidnapped, and murdered their way around the Midwest. Few people expected such horrors to invade their small-town havens, but they did.

"Maybe the traitor isn't a 'true' American,"

Phillip said. "He might be someone with German roots who feels more loyalty to Hitler than to the red, white, and blue."

"How can we possibly find this person?" Eloise asked.

Instead of answering her, Phillip eyed his uncle and carefully chose his words. Most of the details of his last mission, which technically hadn't ended yet, were classified. After the last saboteur was arrested, the FBI had issued a general press release about the eight Germans who'd been caught before they could cause any damage in the United States.

Eloise might be part of this team, but as far as he knew, she didn't have a high enough security clearance for any information beyond what had appeared in the newspapers. "Could there be a connection with those German saboteurs?"

Eloise's eyes rounded, but she didn't say anything. Phillip could almost see the wheels whirring behind her intelligent gaze. So, she had read the sensational news reports but refused to interrupt the conversation to ask questions. A point in her favor for being well-informed and another for discretion. Both points grudgingly given.

"A connection seems unlikely," Richard replied. "But I suppose anything is possible. It's up to you to find out."

"Now I know why you twisted my arm for this mission." Phillip leaned back in his chair.

"I actually had a different reason," Richard replied. "But you were with that operation from its inception, so it shouldn't take you long to ascertain if there is a connection."

"What was your reason then?"

"We can discuss that later." Richard opened a folder and handed two sheets of paper to each of them. "These are copies of letters that may provide national secrets to our enemies."

Phillip scanned the top letter. "This is a letter about a broken doll."

"Is it?" Richard said. "What do you think, Eloise?"

Eloise read through both letters, taking her time before answering. "I can't say for sure, Mr. Whitmer, but this could be an open code. What we call a jargon code. To the casual reader, this letter from Dorothy Walker says she can't find anyone to repair a broken doll."

She focused again on the letter. "I suppose this could be an example of steganography."

"First of all, please call me Richard. Second, I studied code breaking at the academy before either of you were born," Richard said. "Refresh my memory, please."

Phillip made a mental note to thank his uncle later. Though his own stint at the academy was more recent, he'd only taken a basic cryptography course and had no idea what Eloise was talking about—not that she needed to know that. Could he help it if his cases had never involved coded messages before now?

Eloise's eyes sparkled as her enthusiasm for her area of expertise replaced her earlier prickliness. "What we mostly do in cryptology is either encrypt a message or break the code for an encrypted message. At its simplest, that means substituting the original letters with different letters. Or numbers. The encrypted message appears to be a random collection of letters."

She paused as she scanned one of the letters again. "Steganography hides a message within a message. This letter seems innocent enough. But what if the dolls mean something else? Something that only the recipient would understand?"

"Such as?" Richard prompted.

"Perhaps the broken doll is a broken ship."

Phillip tossed the letters on the table. "Or maybe it's simply a broken doll."

Annoyed by his casual dismissal, Eloise glared at him. "Mrs. Walker or whoever wrote this letter says she broke a doll wearing a hula grass skirt. That makes me think of Hawaii. And Hawaii makes me think of . . ."

The room was deathly quiet for a moment then Phillip heaved a sigh. "Pearl Harbor." He turned to Richard. "Who was the recipient?"

"Both letters were addressed to someone in Buenos Aires," Richard said. "Our wartime censors intercepted and forwarded Mrs. Walker's letter to us. It's dated January 27 and has a Seattle postmark. The second letter, supposedly from a Barbara Clark, was postmarked from New York in February. When it was returned as 'Address Unknown,' Mrs. Clark took it to her local post office director, who sent it to us."

"Has anyone talked to these women?" Phillip asked.

"That's your mission." Richard folded his hands on the remaining files in his stack. "First, you'll travel to Springfield, Ohio, to talk to Barbara Clark. Then you'll need to visit Dorothy Walker in Spokane, Washington."

"Ohio?" Phillip narrowed his eyes in confusion. "Didn't you say the Clark letter had a New York postmark?"

"Another puzzle for you to solve." Richard turned his attention to Eloise. "Do you enjoy traveling?"

"I like seeing new sights." Eloise appeared almost giddy at the prospect. "I've never been west of the Appalachian Mountains."

"Just hold on." Phillip raised both his hands. "I'm a trained interrogator. I can do these interviews by myself."

"You're going to talk to these women about their dolls? I think not." Richard tapped the folders. "These are your cover identities."

"Don't tell me," Phillip scoffed. "We're posing as a married couple. Like in that Clark Gable movie." Not even for his uncle would Phillip travel from one end of the country to the other under that scenario.

"I saw that movie," Eloise exclaimed. "*It Happened One Night*, right?"

"Right." Phillip shot an *aha* look at his uncle. "I suppose next you'll hand me a clothesline and a blanket to hang between our beds."

Eloise's eyes widened. *Good.* If his comment shocked her, maybe she'd quit.

"I can't pretend we're married," she stammered. "We can't—I won't."

"See, Uncle? It's not just me."

"Calm down, both of you," Richard admonished. "I personally selected you—the two of you—for this mission because of your particular skills. This has nothing to do with romance, real or feigned." He slid folders toward each of them, a Cheshire cat grin on his face. "But to avoid any hint of impropriety, you are traveling as brother and sister. You're not expected to share the same room, so it's up to you whether you take a clothesline and blanket."

Phillip didn't know whether to laugh or throw a temper tantrum. Not that the latter would ever work with his uncle. He gestured toward Eloise. "She's my sister?"

"To ease the complications of travel and whenever else such duplicitousness is beneficial, yes."

Another sister. Just what he didn't need.

But when Uncle Richard said "jump," the appropriate response from his underlings—which at the FBI included Phillip—was "how high?" He'd go on this mission with his pretend sister. The second it was over, however, he expected Uncle Richard to keep his promise.

CHAPTER FIVE

Eloise pressed her lips together as the reality of Richard's announcement settled within her. Phillip didn't seem any happier about the proposed arrangement than she, but he had the luxury of being related to the person in charge of overseeing their mission—a luxury she didn't have.

Not that anyone cared, but the thought that someone as full of himself as Phillip Clayton could ever be her brother seemed like a sick cosmic joke. She and Allan had a special relationship, one born from loss and instability. They counted on each other when it became clear they couldn't count on anyone else—not even their mother. The loss of Allan had left her bereft and alone, blasting a hole into her heart that would never heal.

And now she was supposed to pretend that she had a similar relationship with this arrogant man who clearly didn't want her as a partner? She wasn't sure she could even pretend to *like* him, let alone think of him as a brother. Under such circumstances, how would they fool anyone into believing they were related?

"I trust the arrangement will be suitable to you, Eloise." Richard's tone seemed genuinely warm. "It's unusual, I know, but the pretense will raise less questions about your relationship. You may encounter strangers who would find it odd for two single people such as yourselves to be traveling together. A sibling relationship allows you to look out for one another without raising undue suspicion."

"I'm not sure who would be paying that much attention to us," Eloise said. "Why do we have to tell anyone anything?"

"Phillip's very presence might raise questions," Richard said. "Some folks may wonder why he isn't in uniform, especially when he doesn't have an obvious disability. Many young men his age have already enlisted. Those who aren't overseas are in training camps, each one doing his part to win this war. People may ask, 'Why isn't he?' I don't fault such people for being curious, but they can't know he's a government agent."

As his uncle talked, Phillip turned his head, and his shoulders tensed. Eloise sensed she'd gotten a glimpse inside him that he meant to keep to himself. He wanted to be one of those young men who were fighting. More than that, he was ashamed not to be. Serving in the States as a trained FBI agent apparently wasn't enough for him. But why not?

"Having a sister by his side could help allay suspicions about him," Richard continued. "For your part, you'll have someone by your side who can keep away any unwanted attention."

"Unwanted attention?" Eloise asked.

"All sorts of men are attracted to pretty young women." Richard gave her a warm smile. "Phillip can ensure no one gets too, shall we say, amorous."

Heat crept up Eloise's throat and flushed her cheeks. She caught Phillip's amused gaze, and he rolled his eyes as if to make gentle fun of his uncle. She held back a nervous chuckle while, at a deeper level, sensing the gesture—simple as it was—acted as a single thread pulling them together.

If Richard had noticed Phillip's subtle eye-rolling, he chose to ignore it. "At the very least, presenting yourself as siblings may keep any uncomfortable questions to a minimum."

"I know how to handle unwanted advances," Eloise said. Her brother hadn't always been around to put a handsy man in his place, and she'd managed just fine, thank you very much.

"I believe that." Phillip leaned forward and folded his hands on the table. "Look, I'm not crazy about this idea either. But, like it or not, it has merit. Traveling across the country can have enough pitfalls without adding any unnecessary complications."

"Have you done this kind of subterfuge before?" Eloise asked him.

"Can't say that I have. Until now, my part-ners have been men." Phillip opened the folder Richard had placed in front of him as he continued. "We pose as salesmen—that's almost always the best cover. Though I've also pretended to be a newspaper reporter. Another time I went undercover as a hobo. Whatever works for the mission."

A hobo? Eloise didn't know whether she could believe him, though she supposed anything was possible. The world had gone topsy-turvy when the Japanese bombed Pearl Harbor. It was as if everyone had followed Alice down her rabbit hole and were trying to make sense of the nonsensical.

Only a few months ago, Eloise had been teaching high school algebra, geometry, and trigonometry. Now she was preparing to decipher a strange letter, which might or might not be written in code, and taking on a new identity while she traveled with a stranger to investigate a possible traitor. So much change in such a short amount of time. A span that included overwhelming grief and tremendous challenges.

"I suppose we can be estranged siblings if that would make things easier for you." He held up a driver's license. "I'm now Phillip Carter. That should be easy to remember."

Eloise opened her folder. A driver's license and social security card rested on top of other papers. Each one displayed her name as *Eloise Carter*. The personal data on the license matched her own—height, weight, date of birth.

The top document provided a bio that listed the names of her fictional parents and one sibling. Phillip Carter.

Never!

Eloise read from the sheet. "I'm still a graduate of Wellesley. Major in math, minor in music. I'm surprised this information is all the same."

"Cardinal rule of deception," Phillip said. "Keep the falsehood as close to the truth as possible. You're familiar with the campus. The professors. No one can trip you up."

"Then why is my hometown different?"

Phillip exchanged a glance with his uncle. "My guess is that you come from a place where everybody knows everybody else."

"True."

"That's the reason."

Eloise nodded, though his answer didn't explain what she was supposed to do if she met someone from their supposed hometown. What if she said something wrong? Codes she understood. Deception with others—that would not be easy.

Richard removed the sheet of biographical information from Eloise's folder to reveal a printed itinerary. "Phillip has other obligations for the next few days. While he's preoccupied, you'll be going to FBI school."

Eloise scanned the itinerary. Tradecraft and investigative technique classes in the mornings. Self-defense and weapons training in the afternoons. A feeling of inadequacy, bordering on panic, washed over her. How could she possibly learn everything expected of her in such a short amount of time? She pushed back from the table, hand on her chest, shoulders gripped with tension.

"If I didn't believe in you," Richard said, "I wouldn't have selected you."

Eloise met his gaze and focused on the kindness in his eyes. "Perhaps you made a mistake."

"My uncle doesn't make mistakes." Phillip's quiet tone softened his words. Eloise stared at him, and he grinned. "At least he's never confessed to any."

An unexpected stirring, a feeling she'd never experienced before, pulsated deep inside her. A feeling she didn't want to experience, not at this time in her life and definitely not with Phillip. Perhaps a sensation she was misinterpreting, one born from grief and disappointments and a desire to do what was asked of her despite her fear that she'd fail.

And yet . . . another thread, one created by Phillip's teasing grin and her odd reaction, connected them. Perhaps enough threads would pull them together to ease her discomfort with him. She hoped so. Otherwise, the next few weeks would be miserable.

"I confess my mistakes to God," Richard said with a good-natured laugh. "That seems sufficient. Unless there are any questions, that concludes our business for today." He handed Eloise a card. "Be at this address tomorrow morning at eight sharp and report to room seventy. Your instructor will meet you there. And if you gain any insights to those letters, share them only with Phillip or me. No one else under any circumstances."

"Of course," Eloise agreed as she scanned the card, which listed the address for the FBI training academy at the marine base in Quantico.

"Pack a bag because you'll need to stay at one of the dormitories on base during your training. All the arrangements have been made. Any questions?" Richard's gaze took in both of them.

"No, sir," Phillip said, and Eloise echoed him though she had a slew of questions she didn't know how to ask.

"Good. My contact information is in your folder. Now, I must get back to my office. Until tomorrow." With that, Richard left them alone.

Eloise slid the new driver's license and social security card into a pocket of her handbag and closed the folder. She was eager to return to the room she shared with another cryptanalyst to review the contents and pack her suitcase. Sensing Phillip's gaze, she raised her eyes to his.

"You must feel like you've been thrown into the deep end of a pool," he said. "I guess you have."

"Thankfully, I'm a strong swimmer."

By the expression on his face, her retort amused him. "Then I guess you don't need any advice from me." He stood and gathered his folder.

Eloise tried, but she couldn't let it go. If she didn't ask him, she'd be awake all night wondering what he hadn't said. "I'm intrigued. What advice do you have?"

His eyes sparkled, as if he'd known she wouldn't be able to resist his baiting. In that instant, he reminded her of Allan. That slightly superior yet good-humored smirk. The unspoken *gotcha!*

Sharp grief pierced her heart like a freshly honed dagger. She tensed her facial muscles so Phillip wouldn't notice her sudden sorrow. She didn't want his sympathy or to give him any reason to remove her from this mission. Because she wanted to do this. She needed to do this. For her brother and, she admitted, for herself.

"Learn everything they teach you," Phillip said. "Take it all in. But—and this is the most important part—be who you are."

"But I'm supposed to be your sister. To play a role."

"Yes. And no." He returned to his seat, seemingly eager to impart his wisdom—a wisdom Eloise coveted. "You're you. A bright and attractive young woman with a dollop of spunk tossed in. That's you. And that's Eloise Carter.

Don't turn her into something she's not or something you aspire to be. She's *you*. Be *you*."

Was his advice valid? Or meant to give her a false sense of security so she would fail? She searched his eyes for any hint of duplicity and found none.

But why would she? He was a trained agent. Trained to lie and to deceive. How could she ever trust him?

CHAPTER SIX

The days of training went by in a blur. For the first week, Eloise attended a personalized series of classes taught by different instructors at the FBI academy. She learned about surveillance and interrogation techniques but also tradecraft activities. She found them interesting but doubted she'd ever be in a situation that required that kind of knowledge.

She'd been transferred to the FBI to help decipher what may or may not be a jargon code and to interview two women who might or might not be involved in sending traitorous information to the enemy. How could either of those tasks require her to know how to tail someone without getting caught or the various methods for marking a drop site? The one-on-one training was intense, but she passed most of her tests with flying colors. The session on following someone without being spotted took more practice than she anticipated. What the instructor called cat-and-mouse training, which included spotting and losing a tail, continued throughout her training period.

On the first day, after a half-hour break for lunch in the training academy cafeteria, Eloise had walked to the firing range for her marksman-ship lessons. She'd never handled a gun before and prayed she'd never be placed in the position to use one against another person. Her first lesson was an abysmal failure, and the instructor, a Lieutenant Boyd, didn't offer her any encouragement. The heavy Smith and Wesson .357 Magnum with its long barrel was difficult to hold and more difficult to aim. Bracing against the expected kickback, an unexpected shock when she first fired the weapon, adversely affected her aim. But relaxing her stance seemed impossible.

After each day's lesson, Lieutenant Boyd marched off the range muttering about women no longer knowing their place. Eloise flushed with humiliation and embarrassment each time. She longed to make a snappy comeback, but her mind always went blank. She hardly slept at night as her mind replayed her failure at the range. Mr. Whitmer might rethink his offer when he discovered she could barely hit the edge of a target. Though why in the world did she need to be a skilled marksman to talk to women about their doll collections?

The following week, a different firearms instructor appeared at the range. He introduced himself as Sergeant Prescott, but he didn't explain why he'd taken Lieutenant Boyd's place. Eloise didn't care enough to ask. Though the sergeant exuded no-nonsense gruffness, he also had the patience of Job.

First, he reviewed the basics of gun safety, a lesson Lieutenant Boyd had glossed over. Then Sergeant Prescott suggested she try a lighter weapon, a Colt semiautomatic. With his guidance and support, Eloise overcame her nerves and consistently shot within the target's boundaries. By the time her training was nearing an end, she was even handling the Smith and Wesson monster with more ease.

Her training regimen also included physical fitness. After she left the range, she joined other female students in calisthenics, navigating an obstacle course, and self-defense tactics. A few of the women excelled at the training while Eloise struggled to go over a high wall with only the aid of a dangling rope. Her final score was acceptable but not stellar. Muscles she didn't even know she had ached from the unaccustomed strain. Obviously, she'd been sitting behind a desk for too many hours for too many days.

Brain, beauty, or brawn.

She knew which category she fit in, and she had no desire to exchange her intellect for either of the other two no matter the inducement. Phillip, on the other hand, definitely claimed brain *and* brawn. According to his dossier—at least the areas that hadn't been blacked out—he was intelligent and intuitive. His superiors wrote glowing reports about his achievements. Though the specifics of any particular mission were also redacted, it was clear he was a valued asset to any team.

His physical training reports indicated respectable scores and race times. Certainly much better than any of hers. But he'd had the benefit of playing football both in high school and college. A quarterback. Just like Allan.

Phillip might beat her in a foot race and on the firing range, but at least she could take dictation for five letters and type them up while he was still looking for a steno pad and pencil. Small satisfaction since he probably had access to a secretary who did that job for him.

Though what did any of it matter? The likelihood that she and Phillip would be jumping hurdles or running races was slim to none. Phillip didn't need to know how to take dictation to do his job, and Eloise didn't need to know how to climb a wall to travel around the country and talk to people.

During her days of training, she never saw Phillip. But Richard Whitmer sometimes appeared at the range or at the edge of the field where they exercised. He didn't attempt to speak to Eloise, but if their eyes happened to meet, he'd tip his hat in her direction. He always stood too far away for her to say anything to him unless she shouted. She sensed he would consider her yelling at him as unseemly, so she simply returned his hat tip with a wave or a nod. Then she did her best to ignore him and focus on the task at hand.

She was imperfectly suited for long marches in the mud and the intricacies of tradecraft. After the training ended, he'd probably send her back to the cryptography unit. Because of the emphasis on "loose lips sink ships" no one would ask her where she'd been or what she'd been doing, so she wouldn't have to confess her failure.

But she'd have to live with it. As she struggled one more time to get over the obstacle wall, she imagined the expression on Phillip's face when his uncle sent her packing. Smug. Arrogant. Good riddance.

With renewed motivation, she clung to the top of the wall with her fingertips and gripped the rope as she pulled herself upward. She wouldn't give him that satisfaction. After flinging one leg over the wall, she straddled it a moment to catch her breath. She could do this. Another deep breath and she slid downward, landed with knees bent, and raced for the finish line.

"You did it," the timekeeper shouted. "With seven seconds to spare."

Take that, FBI Agent Phillip Clayton.

CHAPTER SEVEN

Phillip paced the small room on the fifth floor of the Department of Justice building where he'd been instructed to wait until it was his turn to testify before the closed-door military tribunal presided over by seven generals. Over the past couple of weeks, Phillip had been too preoccupied with Operation Pastorius to think too much about his next assignment. Or maybe he was focusing so much on his current mission because he dreaded even thinking about the next one.

A mission so obscure and unimportant it hadn't even been granted a name. He'd jokingly suggested Operation: China Doll, but Richard hadn't been amused. In his stuffy way, he replied that FBI investigations didn't always require operational names. He'd also explained why he chose Phillip to accompany Eloise on the interviews. The motive boiled down to nothing more than simple pragmatism.

Richard knew, as Phillip did, that the public praise being heaped on the FBI for their capture of the German saboteurs before they'd carried out even one destructive act was due to J. Edgar Hoover's uncanny ability to spin the truth. The men who'd traveled in U-boats from Germany—four to Long Island and four to

Florida—had not been captured because of the Bureau's amazing investigative abilities but because one of the Germans had turned on the others—a little-known fact that Hoover kept out of the press releases.

The one thing worse than German saboteurs on American soil was an American traitor.

If one of Uncle Sam's own was betraying the country, the Bureau needed to find the who, what, and why as quickly and quietly as possible. Richard was adamant that someone like Eloise, with her wholesome, girl-next-door demeanor, was the perfect choice to interview other women.

But a trained agent needed to accompany her on the interviews . . . and that's where Richard's pragmatism came in. As he explained to Phillip, he couldn't send a married agent with Eloise. That could cause unnecessary marital problems. Richard needed an unmarried agent he could trust to act professionally at all times, no matter what circumstances the couple found themselves in.

He needed Phillip.

A knock sounded at the door, and Phillip refocused his thoughts as he buttoned his suit jacket. A military officer led him to Assembly Hall #1, the large room where the tribunal was taking place. Once he was sworn in, he told his story as succinctly and clearly as he could.

He'd been one of the agents who interrogated George Dasch while a stenographer wrote down the German's story. They were in Dasch's DC hotel room, where he'd given them over $82,000 in cash meant to finance the destruction of such important targets as the aluminum plants in Tennessee and vital railway lines throughout the country.

Dasch had betrayed his own team, the men who'd landed on Long Island's shoreline. Then he used contact information written on a white handkerchief in invisible ink to help the FBI agents find the team who had come ashore on a Florida beach near Jacksonville.

Each one of the potential saboteurs had been recruited by the *Abwehr*, Germany's intelligence service, because they had lived in the United States for several years before returning to Germany. Two of them were US citizens. If Dasch hadn't ratted them out, who knew how much havoc they could have created?

And for what?

Phillip understood patriotism and love of country, but he would never understand the motivations of these men who knew firsthand the differences between living in the United States and living in Germany. Did it mean nothing to them that their so-called Führer planned to take over the world? Or was that part of the appeal?

Nah! Their motives had nothing to do with patriotism. Good old-fashioned greed had driven them to undertake their ill-fated mission. They'd been promised exemption from military service and high-paying jobs when they returned to Germany.

The mere thought of the chaos the men could have caused had sickened Phillip when Dasch first confessed the plot, and it sickened him now.

After he was dismissed from the stand, Phillip left the building. At least his part in this chapter of the war had come to an end except for a brief epilogue when the tribunal announced their verdict.

As soon as Eloise finished her classes, they'd be on their way to Ohio. A pretend brother and sister making the long journey by train to talk to a woman about a letter she apparently hadn't written about a bunch of dolls.

Not the reason he'd joined the FBI. Not the reason he wanted to delay his plan B for military service. But he'd promised his uncle he'd do this one last mission before signing up, and his uncle had promised to use his influence to expedite the process.

The tribunal's verdict was announced a few days later. All eight saboteurs were declared guilty. All eight were sentenced to death.

It was the verdict Phillip had hoped for, but he found he couldn't join the others in the assembly hall who celebrated the news. He forced a smile as he shook hands with the legal team and other agents. But all he wanted was to get out of there, to forget about German saboteurs and potential infrastructure disasters. To forget that he was stuck here in Washington, DC, when his buddies were battling the enemy where it counted—in Europe and in Asia.

If he were a drinking man, he'd find the nearest bar, park himself on a stool, and stay there until the alcohol pickled his brain. A jog through the streets of DC would have to suffice, except he wasn't sure he could garner the energy for that, either.

He headed for the exit and found Richard waiting for him outside the corridor.

"Did you hear?" he asked.

"I heard." Richard walked toward the elevator, and Phillip matched his stride. "I have it on good authority that Roosevelt will commute Dasch's sentence to a prison term."

"A reward for turning himself in?"

"Precisely."

"What about Berger?"

When they'd arrived in New York and separated themselves from the other two members of their team, Dasch had told Ernest Peter Berger, who'd been a member of the US National Guard before returning to Germany, of his intentions. Berger didn't accompany Dasch to FBI headquarters, but neither did he try to stop him. Maybe because Dasch threatened to throw him out of a hotel window if he did.

"His sentence will also be commuted." Richard's tone was grim. "Execution for the others will come quickly."

That meant the electric chair. Phillip involuntarily shuddered. They deserved the punishment, a risk they'd accepted when they got in the U-boats that brought them to America's shores. But had Germany sent other unknown saboteurs, ones who hadn't been caught, who were biding their time? Were there other traitors they didn't know about?

"Has Eloise deciphered those letters?" Phillip asked once they were alone in the elevator. "Or are they what they appear to be?"

"She has an idea or two." Richard's expression lightened, as if he were pleased Phillip had asked about Eloise. "I thought we'd have a working session this evening at my home. Would you mind fetching her?"

Phillip wasn't sure he wanted to see Eloise right now. Or more precisely, that he wanted her to see him. Not in his current mood anyway. But his uncle's invitation wasn't exactly a request. More like a polite order. He had little choice. "Better than going on a bender, I suppose."

Richard's eyebrows arched. "A bender? You?"

"Just a passing fancy."

"It's a hard thing," Richard said. "Knowing your actions, your testimony, contributed to men—men created in the image of God—being executed for their actions." He held up a finger. "But that's the key, you see. They chose destruction. And now destruction is coming for them."

The elevator jolted as it reached the ground floor. When the doors slid open, Phillip accompanied his uncle to the exit. He appreciated Richard's efforts to place the blame where it belonged. Yet Phillip couldn't help wondering what he would have done in Dasch's shoes.

Would he have allowed himself to be recruited for such a mission? Would he have betrayed his countrymen to protect his adopted country?

But for the grace of God . . .

CHAPTER EIGHT

As mentally and physically tired as Eloise was after her long days, she spent her evenings studying the two letters and researching possible solutions to phrases she suspected to be in code. That Saturday evening, a couple of women in her self-defense class invited her to go to dinner with them, but she declined. Since most of the dozen or so young women, whose presence at the marine base was a mystery, would have plans to go out on the town, Eloise could take advantage of the rare opportunity for a long soak in a hot bath.

But when she arrived at the dormitory, she found a message waiting for her from Richard Whitmer. His request for a debriefing couldn't be refused. She took a quick bath, pulled her hair into a neat chignon, and donned a pretty floral sundress. Anything else would be too hot. Before leaving the room, she tucked her notes into her handbag.

To her surprise, she found Phillip waiting for her in the dormitory lobby. She noticed him before he noticed her. He leaned against a pillar, his attention focused on one of the windows. Though his shoulders slouched, he didn't appear relaxed. Only weary. Nothing at all like the overly confident agent she'd met several days before. Perhaps the matter he had to attend to while she was in training hadn't gone well. Eloise supposed she'd never know. Seemed like everyone had their secrets these days.

Loose lips sink ships was more than a slogan on a poster. Decoded messages often delivered the tragic news of another ship lost to U-boats as it tried to deliver needed supplies to England.

As if he sensed her presence, he turned her way. His shoulders straightened as a welcoming smile brightened his expression. The transformation from carrying the weight of the world and not having a care in the world was seamless.

"My uncle sent me to fetch you," he said lightly. "I hope you don't mind."

"Not at all." Eloise matched his tone. "I suppose we need to get used to traveling together."

"It's too bad we can't drive to Ohio and beyond. Then we could set our own schedule instead of following the dictates of bus and train timetables." He offered his arm, and Eloise took it as they walked toward the door.

"I imagine traveling by car would be more comfortable," she said. "I took a bus when I moved here. It wasn't at all relaxing with so many stops and starts. And it was scorching hot even with the windows down."

"Did you ever consider turning back?"

"Not even once." Though she hadn't been

sure what waited for her when she arrived in the capital, she knew without a doubt she was needed here. She had picked up her brother's fallen mantle, and she was determined to do everything in her power to bring this war to an end as quickly as possible. Only a swift victory would protect others from experiencing the same grief she had known.

Phillip chuckled as if at a joke known only to him. "Spunk. It should be your middle name."

"Maybe it is."

"I've read your file, remember?" He leaned close and whispered, "Eloise May. Very pretty."

Eloise flushed at the compliment then inwardly chided herself for such silliness. This was a working partnership not a date. "Why the flattery?"

"Why not?"

"I know your middle name too." That and his birth date and alma mater. The thin file also contained his training scores and a few letters of commendation with specific details blacked out. Instead of trying to decipher the heavily redacted documents, though, she'd mostly focused on his photograph. He stared at the camera, his mouth set in a straight line, yet there was something playful in his expression. As if he found it hard to be serious for this oh-so-serious photo. "Phillip Richard Clayton," she continued. "I assume you're named for your uncle."

"Give the girl a prize." Phillip opened the door, and they stepped out into the balmy evening. The sun hung low in the western sky as if reluctant to let go of the day.

"A year ago on an evening like this," Phillip continued, "we'd be on our way to a movie or to dinner and dancing. I don't know about you, but I miss those days."

"Me too." Eloise's tone sounded more wistful than she had intended. But he was right. Saturday nights used to have a special, festive quality about them. Now, the days seemed to run together with only Sunday as a consistent day for worship and rest. Even that was difficult when codes and alphabetical patterns invaded Eloise's thoughts during an overly long sermon.

Phillip suddenly stopped. "Then why not?"

"Why not what?"

"Why not go to a movie? Or dancing, your choice."

"Because your uncle is expecting us. I have information to give him about those letters."

"Great." He started walking again, his pace slightly faster now. "We'll stop in for a few minutes, and then we'll go out on the town."

Eloise scurried to keep up with his long stride, not sure whether she should put an end to his madness or go along with it. She sensed he needed a break from the harsh realities of whatever he'd been involved with the past couple of weeks. But she couldn't bail out on his uncle even if he could.

Once again, he suddenly stopped, and she almost bumped into him. He grabbed her by both elbows. "Nothing is going to happen tonight unless you know the name of the traitor. Do you?"

"All I have are a few ideas on what the letters might mean."

"The operative word being *might*. Trust me, whatever you tell him will need to be corroborated and verified. It's possible Uncle Richard would make a phone call or two, but no one's going to be arrested tonight. Probably not tomorrow either."

Phillip's mood shifted as he let go of her arms and stared toward the horizon. "December seventh. That's the only time I knew him to go to work on a Sunday."

Eloise's mind went back to that tragic morning. A gentle snowfall had blanketed the tree-lined streets, presenting a picture that could have graced a Currier and Ives Christmas card. After church, she and her mom joined friends at a local diner. They were enjoying warm slices of apple pie served with generous helpings of vanilla ice cream when the attack was announced on the radio. The clatter of dinnerware and buzz of conversation quieted, the eerie silence somehow louder than the earlier commotion.

Someone turned up the volume on the radio. As the announcer repeated the news, Eloise stared at her mother, who stared at her uneaten dessert. A single tear rested on her cheek. Eloise blinked back her own tears and squeezed her mother's hand. Her touch was the only comfort she could offer.

She didn't trust her voice now any more than she had then.

"A day of infamy," Phillip said.

Eloise swallowed the lump in her throat and prayed she could respond without sounding too emotional. Without thinking, she gripped Phillip's arm. "Never to be forgotten."

A tense quiet settled over them. Eloise struggled to stop the flood of memories that threatened to wash over her. Now wasn't the time to relive the arrival of the dreaded telegram or the flag-draped casket.

"That settles it." Phillip gently prodded her shoulder with his. "We're definitely putting the war behind us for a few hours."

Eloise wanted to agree. A break sounded heavenly, and she was grateful for his efforts to lighten the mood. But . . . "You can get away with ignoring your uncle. I can't."

"Are you accusing Uncle Richard of nepotism?" Phillip teased, his boyish grin a charming alternative to his previous gloom. "He'd be devastated."

"That's not what I meant." Eloise couldn't help but return his smile. "And you know it."

"Let's find a phone."

"There's one in the lobby."

"Perfect." He grabbed her hand, and they hurried back to the dormitory.

Eloise wandered to a plant stand near the window so Phillip could make the call in private. She didn't want to stare at him, but this seemed a good opportunity to practice reading body language, one of the skills she'd been introduced to in her accelerated course.

He appeared relaxed as he chatted, his expression open and warm. Very different than when they first met. Then a wall had surrounded him— one with a sign that said *No girls! Keep out!* Just like on her brother's tree house. Not that Eloise had ever paid attention to the message. As long as she climbed the tree with a bag of sandwiches or a box of cookies, she was welcomed.

That wall had dissipated, though now Phillip seemed driven by a nervous energy she hadn't noticed before. What had he been up to while she was taking classes and learning to fire a gun? Would he tell her if she asked?

She plucked brown leaves from a purple African violet. When he chuckled, she glanced his way, and he gave her a thumbs-up. Nepotism or not, he and his uncle obviously had a close relationship. For the first time, she was struck by the handsome line of his jaw and the playful gleam in his eyes. Her pulse quickened, and she feigned interest in a vining philodendron so he wouldn't see the flush in her cheeks.

The call ended soon after. "Permission granted," he said as he came toward her. "As long as he gets to select the movie. Care to take a guess?"

Eloise reflected on the movies she'd heard her colleagues talk about in recent weeks. "Is he a baseball fan? I think there's a movie playing about Lou Gehrig."

"What true blue American isn't a baseball fan? And you're right. It's called *Pride of the Yankees*. But you're also wrong. That isn't the one."

"The new Superman movie? *The Three Stooges*?"

Phillip shook his head, and his grin widened. Eloise was at a loss. "I give up."

"Have you seen *The Postman Didn't Ring*?"

Of course, that would be the one Richard chose for them. The distinguished gentleman apparently had a good-natured ornery streak. "I've seen previews for it," she said. "Missing letters found in an attic."

"Two people traveling across the country to deliver them." Phillip chuckled. "He thought we might learn a thing or two."

"Do those two people pretend to be siblings too?"

"I guess we'll find out." He checked his

66

watch. "But we need to hurry, or we'll miss the cartoons."

His boyish excitement caused Eloise's heart to turn cartwheels, which was not something she wanted to happen, especially not with someone as temperamental as Phillip was proving to be. Stony-cold serious one day, fun and games another. Except that wasn't quite fair. He'd seemed troubled when they met in the lobby. The boyish persona hid something deeper—something he wanted to avoid thinking about for a few hours.

Her heart, also in need of a reprieve from grief, merely responded to his liveliness with a buoyancy of its own.

Instead of spending her evening nervously briefing a higher-up in the FBI, she'd be enjoying a movie with a strangely mercurial FBI agent. That getting-to-know-you awkwardness between them still existed, but at least this wasn't an official date, though it was certainly a step up from a blind date. With neither of them harboring any romantic notions, however, she could relax. Laugh at the cartoons. Enjoy the popcorn. And escape into another world where young men weren't killed by bombs and mothers didn't cry themselves to sleep every night.

CHAPTER NINE

The movie, an entertaining mix of over-the-top comedy, small-town shenanigans, and a hero-gets-the-girl love story, was a welcome break from glum thoughts about traitors and saboteurs. Phillip also appreciated having an attractive young woman to share his bucket of popcorn. He had no romantic designs on Eloise, but what red-blooded American male didn't enjoy the company of a good-looking gal who turned the heads of other guys?

An interesting observation about Eloise, though. She didn't seem to notice the masculine attention.

The invitation to the movie had been on the spur of the moment. Just like the episode with the crayons a few weeks ago, he couldn't say what prompted him to suggest such a thing. But he'd needed this evening. He guessed she did too.

Spots of light from streetlamps and auto-mobiles softened the darkness that had descended around them. Blackout rules weren't as strict here in the States as they were in England. Phillip hoped they never had to be. Especially when a flashing neon sign on the corner caught his attention, giving him an excuse to postpone saying good night for a while longer. He wasn't ready to return to the tiny two-room apartment he called home. Once he stepped across that threshold, the details of the military trial would descend upon him as he replayed his testimony, second-guessed what he'd said, heard again the solemn pronouncement of the tribunal's death sentence.

He shoved away the gloomy thoughts. Not yet. Not here.

"I don't know about you," he said, forcing a grin, "but I'm starving. Why don't we stop by that diner before calling it a night?"

Eloise looked toward the vertical sign with its flashing green letters spelling out the words ROSIE'S CAFÉ. He'd been prepared for her hesitation. After all, she'd expected to spend this evening talking over letters and plans with Richard, not on a . . . well, it wasn't really a date . . . but she hadn't been expecting to spend the evening with him. He hoped she didn't regret it. He certainly didn't.

Even though he preferred to go on this cross-country mission without a civilian as his part-ner—no matter how skilled she was at breaking codes and talking to other women about dolls—their time together outside of work seemed to have eased a lingering tension between them, a tension that was mostly his fault.

Perhaps that was why Richard so quickly agreed to Phillip's request to postpone the planned debriefing. A suspicious notion popped into Phillip's head. Had this been his uncle's plan all along? He certainly did have the movie times conveniently at hand. That old geezer.

"I wouldn't mind a bite to eat," Eloise said, breaking into his thoughts. "I have time before the academy's curfew, and it's such a lovely evening. I'm not ready for it to end."

From someone else, Phillip would have interpreted that last sentence as flirtatious. But he didn't have to read Eloise's mind to understand she was as reluctant as he to return to an empty room.

"Me either." He offered his arm, and she tucked her hand in the crook of his elbow.

Once inside the diner, Phillip led the way to a corner table and pulled out the chair for Eloise. He took the seat with a view toward the entrance.

"I know what you're doing," Eloise said, a sly tone in her voice.

"What am I doing?"

Instead of answering, she tilted her head and gave him a long, knowing look. He suppressed a chuckle. "What can I say? It's a habit."

"Always watching. Always assessing. Do you ever tire of being on guard?"

A waitress wearing a blue apron over a white uniform brought water glasses and menus to the table. She spouted off the evening special of pork chops with corn on the cob and promised to be back soon to take their order.

"I've eaten here before," Phillip said, grateful that the waitress's appearance had interrupted the conversation. He didn't like admitting it, but yes, sometimes he tired of "being on guard." However, what choice did he have?

He was too young to have participated in the public enemy era of the early 1930s. The shootouts, captures, and deaths of such notables as John Dillinger, Baby Face Nelson, and Pretty Boy Floyd had clinched the reputation of the FBI as a highly trained force of skilled and tireless agents whose only purpose in life was to rid the world of criminal scum.

But in the early years of this new decade, the public faced a new and more frightening danger that only a few knew about—enemy saboteurs who hid in the shadows while hatching their destructive plans.

"What do you recommend?" Eloise asked. Her voice once again pulled him from his thoughts. Somehow, he sensed she knew that. At least she hadn't returned to her original question.

"I like the meat loaf." He put extra oomph in his response as if to prove he could relax. "The roasted chicken is good too."

After a bit of back-and-forth debating, they both settled on the chicken. Phillip gave their orders to the waitress when she returned.

"I suppose we'll be eating together all the time once we start traveling." A flush crept up Eloise's neck. "I mean, of course we will. It's strange to think about, that's all."

"Maybe sooner than that." Phillip folded his hands on the table. "We have to pay a price for tonight's freedom from the grind of work."

"What price?" Her tone revealed she was intrigued.

"Richard requests our presence at dinner tomorrow. After church, of course. Apparently, he's breaking his 'no work on Sunday' rule to hear what you have to say."

Eloise's cheeks reddened, and her eyes grew large with panic. "Why didn't you tell me this sooner?"

"Because I needed a diversion. And I think you did too."

"You're right." The color in her cheeks slowly subsided, but the panic didn't quite leave her eyes. "The last few days have been . . . intense." Her lips, a flattering shade of pink, turned down at the corners, and her shoulders drooped.

"That bad?" he asked gently, suddenly eager for her to confide in him, though he couldn't explain why. Perhaps because he needed to know her, to understand her. Partners worked best when they could anticipate the other's moods and knew how to respond to them. That kind of relationship took time, but time was a luxury they didn't have.

"I did well on the written and observational

tests." She perked up as she shared that news. Then she leaned forward and whispered, "Am I allowed to tell you that?"

He grinned, touched by her eagerness not to make even the simplest faux pas. "It's fine," he whispered back. "What about the obstacle course?"

"I barely passed. We both better pray I don't have to scale a wall in a hurry."

Phillip leaned back and laughed. She stared at him, hurt in her eyes, but he couldn't help himself. The image he had conjured of her stuck on a wall like a hapless fly was too funny. "I'm sorry," he managed to say before bursting into another round of laughter.

"It was humiliating," she said, crossing her arms and glaring at him. "I've spent the past months sitting behind a desk staring at message printouts of jumbled letters and numbers, and now I'm expected to be a . . . a . . . Tarzan."

Phillip laughed again, and after a moment, Eloise did too. The laughter subsided when the waitress appeared with their meals and an amused look in her eyes.

"I'm sure you did fine," he said to Eloise after the waitress left them. "No one expected you to pass everything with flying colors."

"I did," she admitted as she placed her napkin in her lap.

With the bout of uncontrollable laughter out of

his system, he gave her a reassuring smile. "Do you mind if I say grace?"

Surprise flickered in her eyes. It was there then quickly gone. He guessed she hadn't considered him to be a praying man. "Please do," she said quietly then bowed her head.

He said a simple prayer, asking God's blessing on their meal and on their work. She echoed his amen then accepted the butter dish he held out to her.

"How did you do with marksmanship?" he asked, keeping his tone conversational and, fingers crossed, hoping she'd done well. She might not forgive him if he laughed at her again.

"Not much better than the obstacle course." She frowned as she buttered her yeast roll then set the knife on the edge of her plate. "What if I'm not the right person for this mission?"

Her crestfallen expression did something to Phillip's insides that he couldn't explain. The urge to console her, to hold her, swept over him and tied his stomach into knots. He hadn't wanted her as a partner, but her admission somehow changed that. Or maybe it was the emotional merry-go-round he'd been riding the past few days that had his sympathy on overdrive. His disappointment over the failed appeal. The skepticism of being paired with a civilian. His unsettled despondency over the Operation Pastorius trial.

It could be all those things or none of those

things. He didn't have time to sort out his thoughts. All he knew was that she needed to be the one to go with him. Richard, as always, was right. She couldn't back out. Not now.

"Who was your instructor?" he asked, doing his best to keep his tone conversational.

"The first week, it was Lieutenant Boyd." She heaved a deep sigh as if preparing herself for his disappointment. "I did everything wrong. It was awful."

Phillip snorted. Boyd was a skilled marksman, but he didn't have the best temperament for teaching novices how to shoot. His expectations were high, too high for beginners. "He's used to working with experts. Making the best even better, I guess you could say."

"He definitely wasn't happy teaching me. I don't think he likes women." She stared at him, as if challenging him in some way he didn't understand.

The truth was Boyd liked women very much. Too much. But Boyd believed men and women had distinct roles. He didn't like females encroaching on his territory. Phillip didn't plan to share any of that with Eloise. She might believe he thought the same. With four sisters at home, two older and two younger, Phillip valued the talents and expertise women could offer their country. They were needed now more than ever to fill the gaps left by the men who'd gone away from home to fight.

75

"You said you had Boyd the first week. Did he give up on you?"

"The second week this other instructor showed up. Sergeant Prescott. I liked him much better."

"I've worked with Prescott. He's a good man. He can be stern, but he has a heart."

"He is definitely patient. At least now I can hit the outer rim of the bull's-eye."

"All you need is more practice."

"Why?"

Startled by her determined tone, he lowered his fork. "What do you mean, why?"

"I don't want to carry a gun, Phillip. I don't want to shoot anyone. I can't."

"You probably won't have to. But this is a skill you need. Just in case."

"In case what?" She leaned toward him and lowered her voice. "Someone who collects dolls decides to shoot us?"

"We don't know what's going to happen on this trip. The most unlikely person could be a threat." Phillip paused to figure out what to say to make her understand. "I know it's hard, and I hope it never comes down to a shooting match between you and someone else, but if it does, in case it does, you need to know how to protect yourself." His voice became too adamant, too pleading. He took a deep breath. "You owe it to your family. And to . . . to the Bureau."

He'd bit his tongue from saying she owed it

76

to him. She owed him nothing except to do her job and to do it well. If there was any shooting to be done, he could take care of it. But that didn't change anything. She needed to be comfortable with a gun in her hand.

"After we meet with Richard tomorrow, I'll take you to the range myself."

"That isn't . . . you don't need to do that."

"I promise you. I have even more patience than Prescott. And I'm nothing like Boyd."

He gave her his lopsided grin, one specially designed to get his way with his sisters. "It'll be fun. You'll see."

"Or it'll be a colossal waste of time."

"How about I tell you what happened to me on my first day of obstacle training? It might make you feel better, but you have to promise not to laugh." The story he spun was about one-fourth fact and three-fourths fiction, but it did the trick. Maybe having Eloise along for the mission wouldn't be such a bad thing after all, though he wasn't yet ready to admit that to Richard.

CHAPTER TEN

By the time they had arrived at the dormitory, Eloise had agreed to Phillip's plan to attend church the next day with him, Richard, and Richard's wife, Patricia. She'd visited several of DC's churches since arriving in the city. Though she was strong in her own doctrinal beliefs, she appreciated the opportunity to worship in a variety of magnificent cathedrals and historic churches.

During the service, she sat between Patricia and Phillip, soaking in the gracious hospitality that made her feel less like an outsider and more like a family friend. When they stood for the closing hymn of "How Great Thou Art," Eloise's soprano and Phillip's tenor blended beautifully. The harmony of their voices seemed to wrap around them like a snug cocoon, a near-mystical experience that thrilled Eloise to the tips of her toes.

After the final prayer, Phillip whispered, "We'll sing duets when we travel. It'll be a great way to pass the time."

Eloise nodded agreement, feeling a deep satisfaction that he'd been as moved by the intermingling of their voices as she had been.

Dinner was a scrumptious affair. The one rule

seemed to be no shop talk. Patricia wouldn't allow it and gently admonished both her husband and Phillip if either one veered too close to any work-related topics. Instead, the talk centered around the movie that Phillip and Eloise had seen the night before, the beauty of the cherry blossoms in the spring, which Eloise had missed, and the must-see sights in the nation's capital.

After dessert, Richard rose from the table and pulled out his pocket watch. "You'll excuse us for an hour or so, my dear."

"Of course, darling." Patricia stood and grasped Eloise's hand. "It's been simply a delight to meet you. I hope you'll come again."

"I'd love that. Thank you for your hospitality. For everything."

Patricia widened her smile to include Phillip then glided from the room. Eloise wasn't sure she'd ever met anyone with as much poise and elegance. Beside this sophisticated woman, she felt clumsy and dull.

Before she could allow herself to fall further into such thoughts, Richard gestured toward the opposite doorway. "Shall we?"

Eloise preceded the men into the room, a square study lined with bookshelves and dominated by a huge desk. A nearby easel held enlarged copies of the two letters. She darted a glance toward Phillip, but the harmonious tenor and congenial dinner companion had disappeared behind the facade of the no-nonsense FBI agent. She took her cue from him, determined to present herself as a professional though she felt like a fraud. Did she really have anything to offer his powerful uncle that could be helpful?

She breathed a silent prayer. She could do this.

Richard settled himself behind his desk, and Phillip took a seat across from him. After taking a deep breath, Eloise squared her shoulders and stood by the easel.

"This typewritten letter, dated January 27, 1942, was allegedly sent from Dorothy Walker of Spokane, Washington, to Señora Ines de Molinali in Buenos Aires, Argentina." She was telling them information they already knew, but the introduction helped settle her nerves. "The postage was incorrect, so it was examined more closely. In February, the censors forwarded it to the FBI."

She pointed to the second paragraph. "This is the important part of the letter. It says:

'I must tell you this amusing story, the wife of an important business associate gave her an old German bisque Doll dressed in a Hulu Grass skirt. It is a cheap horrid thing I do Not like it and wish we did not have to have it about. Well I broke this awful doll last month now the person who gave the doll is coming to visit us very soon. I walked all over Seattle to get someone to repair it, no one at home could or would try the task.

Now I expect all the damages to be repaired by the first week in February.'"

Eloise glanced at each man in turn. The moment had come to prove her value to the team.

"I'm convinced it's a jargon code," Eloise said. "The doll refers to a warship that was damaged at Pearl Harbor and taken to the Puget Sound navy yard for repairs."

"Do you have any proof?" Phillip asked. "It still sounds to me as if you're simply substituting a possible meaning where none exists."

"What about the second letter?" Richard asked. "The one written by Barbara Clark, who told the local postal director she didn't write it or mail it."

Shaken by Phillip's lack of confidence, Eloise gave Richard a weak smile. At least he seemed to believe her. "As you know, it was also sent to Señora Molinali. Same address as the first letter. Also typewritten. Argentina sent it back to the sender. Apparently, Señora Molinali moved without leaving a forwarding address."

"This is the letter with the New York postmark, right?" Phillip asked.

"Yes. But Mrs. Clark lives in Springfield, Ohio." Eloise turned her attention to the letter. "I find this one the more enlightening of the two, particularly this passage:

'You asked me to tell you about my collection a month ago. I had to give a talk to an art club, so I talked about my dolls and figurines. The

only new dolls I have are THREE LOVELY IRISH dolls. One of these three dolls is an old Fisherman with a Net over his back—another is an old woman with wood on her back and the third is a little boy. Everyone seemed to enjoy my talk. I can only think of our sick boy these days. You wrote me that you had sent a letter to Mr. Shaw, well I want to see MR. SHAW he distroyed Your letter, you know he has been Ill. His car was damaged but is being repaired now. I saw a few of his family about. They all say Mr. Shaw will be back to work soon.'"

Phillip joined her at the easel and peered at the letter. "Any ideas on why some of those words are capitalized?"

"The capitalization definitely draws attention to them." Again, Eloise pointed to each phrase as she discussed its possible meaning. "I've studied naval ships and naval terms as part of my code training. The 'fisherman with a net over his back' could refer to an aircraft carrier. They have anti-torpedo nettings on their sides."

"Interesting interpretation." Richard nodded approval.

"And the old woman?"

"The old woman carrying wood could refer to an older battleship, one made out of wood."

"What about the third ship?" Phillip's tone suggested he was playing along but still not convinced. "The little boy?"

"I can't be sure of that one. But my guess is that it's a destroyer."

The corners of Phillip's lips turned up into a spontaneous grin. "Because little boys like to destroy things?"

"Because of the reference to Mr. Shaw." Eloise beamed as her excitement grew. This was the moment she'd been waiting for—the vital information she wanted to give Richard. Information that would prove to Phillip that she knew what she was doing. "The USS *Shaw*, a destroyer, was in dry dock at Pearl Harbor. About two weeks before this letter was written, it was undergoing repairs in San Francisco."

"Are you sure about that?" Phillip asked doubtfully.

"Absolutely." She held his gaze, refusing to back down from his skepticism. "I have contacts in the navy, you know. And don't worry. I didn't say why I wanted to know."

Phillip pressed his lips together and slowly nodded. " 'Mr. Shaw will be back to work soon.' I admit it's clever."

"Perhaps a little too clever." Eloise turned back to the easel. "My guess is that *distroyed* is purposefully misspelled to draw attention to it. And then look at the next word. *Your* is capitalized when it shouldn't be." Eloise jabbed at each word as she said it. " 'Distroyed Your.' Run the words together and you get—"

Together, she and Phillip said, " 'Destroyer. ' "

"What do you think of the jargon code now?" Eloise asked him. She tried but failed to keep a sense of superiority from her tone. Phillip didn't seem to notice. He leaned back in his chair with a satisfied smile on his face.

"I think you're a genius."

Eloise's cheeks warmed at his praise, but she didn't let her embarrassment spoil her sense of accomplishment. She shifted her gaze to Richard. He finished jotting a note and placed his pen in the holder. "Good work, Eloise. I will need to confirm your information about the USS *Shaw*. Protocol, you understand, not because I doubt you. I believe you interpreted this letter correctly."

"Thank you, sir."

"With this information, I believe we need to speak with Mrs. Clark and Mrs. Walker as soon as possible." Richard settled back into his opulent leather chair. "I'll have my secretary make your travel arrangements. You'll need to be prepared to leave at a moment's notice. Both of you."

Eloise widened her eyes. "You mean we're leaving today?" She wasn't prepared to go any-where, especially not a trip that could last a week or longer. A few of her belongings were at the academy dormitory at Quantico, but everything else was in her room behind the Francis Scott Key Bookstore. She needed time to handwash her unmentionables and brush her traveling suit.

"More likely on Tuesday," Richard said. He smiled as Eloise let out an audible sigh of relief. "By the way, I received your test scores and instructor evaluations. I must say I'm very pleased, especially considering how much training was crammed into such a limited amount of time."

Surely, he was kidding. But nothing in his expression indicated that he was anything but sincere.

"Did Boyd give her a good evaluation?" Phillip asked, sounding strangely annoyed. Eloise hoped he wouldn't tell his uncle what she'd said about Lieutenant Boyd not liking women. Why had she told him about that awful experience?

Richard shrugged. "Prescott's report was the more pertinent of the two since he spent the most time with Eloise. He said she is a willing student who paid close attention and made significant improvement. However, he does recommend additional time on the range."

Thankfully, there wouldn't be time for that. No sooner had the thought flitted through Eloise's mind when Phillip spoke up.

"We could go this afternoon."

Eloise widened her eyes. "I don't see how. I need to go back to the base then to my room."

"No more training," Richard said. "It's the Lord's Day. Time for rest and reflection."

And time to ready herself for an assignment

she'd never have dreamed possible. Everything about the past few weeks, all that she'd learned and studied, seemed surreal somehow, as if the long days had been a strange dream. The future appeared just as surreal. In a day or two, she'd be traveling with a man she barely knew on their hunt for a possible traitor.

She wished everything that had happened this entire year had been a dream. That she would suddenly wake up in her own bedroom in her own home in Camden Falls. Awaken to the mouthwatering aroma of sizzling bacon, freshly baked muffins, and hot coffee. That she'd join her mother at the breakfast table. And, most important of all, that Allan would be there too.

But no. That longing was the fantasy. God had planted her feet on an unusual and perhaps even dangerous path. She prayed He'd never leave her side while she was on it.

CHAPTER ELEVEN

They arrived in Dayton, Ohio, the nearest metropolitan area to Springfield, in the middle of the night after more than twelve hours on the train. Reservations had already been made for them at a nearby hotel. Eloise practically fell into bed but arose early so she'd be ready in plenty of time to meet Phillip in the lobby. Richard's secretary also had arranged a car for them.

The drive took less than an hour. Mrs. Clark lived in a well maintained bungalow on a tree-lined street on the outskirts of the large town. Neatly trimmed hedges bordered the property lines, and flowers adorned the entryway. A blue star banner with two blue stars hung in the window.

Eloise pasted on a smile while Phillip rang the bell. The woman who opened the door wore a floral apron over a lavender-checked shirtwaist dress. Her eyes narrowed as she took in the two strangers on her doorstep.

"You're wasting your time." Her voice had a good-humored lilt that softened the harsh words. "I have pies in the oven, and I'm not in a buying mood. Now Mr. Bleeker, over there across the street, he'll buy just about anything from anyone who has a mind to sit a spell with him. You might try persuading him to part with his money."

"We aren't selling anything, ma'am." Eloise widened her smile, hoping to gain the woman's confidence. Or at least time to explain their presence before she shut the door in their faces. "We're looking for Barbara Clark. It's about a letter that was sent to Argentina."

"I'm Barbara Clark." She folded her arms across her ample chest. "How do you know about that letter?"

Phillip held up his badge and introduced himself. "I'm with the FBI. This is my colleague, Eloise Marshall. We have a few questions to ask."

"Then I expect you best come on in." Once they were inside, she removed her apron and patted her hair. "If I'd known I was going to have company today, I would have put those pies in the oven earlier. I've raised three young'uns, and I found that asking and answering questions always goes better when all those involved are eating pie. The best I can offer is coffee and perhaps some leftover muffins from breakfast."

"Thank you for your hospitality," Eloise said. "But we're fine. If we could just talk to you a few moments?"

"Of course, of course. Please have a seat. Keep an ear out for the timer, will you? A burnt pie may be better than no pie at all, but I'd rather that didn't happen."

"We'll be sure to listen for it." Eloise perched on the edge of the sofa.

Phillip pulled a folded piece of paper from an inner pocket of his suit and handed it to Mrs. Clark before taking a seat beside Eloise. "This is a copy of the letter you gave to the postal director here in Springfield."

Mrs. Clark unfolded the paper and squinted through her spectacles at the words. "That's right. It was the strangest thing, having a letter returned to me that I'd never written. How would I know anyone who lives all the way down there in Argentina? The strangest thing that's ever happened to me. And that's saying a lot considering I've had all kinds of strange things happening to me over the years. That's what makes life fun, isn't it?"

"It sure is, ma'am," Eloise agreed. "Do you know who might have written it?"

"Can't say that I do. I remember the envelope had a New York City postmark. Well, heavens, child, I've only been to New York City once in my life. And it definitely wasn't to mail any letter to Argentina. Oh, no. I went to see one of those Broadway shows you hear about on the radio. Have you ever been to one of those Broadway shows?"

"I haven't had the pleasure, though I hope to visit someday."

"Do try to go. It's such a grand place." Mrs.

Clark returned her attention to the letter. Eloise sensed Phillip was about to speak so she placed her hand on his arm. The older woman reminded Eloise of a friend of her mother's. The same no-nonsense yet affable personality. If they let her guide the conversation, she might be more forthcoming.

"I did think it odd that the letter mentions a sick boy," Mrs. Clark said.

"Why is that?" Eloise asked.

"Because of my nephew. He has an incurable brain tumor." She gazed at Eloise, concern in her eyes. "How could the person who wrote this letter know that?"

"Perhaps it was written by someone you know."

"Who used my nephew to pretend to be me? That is a lowly thing to do. A lowly thing."

"I agree with you. It's one reason we want to find out who did this." Guilt tugged at Eloise for the little white lie. She'd glossed over the sentence about the sick boy, supposing it to be a reference to another damaged ship. But Phillip had warned her that they were not there to provide information—only to get it. Mrs. Clark couldn't know that the letter may be jargon code written by a traitor.

"I suppose that's why it was typed instead of written out." Mrs. Clark studied the handwritten signature at the end of the letter. "It looks like my writing, but I swear to you it's not. I never signed this. And if I'd written it, I would have written the whole thing. I don't know how to type and don't see any need to learn. Not at my age. That's more for the younger gals."

Her sharp eyes seemed to be appraising Eloise. "It's amazing what a young woman can do these days. Taking the place of the men, they are. Stepping up and doing a man's work. It's not how it was when I was kicking up my heels and going out on the town with Mr. Clark during our courting time. Such peaceful days they were. A woman could teach school or be a nurse, but there weren't many other options. Besides, those typewriters seem like such noisy machines, don't they?"

"Yes, they are," Eloise said, secretly amused by the older woman's assessment mingled with memories of her younger days and how she meandered from one topic to another and back again.

"Whoever wrote this seems to know a great deal about dolls," Eloise continued. "Are you a collector?"

Mrs. Clark actually blushed. "I have a few. Not in this room, mind you. Mr. Clark wasn't such a fan of my hobby. He always said he couldn't abide all those eyes upon him." She relaxed in her chair, smiling to herself as if lost in the past. "As if any of those dolls were watching him. He had quite the imagination, Mr. Clark did.

But he didn't really mind me keeping them. You should see the shelves he made. He was quite the craftsman, I tell you."

"Could we?" Phillip asked. "See his shelves, I mean."

"I don't see why not." Mrs. Clark returned the note to him as she stood. "They're in the spare room. Now it wasn't a spare room when all the children were still at home. But once we had it as a spare, well, then, it didn't need to be empty, did it? Come with me."

She led them down a short corridor and into a small bedroom. Custom-built shelves lined two walls, and a large bow-front cabinet with glass doors dominated another one. Multiple dolls were artistically displayed on the shelves and behind the cabinet doors.

Eloise hardly knew where to look first. The beautiful costumes, made of a variety of fabrics and adorned with ribbons, lace, feathers, and buttons, took her breath away. She glanced toward Phillip and stifled a laugh at the horrified expression on his face.

He scanned the shelves. "Are any of these Irish dolls?"

"I have this one." She pointed to a porcelain doll wearing an emerald-green silk dress. A matching cloche with black and silver feathers perched on top of her red curls, which were tied with a tartan ribbon. "Isn't she lovely?"

"She's beautiful," Eloise agreed. "I don't think she's one of the dolls mentioned in the letter though."

"Those dolls are puzzling." Mrs. Clark tilted her head. "A fisherman, a woman with wood on her back. A little boy. Are they supposed to be a set of some kind?"

"We hoped you could tell us."

"I've never heard anything of the like." Mrs. Clark pointed at a barrister's bookcase nestled between two windows that contained a row of books and stacks of magazines. "I read those from cover to cover as soon as they arrived, but I don't recall reading anything about three Irish dolls like those talked about in that letter. They are a mystery, and I am sorry not to be able to help the FBI."

"Please don't apologize." Eloise rested her hand on the woman's arm. "You've been a tremendous help. And your dolls are absolutely beautiful."

"They do bring me joy. Especially now that Mr. Clark is gone. Though I'm a member of the Springfield Art Circle, and that does keep me busy—attending the art shows and the exhibits that come around from time to time."

"If you ladies don't mind," Phillip said, "I'm going to step outside for a few minutes."

"Are you wanting a cigarette? There's no need to go outside for that. The dolls and I don't mind a little tobacco smoke. It's one of those things I miss now that Mr. Clark has departed."

"Please accept my sympathies," Phillip said. "But, no, I'm not going out to smoke. Just thought I'd leave you ladies to talk about"—he waved his finger around the room—"all of this. I'm sure Eloise would like to know more about your collection." He gave her a pointed look. His unspoken message couldn't have been clearer.

"Oh, yes." She gestured toward a shelf of porcelain dolls wearing elaborate wedding dresses. "These must be very special."

"Among my favorites." Mrs. Clark led Eloise toward the shelf.

Eloise glanced at Phillip over her shoulder. He gave her a nod and left the room. His approval buoyed her confidence, but uneasiness overshadowed those good feelings. While she distracted Mrs. Clark, who seemed to be innocent of any wrongdoing, Phillip would be scouring her home for any evidence that she was lying to them.

When Eloise had role-played distractions with her tradecraft instructor, it had all seemed like a fun game. The reality, especially with someone as unassuming and down-to-earth as Barbara Clark, seemed unnecessarily deceptive.

Maybe Eloise should have stayed in the code room where each puzzling message had a definite solution. Where each number or letter corresponded to another specific number or letter. As difficult as it could be—as it often was—to decode an encrypted message, looking beyond a person's words and demeanor to see the truth in their hearts was infinitely harder.

Eloise believed Barbara Clark to be a typical Midwestern housewife. But what if she were part of a treasonous plot? Impossible. If so, she wouldn't have turned the suspicious letter in to the post office. That action alone proved her innocence.

Didn't it?

CHAPTER TWELVE

Though he'd feigned indifference, Phillip couldn't get away from all those staring dolls' eyes fast enough. They gave him the creeps, as if they stared into the depths of his soul. Even though he knew that wasn't possible, he understood why Mr. Clark hadn't wanted his wife's collection spilling into other rooms in the house.

All four of his sisters had their favorite dolls, and he had never minded them. But then again, they'd been played and slept with, loved and cradled and dragged and tripped over. They were nothing like these costumed creatures whose only purpose was to . . . what? He didn't even know.

Apparently, Richard had been wise to send Eloise along with him. Not that Phillip was ready to tell his uncle that. He also had to admit she'd been a welcome companion on the long train trip from Washington, DC, to Dayton. Not overly talkative. Congenial. Excited about traveling across the country.

The tickets were in the names of their false identities, and the brother-sister cover story worked out great. No one seemed overly interested in them, and they mostly kept to themselves. They ate their meals in the dining car with an Amish couple who weren't interested in conversing with the *Englisch*.

When they first entered Mrs. Clark's home, Phillip had surreptitiously scanned the room, which was crowded with upholstered chairs and wooden tables with shelves but no drawers. A rolltop desk tucked in a corner was the only place in this room that might hide incriminating evidence.

He quickly searched through its cubbyholes and drawers but found little of interest. Mrs. Clark's checkbook register didn't reveal anything out of the ordinary. Her savings account had a more-than-respectable balance but not enough to arouse suspicion. He found a ledger that detailed transactions involving her doll collection—ones that she'd bought and sold over several years. The same drawer where he'd found the ledger also contained a folder with legal documents. Birth certificates for Barbara and her husband. The deed to her home, which was hers free and clear. The title to her car, a 1935 Studebaker.

There was nothing to indicate what Mr. Clark had done for a living, though he'd apparently made good money. True, the house was a modest one, but it was well-maintained and the furniture, even though there was too much of it in Phillip's opinion, was of fine quality. He needed to ask Mrs. Clark about her husband and pray she didn't fall apart on him. Widows seemed to have a habit of tearing up whenever they talked about their dearly departed. Even the ones who didn't seem to like their husbands very much when they were alive seemed to become upset when the subject was broached. At least that's what he'd noticed growing up and as an agent.

He wandered into the kitchen. The aroma of baking pies made his stomach rumble. Maybe he should have accepted Mrs. Clark's offer of those breakfast muffins. Except for a mixing bowl and a few other items near the sink, the kitchen was as immaculate as the rest of the house. Four chairs surrounded a round oak table covered with a cheery floral cloth. He opened a few drawers and cabinets but found only what he'd expect to find in a kitchen.

The window over the sink provided a view into the backyard. A tool shed stood in a rear corner. To one side, a victory garden boasted rows of sweet corn and vining tomatoes. He also recognized green beans, cabbage, cucumbers, and squash.

Hearing voices coming his way, Phillip eased out the back door, closing it softly behind him, and jogged around to the front. Hands tucked in his pockets, he leaned against the fender of the borrowed car and whistled a tune. Mrs. Clark would never know he hadn't been here the entire time patiently waiting for Eloise to join him.

He straightened as both women emerged from

the house. Eloise carried a small cardboard box. "Mrs. Clark wants to help our investigation in any way she can. These are the letters she's received from other doll collectors. Maybe there will be something to help us." Her tone sounded hopeful, as if she couldn't wait to dig into the correspondence.

"That's very kind of you," he said to Mrs. Clark as he took the box from Eloise. "On behalf of the FBI, let me thank you for your cooperation and your loyalty to your country."

"Who else would I be loyal to?" she replied. "Two of my sons and a son-in-law are overseas, though no one can tell me where."

"I'll pray for your family," Eloise said. "Thank you again. For everything." She headed for the car but paused when Phillip didn't join her.

"I've been admiring your home," he said. "Nice place. The kind of place I'd like to own someday."

"Yes, well, it's been my home since Mr. Clark carried me over the threshold. Seems like only yesterday we were that young and foolish. Time has a way of passing by when you're not paying any attention."

"That's true." Phillip took a long, admiring look at the house. "What kind of work was Mr. Clark in, if you don't mind me asking?"

"Insurance sales. Unlike so many others, we made it through what they're calling the Great

Depression without too much harm. What a time that was."

"We should probably go now," Eloise said. "Thanks again, Mrs. Clark."

"Before we do," Phillip said, "I'd like to express my condolences for your loss, Mrs. Clark."

"What loss?"

Stunned by the question, Phillip narrowed his eyes. "Of your husband."

"I didn't lose my husband." Her voice hardened, and her face flushed.

"I . . . I'm sorry," Phillip stammered then glanced at Eloise, though he couldn't say why. For support? For help? He was certain Mrs. Clark had referred to her husband in the past tense more than once. "I got the impression . . . I mean, for some reason . . . I thought you were a widow."

"He's gone to Virginia, though no one knows what got that notion into his head, and no one cares either. I hear from him now and again. But I didn't *lose* him." She crossed her arms. "You might say he lost me when he came home one too many times smelling of the drink. We all make our choices. He made his and I made mine."

Phillip had no idea how to respond. He'd certainly stuck his foot in his mouth, but how did he get it out?

Eloise stepped around him and touched Mrs. Clark's arm. "You've been a great help to us today. I'll do everything I can to be sure your

100

letters are safely returned to you. Goodbye now."

"Thank you for that assurance, honey. Now you take care of yourself." Mrs. Clark shifted her gaze to Phillip, and the smile she'd given Eloise turned into a frown.

Eloise tugged on his sleeve, and he followed her to the car with a backward glance. Mrs. Clark glared after him.

"I should apologize," he said softly.

"We should go." Eloise tugged on his sleeve again.

As he opened her car door, she waved to Mrs. Clark. "Goodbye. Take care."

Mrs. Clark returned the wave. "You too."

Phillip half-raised his hand, but Mrs. Clark turned on her heel and marched back into her house. Eloise tilted her head as she slid into the seat, but he definitely heard a giggle. He handed her the box of envelopes and closed the car door. As he rounded the car to the driver's side, he sensed he had totally lost control of this situation, but he wasn't sure how. Anyone hearing Mrs. Clark talk about her husband would have made the same assumption he did, wouldn't they?

He eyed Eloise as he slid behind the steering wheel, but she was engrossed with the contents of the cardboard box. More accurately, she was pretending to be engrossed with the contents while her shoulders shook with silent laughter.

He cranked the ignition and backed out of the

driveway. "Enough," he finally said. "Just tell me what happened when you were alone with the kindly Mrs. Clark."

"She took a shine to me." Eloise's radiant expression showed she was pleased with herself. As she should be, considering she'd given him time to search through at least a couple of rooms. It was impossible to search the other bedrooms with Mrs. Clark there, but he doubted he'd have found anything incriminating even if he had. Eloise had also managed to get the letters. The odds were against finding anything useful in them, but they couldn't afford to ignore any possible leads, no matter how slim.

"Bonded over creepy dolls, did you?" he teased.

"More like over men."

Phillip gave her a sideways glance. Her eyes still shone with humor. "So, you knew about the husband," he said. "You couldn't have given me a signal? A sign? Something?"

"I tried to get you to leave, but you insisted on being a gentleman."

"That doesn't usually get me into trouble."

"Nor should it. I think it was admirable of you to offer your condolences."

"Be honest. Didn't you think she was a widow from the way she was talking?"

"I did. Luckily, she told me about Mr. Clark's exploits before I made the same mistake you did." She paused, apparently for dramatic effect. "He's a moonshiner."

"You're kidding me."

"I am absolutely not."

"So that's where she gets her money. She's got quite a bit socked away in a savings account."

"She refuses to take his 'ill-gotten gains,' as she called them. She told me her husband was a respectable businessman who managed to keep his head above water for a couple of years after the stock market crashed. But seeing what had happened to his friends and colleagues changed him. So many of them were ruined through no fault of their own. Eventually, he decided to give up the conventions of society and make his own way." Eloise lowered her voice to a conspiratorial whisper. "And he always did love to drink."

"What a story." Though not much could surprise him. Any agent who'd been in fieldwork for any length of time soon learned not to make assumptions about anyone—a lesson Phillip had temporarily forgotten. He maneuvered onto a main highway and headed west.

"Aren't we going back to the train station?"

"We're going to the Indianapolis FBI office to drop off those letters."

"But I want to read them."

"We'll both read them. Then we'll send them to Richard for analysis."

"What kind of analysis?"

"We've got experts who can tell if any of the letters were typed on the same typewriter as the Clark letter. If we find the typewriter itself, then that gives us evidence against the traitor."

"How do they do that?"

"Not my area of expertise. It has something to do with the individual letters, how they hit the paper, that kind of thing. Amazing how accurate they can be though." He grunted as he slowed to take a curve. "Not the kind of work I'd want to do, but I'm glad somebody does."

"I'm not sure it's much different than my job. Staring at messages. Trying to find the patterns in what looks like a random combination of letters and numbers."

Another job Phillip was glad he didn't have to perform. He couldn't imagine being stuck in an office all day every day. He'd go stark raving mad within a week. After being on the road, conducting interviews, and tracking down a traitor, Eloise might feel the same. That thought led him back to something she'd said earlier.

"What men?" he asked. From the corner of his eye, he noted her perplexed expression. "You and Mrs. Clark bonded over men. Plural. Her husband and who else?" It wasn't until the question was out of his mouth that he realized how intrusive it sounded. They had talked about various topics while on the train, but both had steered clear of anything too personal. Not even their families.

"Stuck my foot in my mouth again, didn't I? Twice in less than an hour. Must be a record."

"She asked why I wasn't married." Dots of pink highlighted Eloise's cheeks. Phillip realized he wanted to know the answer to that question too, but he didn't dare ask it. Instead, he stayed silent, hoping she'd fill in the silence with an explanation. Did she have a beau who'd gone overseas? Someone who had asked her to wait for his return? Or had his leaving driven them apart? She was too attractive not to have caught some man's attention.

What did you tell her? Phillip wanted to shout out the question. Seconds passed and she said nothing. That nothing seemed to speak volumes, but Phillip couldn't decipher the message. He gave her another sideways glance. She stared out the windshield, seemingly deep in thought, slightly turned so he could only see her profile.

Her mood had turned pensive with the change in the conversation. There was something vulnerable in her expression, as if she were no longer inhabiting the same world he did but was caught in the past. The softness of her jaw, the uneasy set of her shoulders, reminded him of Nancy. How often had he caught her pining for a love that couldn't be? Who was the man, if such a man existed, who had hold of Eloise in much the same way?

A strange feeling irked its way from his gut to

his heart. Jealousy? No, it couldn't be. Maybe an odd kind of protectiveness. Similar to how he felt for his sisters when their hearts were bruised.

Except the feeling went beyond that—he couldn't hide from that truth no matter how much he wanted to. And yet he didn't want to acknowledge it either. He couldn't. The mission was too important to give in to any silly romantic impulses. They were brother and sister, at least as far as the mission was concerned. They were themselves only when conducting their interviews.

He had to regard her as a sister. This minute, today, and always. He was too much of a professional to do anything else.

CHAPTER THIRTEEN

The Doll Woman shook her head at the *New York Times*'s bold headline announcing the military tribunal's sentencing of the German saboteurs who had been captured by the FBI. She had no sympathy for the condemned men. Obviously, they were incompetent fools, or they would not have been caught.

Who cared about the Germans anyway? Despite the fact that both her parents were of German descent, she certainly did not. She considered it her good fortune that Otto and Elizabeth Blucher had moved from eastern states to settle in Sacramento before their children were born. Her childhood, and that of her younger brother, was as sunny as the weather.

That fortune changed for the worse when Elizabeth succumbed to tuberculosis less than a year after the Doll Woman received her Bachelor of Arts degree from the Farm, the colloquial name for Leland Stanford Junior University. A brief four years later, she was working for a San Francisco bank and planning her first wedding when Otto died in a tragic accident. He'd been crushed beneath the wheel of a car.

That first brief marriage ended in divorce, as did her second—also fortunate events. Her third marriage to the owner of a produce commodity brokerage company, one that catered to Japanese clients in California's Imperial Valley, allowed her to step into a world she'd idolized her entire life.

In the years preceding the war, she'd cultivated deep relationships within the Japanese-American Society. At social gatherings attended by important government officials and dignitaries, she dressed in authentic Japanese attire. Oh, how she adored wearing the traditional costumes while Japanese musical recordings played in the background. Dressing her small frame in the gorgeous silks and vibrant colors fed her soul like nothing else in the world. She'd stand before the full-length mirror, turning this way and that, to ensure perfection. Her husband, Lee, often teased that she became his own personal doll in her silk costumes.

The Pearl Harbor attack that shocked and horrified her neighbors had not come as a surprise to her. Instead, she'd been taken aback—and honored—that her Japanese friends asked for her assistance in finding out the extent of the damage to the US Navy beyond what was being reported in the newspapers and on the radio.

Those days of visiting dignitaries at the Japanese consulate and entertaining highly ranked government officials had ended abruptly as Americans unfairly blamed innocent people for what their emperor had chosen to do—what he had a right to do to protect his nation's interests. Why could no one see this as clearly as she did?

The Doll Woman tossed the hateful newspaper on a side table in the bedroom of her Madison Avenue apartment. War or no war, and despite Lee's recent death, she planned to attend this evening's private dinner at the Nippon Club. Her dear friend, Kaname Wakasugi, the Japanese consul general, was rumored to be attending. It might be her last chance to spend time with him before he returned to Tokyo. If only she could persuade him to allow her to accompany him. What a wonderful adventure that would be.

She perched on her bed and stared at the painting hanging above the fireplace. The landscape, depicting a Japanese home with cherry trees and koi ponds in the walled garden, had been a gift from a Japanese naval attaché she'd befriended when she became a member of the Japanese Institute of New York. He had already been expelled from the United States; but before his departure, he'd asked the Doll Woman for a favor—one she had not hesitated to oblige.

Passing along information about the navy's ships and shipyards proved her loyalty, and she had no doubt she'd be handsomely rewarded beyond the money she'd already received. She closed her eyes and imagined the home in the landscape as her own. What days of tranquility and peace! She could still own a doll shop, of course, if she wanted; though perhaps she would set aside all thoughts of business and commerce to focus instead on throwing lavish parties for the elite of Japanese society. She might even set up a kind of salon similar to those New York gatherings where sophisticates discussed the issues of the day and looked down their noses at those too pedestrian to accept their liberal points of view.

What a tremendous life that would be. And it might soon be hers.

She returned to the apartment's kitchen, where her typewriter, a portable Underwood, rested on the table. She took a seat, rolled a sheet of paper into the machine, then consulted the guidebook her handlers had provided. Apparently, the code they'd created was successful. She'd already sent out several letters using the names and return addresses of a few of her clients. Though she'd at first been nervous that the scheme wouldn't work, months had passed since her first batch of letters were mailed, and the consequences had been nil. She no longer had any fear that the letters could be traced back to her. Señora Ines de Molinali, if she even existed, had undoubtedly received her updates and passed them along to those who could benefit from their contents.

The Doll Woman's deception remained undetected, and she could sleep at night knowing she was doing her part to bring this war to a quick end. She was doing so by helping those considered as the enemy by most of the country's population.

Pshaw!

The Doll Woman knew better. Someday, in the far future, perhaps her contribution would become common knowledge. She'd be remembered as a heroine. Books would be written about her. Her fame would live long after she passed from this earth.

A satisfied smile stretched across her red-painted lips. Such a legacy. And it had been given to her.

CHAPTER FOURTEEN

Eloise read the last letter from the box Mrs. Clark had given her and handed it to Phillip. They had rented two adjoining rooms at a roadside motel on the eastern outskirts of Indianapolis, registering at the front desk as the siblings they weren't. Now they were seated across from each other at the tiny round table in Eloise's sparsely furnished room.

As she opened each letter, Eloise listed the name and address of the sender, the date of the letter, and the postmark information in her steno pad. Mrs. Clark had kept the letters in chronological order, and that's the way Eloise insisted on reading them. Phillip had disagreed, preferring to delve immediately into the envelopes postmarked from New York since the letter supposedly written by Barbara Clark had been postmarked from there.

"Reading them chronologically may show connections we'll miss if we read them willy-nilly," she'd insisted. He'd laughed at her for saying "willy-nilly," but to her surprise he conceded her point with a flippant, "You're the code breaker."

She hoped he'd agreed because he respected her expertise. But what if he only agreed because he wanted her to fail? She tried to reason away scles. "So, no. It wasn't a waste of time."

But none of the letters sounded suspicious.
ppose one of them, maybe more than one,
ld include jargon code." Her voice faded
y. What if she had missed something? She'd
er forgive herself if the answers were in the
and she'd overlooked them.

Nothing stood out to you, though? Right?"

Nothing." She grabbed the box and removed
one with the earliest date. "I'll read them
in. Just to be sure."

You don't need to do that."

Yes, I do." She unfolded the lined sheets
orated with a floral border.

hillip reached across the table and placed
hand on her arm. "Let's go to supper first.
netimes it helps to take a break. Give yourself
e distance from the letters so you can come
k to them with a fresh outlook."

'm not hungry."

am." He pushed away from the table and
tched as he stood, extending first one arm
then the other. "You have ten minutes to get
ly. Hurry up or I'll leave without you." He
k the box and the letter. When he reached the
n door, he glanced back. "I mean it, Sis."

efore she could reply, he shut the adjoining
r behind him. But the closed door didn't
vent her from hearing his amused chuckle.

er stomach made a rumbling noise, forcing

that notion before it took root. Afte
failures on her part affected him too.
mission.

His plan wasn't a bad one. If one o
York letters provided information the
there would be no need to read all the
that notion bothered her even more tha
them out of order. Unread letters
incomplete task. She *needed* to read
even if the first letter gave them incon
proof of the traitor's identity, before
was handed over to the FBI field offic
morning.

As Phillip scanned the last letter, Eloi
down the list she'd created. The letters
her an important introduction into the
doll collectors. The women discusse
dolls they'd bought and sold, gossi
prominent members of the avocation, a
personal information. But none of the le
any indication of being anything other
they seemed to be—correspondence
women who enjoyed the same hobby.

Phillip tucked the last letter into its
and returned it to the box.

"Was that a waste of time?" Eloise as
"Did you learn anything about collecti
"Quite a lot, actually. Did you?"
"More than I ever wanted to know
rubbed the back of his neck as if to

that notion before it took root. After all, any failures on her part affected him too. And their mission.

His plan wasn't a bad one. If one of the New York letters provided information they needed, there would be no need to read all the rest. But that notion bothered her even more than reading them out of order. Unread letters meant an incomplete task. She *needed* to read them all, even if the first letter gave them incontrovertible proof of the traitor's identity, before the box was handed over to the FBI field office the next morning.

As Phillip scanned the last letter, Eloise glanced down the list she'd created. The letters had given her an important introduction into the world of doll collectors. The women discussed specific dolls they'd bought and sold, gossiped about prominent members of the avocation, and shared personal information. But none of the letters gave any indication of being anything other than what they seemed to be—correspondence between women who enjoyed the same hobby.

Phillip tucked the last letter into its envelope and returned it to the box.

"Was that a waste of time?" Eloise asked.

"Did you learn anything about collecting dolls?"

"Quite a lot, actually. Did you?"

"More than I ever wanted to know." Phillip rubbed the back of his neck as if to ease his muscles. "So, no. It wasn't a waste of time."

"But none of the letters sounded suspicious. I suppose one of them, maybe more than one, could include jargon code." Her voice faded away. What if she had missed something? She'd never forgive herself if the answers were in the box and she'd overlooked them.

"Nothing stood out to you, though? Right?"

"Nothing." She grabbed the box and removed the one with the earliest date. "I'll read them again. Just to be sure."

"You don't need to do that."

"Yes, I do." She unfolded the lined sheets decorated with a floral border.

Phillip reached across the table and placed his hand on her arm. "Let's go to supper first. Sometimes it helps to take a break. Give yourself some distance from the letters so you can come back to them with a fresh outlook."

"I'm not hungry."

"I am." He pushed away from the table and stretched as he stood, extending first one arm and then the other. "You have ten minutes to get ready. Hurry up or I'll leave without you." He took the box and the letter. When he reached the open door, he glanced back. "I mean it, Sis."

Before she could reply, he shut the adjoining door behind him. But the closed door didn't prevent her from hearing his amused chuckle.

Her stomach made a rumbling noise, forcing

her to admit her hunger. And she supposed he was right that it was a good idea to step away from the letters. When she read them again, she would be even more alert to any hint of a correspondent using a jargon code.

She brushed her hair and pinned her cloche hat at a jaunty angle. After applying a fresh coat of lipstick, she pulled on the jacket matching her skirt. When Phillip knocked on the adjoining door, she was ready for another entertaining evening with the man she once considered insufferable. She was learning he was anything but that.

Early the next morning, Phillip ushered Eloise into the FBI field office building in downtown Indianapolis. During the three-hour drive from Springfield yesterday, he'd called during a gas stop to let Special Agent in Charge Reed E. Vetterli know he'd be coming by. The person who answered the phone promised to relay the message. Hopefully, Vetterli would be there. Phillip didn't want to give the letters to anyone else, but if Vetterli wasn't around, he'd have no other choice.

He flashed his badge at the middle-aged woman staffing the receptionist's desk. He figured she was probably the same no-nonsense woman he'd talked to on the phone the day before.

"Agent Phillip Clayton." He gestured toward Eloise. "My associate, Eloise Marshall."

"I know who you are, Agent Clayton." She stood and extended a hand. "All of us have been following the Operation Pastorius case with great interest. To think that the Germans thought they could get away with such a scheme. You deserve the gratitude of all Americans for bringing them to justice."

Heat crept up Phillip's neck. He avoided glancing at Eloise, though he felt her eyes upon him. The mission had never been far from his mind—especially since the execution date was imminent—but he'd never brought it up. He'd been tempted to a couple of times, especially on the train ride from Washington, DC, and even yesterday on the drive from Springfield. During those long hours of inactivity, his mind tended to brood on his interview with Dasch, the capture of the other men, and the testimony he'd given before the tribunal.

But how could he explain to a stranger the mixed feelings he'd had about the sentencing? If he had a mission to blow up a munitions factory in Germany, he'd do it and be hailed a hero here at home. Should a man lose his life for serving his country? In war, the easy answer was yes. The nationwide publicity could dissuade other secret agents from carrying out sabotage.

And yet . . . this was a man's life. A man created in the image of God.

The receptionist still smiled at him, but the

tilt of her head and the sharp look in her eyes indicated she was studying him. Out of politeness, he shook her hand. "I can't claim all the credit," he said with a forced laugh. "Agents from different field offices worked together to get the job done. Thankfully, we apprehended the saboteurs before they could do any damage."

"Modest." The woman turned her gaze to Eloise. "The best agents always are."

Phillip awkwardly cleared his throat before Eloise could respond. "I left a message for Reed Vetterli," he said. "Is he here?"

"He's expecting you." She returned to her seat and picked up her phone. "I'll let him know you've arrived." While she used the phone's intercom system to contact Vetterli, Phillip pulled Eloise away from the desk.

"I didn't know I was working with a hero," Eloise whispered.

Phillip scoffed. "I'm no hero. One of the saboteurs turned himself in. If he hadn't . . ." There was no need to finish the sentence. Eloise was a bright girl. She could imagine the carnage that might have occurred.

"I didn't read that little detail in any of the papers."

"Of course not." Phillip kept his voice low. "A bit of a black eye for the Bureau if people knew we hadn't uncovered the operation on our own."

Eloise's eyes narrowed as she stared at him.

Her lips were pressed together, and her intensity heightened his internal antennae.

"What is it?" he asked.

"You're not a hero."

He frowned, and her lips turned up into a gentle smile.

She leaned toward him. "But you are heroic."

He stared at her, not sure how to respond, but her attention was now focused on the portrait of E. L. Osborne, the first special agent in charge when the Indianapolis field office opened in the twenties. Phillip sensed Eloise knew exactly what she was doing—knocking him down then picking him up again. And now feigning disinterest. Exactly like something his youngest sister, Janie, would do.

"Agent Clayton?" the receptionist called for him. "Special Agent in Charge Vetterli will see you now. He's waiting for you in his office."

Grateful for the distraction, Phillip tugged on Eloise's sleeve. "Let's go." He led the way down a long corridor to Vetterli's suite. A secretary greeted them then ushered them into the inner office.

Vetterli stood behind his desk. "Phillip. How good to see you again. Come in, come in." His smile widened at the sight of Eloise. "Who's your companion?"

Phillip made the introductions, and he and Eloise took seats opposite Vetterli.

118

"Good news about those German saboteurs," Vetterli said. "I'm a trifle miffed none of them made their way to Indianapolis. It would have been a pleasure to participate in the hunt."

Phillip puzzled over what to say. *Better luck next time?* God help them, there would never be a next time.

"Here's your opportunity to help on a different matter," he said. "We suspect someone is sending information about the damage done to our ships at Pearl Harbor to either the Germans or the Japanese."

"Do tell." Vetterli leaned forward with interest. "What prompted this?"

"A couple of letters that appear to be written in what's known as jargon code." Phillip handed copies of the letters supposedly written by Barbara Clark and Dorothy Walker to Vetterli. "Eloise is a trained code breaker with the US Navy. She believes certain words in the letter refer to specific ships."

"Is that so?" Vetterli scanned the two letters. "Which words?"

Phillip turned to Eloise. "You're the expert."

For the next several minutes, Eloise explained to Vetterli about the letters and her possible explanations. Then Phillip briefed him on their visit to Barbara Clark's home.

"She gave us these letters." Phillip placed the box on Vetterli's desk. "We read them yesterday, and they seem innocent enough, but with the stakes this high, we can't afford to leave any stone unturned."

"What do you need from me?"

"First of all, copies of the originals that Eloise and I can take with us."

"And second?"

"The originals shipped to headquarters for analysis. Hopefully, the geniuses in forensics will find something useful."

"I'll select the courier myself," Vetterli promised.

"That'd be great," Phillip replied. "The package needs to be given to Richard Whitmer. No one else."

"Of course." Vetterli called in his secretary and gave her instructions to make duplicates of the letters. Once she'd left, he turned again to Phillip and Eloise. "You're obviously not returning to DC. May I ask where you're headed next?"

"Mrs. Walker lives in Spokane," Eloise said. "We're going there to interview her."

Vetterli leaned back in his seat. "That's a long trip."

"Tell me about it." Phillip propped his ankle on his opposite knee. "You must have a train schedule around here. Any tips on which route to take to the northwest corner of the country?"

"I do. But how would you like to fly instead?"

Phillip widened his eyes. Had he heard Vetterli

correctly? "That would be . . ." Words momentarily failed him. "That would be terrific."

"No, it wouldn't." Eloise's defiant tone cut Phillip to the quick.

"You don't want to fly?" He was astounded.

"No."

That was it. Simple. No nonsense. *Finis.*

He could pull rank on her, giving her no choice. Or he could beg. He wasn't too proud to do that, not if it meant he could fly.

Vetterli tried to hide a smile as he shifted his gaze from Eloise to Phillip. "I happen to know that a military transport is leaving from our local training camp for Seattle in a couple of hours. Maybe I can pull a few strings to get you on board. It's up to you."

Phillip gazed at Eloise until she faced him. "I've never been on a plane before," she said.

"Neither have I." He put as much enthusiasm in his voice as he could muster, not that he had to try very hard. He didn't know when he'd last been this excited. "It will be an adventure. Something to tell your grandchildren."

"Unless the plane crashes and I die," she retorted.

"That won't happen," he insisted.

She turned to Vetterli, eyebrow arched.

"The pilots are highly trained," he said. "And it'll save you from spending days on the road."

"You'll see, Eloise." Phillip covered her hand

121

with his. "It'll be fun." If she didn't say yes soon, he'd drop to his knees in front of her. *Please say yes before I totally humiliate myself.*

She closed her eyes and shook her head no. Phillip's heart fell to his stomach. If only he could make her understand how important this was to him, but that would mean telling her about his broken dream of becoming a pilot, of the colorblindness that kept him from doing so.

"Yes."

It seemed to Phillip that she breathed the word instead of saying it. Or had he imagined what he wanted to hear?

His grip on her hand tightened. "Did you say yes?"

"Yes." She released a deep breath and pulled her hand away. "I said yes."

Phillip barely stopped himself from jumping to his feet and letting out a loud hurrah. His smile was so big that his cheeks hurt. He didn't care. He was going to fly.

CHAPTER FIFTEEN

Saying yes to the plane trip had proven to be a wise decision. The experience wasn't nearly as frightening as Eloise had expected it to be. At least not once she got over the initial shock of being among the clouds. She also was glad she'd said yes for Phillip's sake. The captain invited him to spend time in the cockpit. He couldn't stop talking about how much fun that had been. Still, she was glad to have both feet back on the ground.

Today they sat around Dorothy Walker's kitchen table. A petite woman with graying hair and round spectacles, she scanned the letter that the censors had forwarded to the FBI last February, six long months ago.

"I know nothing about this," she said, her voice wavering. "The signature is similar to mine, but this letter is not from me."

"We believe you," Eloise said soothingly. "We're not here to upset you, but we do have to ask a few questions."

"Of course. I understand." Mrs. Walker pointed at the next to the last paragraph. "Though this is true."

Eloise scanned the words. *I do hope you can read my typing, I am trying to learn to type so I can be able to type records for the Red Cross.*

"You're learning to type?" Eloise asked.

"It's a way for me to be of service. But I would never have said it like that. 'I can be able to type.'" She pushed the letter away. "That's atrocious grammar."

"Who knows about the typing lessons?"

"Just about everyone, I suppose. It's not a secret." Mrs. Walker crumbled the cookie on her plate into pieces. "I don't know why anyone would use my name for something like this. It makes me feel . . ." She shivered.

Eloise laid a comforting hand on the woman's thin arm. "I know this is difficult. But can you think of anyone, maybe someone who has a grudge against you for some reason, who might have done this?"

Mrs. Walker's lips formed a worried line. "I live a quiet life with a small circle of friends. We've known each other since we were young mothers together, and most of us attend the same church. I just can't see any of them writing a letter like this or being involved in something nefarious."

"Do your friends also collect dolls?" Phillip asked.

"Three or four of us do. The rest have other hobbies." She folded her hands in her lap, no doubt to stop their shaking. "Quilting. Knitting. Gardening. The usual things. Though we're all gardening now. Anything we can do to contribute."

124

They chatted a little longer, but Mrs. Walker could tell them nothing that was helpful. Eloise asked if she had correspondence with other doll collectors, but Mrs. Walker said no. She was too busy to write to anyone except family and faraway friends.

The next day, they made the long trip from Spokane back to the FBI's Seattle field office. Neither of them had much to say on the hours-long drive. It didn't seem like they were any closer to finding proof that Eloise's assessment of the jargon code was correct. She had no idea what they were supposed to do next. She'd been a failure when she longed to be a success. Not for her own glory but to ensure that, if there was a traitor, he was caught. To prevent any more information about the US Navy falling into the hands of their enemies, whether they be German or Japanese.

When they arrived at the field office, an agent informed them that Richard Whitmer, some bigwig from headquarters, had left a message for Phillip to return his call. The agent didn't seem to realize that Richard was Phillip's uncle, and Phillip didn't tell him. Perhaps that's the way he wanted it—to make it in the FBI on his own merit and not because of his uncle's position. Eloise admired him for that and for other things.

He treated her with respect despite her lack of investigative experience. She'd read the printed copies of what they were calling the Clark correspondence several times, especially the ones postmarked from New York, paying close attention to any unusual spellings or odd capitalizations. But nothing seemed to stand out. Nothing seemed off or strange. But Phillip never criticized her or made fun of her. He'd even read the letters once more, though he had no better luck than she did.

The agent directed Phillip to an office where he could make his call in private. Eloise hesitated, unsure whether she should join him.

"Stay here," he said, answering her unspoken question. "This won't take long."

She nodded agreement while swallowing her disappointment. They were supposed to be equal partners on this mission, so anything Richard had to say to Phillip about the case should be said to her too.

Phillip disappeared down a long corridor while Eloise stayed in the reception area. As she waited for his return, a freckle-faced man with a shock of red hair beneath his fedora and a slight limp came through the door. He gave Eloise a too-long glance before making his way to the front desk. She turned away, uncomfortable with the man's appraisal, then realized her response wasn't that of a trained operative. She straightened her shoulders and faced his direction. He was bent forward, hands on the desk, as he talked quietly to the thirty-something woman sitting near a bank of phones. From the expression on the woman's face, she was swatting away the man's attempt at flirting without any effort whatsoever.

Eloise swallowed a sigh. That was a gift she wished she had. Despite what she'd told Phillip about her ability to handle men, she often felt like she was to blame for a man's unwanted attentions and apologetic for any rebuffs she made. Even her brother had chastised her for being so foolish, but that hadn't affected her inability to get over her discomfort enough to take a different approach.

The woman said something and rolled her eyes. The man merely laughed then eyed Eloise again. She refused to look away but prayed Phillip would return soon. She didn't like the awkwardness of not knowing whether she should sit or stay standing or what she would say if the man made an unwelcome comment to her.

Thankfully, he didn't. Instead, he tipped his hat in her direction then headed down the same corridor that had swallowed up Phillip.

Eloise dropped into a chair where she could see both the front door and the corridor door. That's what Phillip would do. Line of sight on two entrances and, as a bonus, the receptionist's desk. Eloise picked up the front section of the local newspaper, which lay on a nearby table. None of the articles held her attention, and she found herself reading paragraphs twice without knowing what they said.

She flipped one page and then another. As she started to turn one more, a photograph near the lower corner caught her eye.

No! It couldn't be.

A sick feeling swirled in her stomach, and she fought the urge to vomit. With careful movements made more deliberate by her painstaking attention to detail, she folded the newspaper in half then in half again.

The photograph and accompanying article took up most of the quarter page. Hot tears stung Eloise's eyes. The corridor door opened, startling her, and two men walked through. Her sudden dread collapsed into relief that neither of them was Phillip. Without thinking, she gripped the newspaper and fled from the building.

Once outside, the humid heat beat upon her. The field office was located in the Vance Building where Third Avenue intersected Union Street. The nearby buildings, housing a variety of stores and offices, formed shadowed alleyways that trapped the damp ocean air between their stone and concrete walls. Eloise pushed against the heat, unaware of her path, only aware that she was moving, that she needed to keep moving because if she stopped, she'd have to think about the photo she'd seen, the headline she had read. The article itself—she'd been too shocked to read it. Only a few words had popped out at her. She stopped at the crosswalk in a robotic trance, then trudged on without a thought of where she was going or what she was doing.

When the sidewalk eventually ended, she turned the corner, suddenly aware that she had entered an area of tenements and fleabag hotels. A different kind of dread gripped her, and she turned on her heel to retrace her steps. She walked slower now and realized her cheeks were damp from tears she hadn't realized were falling.

Weary with emotion and weighed down by the relentless heat, she paused in the entryway of the first department store she came to and leaned against the brick wall. With the newspaper tucked beneath her arm, she pressed her fingers against her eyes. Surely this was a mistake. There *had* to be a mistake. Even as doubt crept in, she couldn't bring herself to look at the photograph again. Not yet.

Customers exited the store, and she turned away from their curious stares, crossing her arms around her body to give her the strength to stay on her feet. After they passed by, she entered the store.

The interior was cooler than the street but not by much. Eloise edged around the perimeter, avoiding eye contact with any of the salesclerks, until she found the elevators. After descending to the basement, she made her way to the ladies' room. A vanity stretched along one wall, and she lowered herself onto the stool. The person in the

129

mirror stared at her, eyes wide and shimmering with tears, cheeks smeared with mascara, her hat askew.

She looked a mess.

She was a mess.

The turmoil twisting her insides scared her with its vehemence, as if a monster had awakened within her and was determined to get out or to destroy her in the attempt. She'd experienced strong emotions before—and not that long ago—but this painful angst was something entirely different than the overwhelming grief that assailed her when Allan died.

Raw anger fed the monster along with a stabbing pain to her heart she hadn't thought possible to endure. She feared giving in to the monster, knowing it could devour her, but she wasn't sure she had the strength to fight it.

She plopped the newspaper on the counter, the photograph facedown so she didn't have to see it, then unpinned her hat. She carelessly dropped the pins onto the counter. One bounced to the floor. She reached for it, stretching her fingers toward it while balancing herself on the stool, then she overreached and fell—hard—to her knees. A small tear appeared in her nylon stocking.

No, no, no!

This last indignity was too much. She sat on the hard floor, arms wrapped around her shins, head on her knees, and rocked back and forth as hot tears flowed. The rhythmic movement somehow seemed to calm her monster even as all reason escaped her. She seemed to have no thoughts; instead, she was lost in a swirl of wordless emotion.

As her mind settled, her heart turned to a despairing prayer.

Why?

It was a question that must have been asked by anguished souls since the beginning of time. Wouldn't Eve had begged God for an explanation of why he'd placed the Tree in the Garden? And again when Abel was found murdered in a field or when Cain was marked by God?

"I don't understand, Lord." Eloise shook her head. "I will never understand."

The restroom door creaked open. Eloise grabbed at the pin and rose to her feet. The two women who entered glanced at her with questioning gazes then at each other.

"I'm fine," Eloise said before either of them could speak. Doing so gave her control of the conversation and, hopefully, would prevent her from experiencing the horror of falling apart in front of strangers. "I had startling news, that's all. I'm better now."

The older woman dug in her purse and pulled out a man's handkerchief. She handed it to Eloise with an apologetic smile. "I always carry one of my husband's handkerchiefs in my purse along with my dainty lace ones. Those little feminine squares aren't meant to soak up the kind of tears we find ourselves crying these days."

"Isn't that the truth?" the younger woman said. Tears glistened in her eyes, and she blinked them away. "It seems there's nothing for us to do but trust in God."

Eloise bit her lip as she accepted the oversized handkerchief. Trusting in God wasn't easy when a person's world was falling apart. But the woman was right. What else could she do? Throw away her faith entirely because life hadn't turned out the way she thought it should?

As tempting as that might be, she couldn't do it. Without her Heavenly Father beside her, she'd be lost in a slough of despondency without any hope. She might only be holding on to her faith by a thread, but that thread was strong. God wouldn't let her go, so the choice was hers—to hold on with all her might or to let her faith slip through her fingers.

She refused to let go.

The older woman led Eloise to a sink. "Wash your face now. We'll stay with you as long as you wish."

"Thank you." Eloise wanted to say more, to let these women know how much she appreciated their thoughtfulness. But she wasn't sure she could trust her voice. She took a deep breath and whispered again, "Thank you."

She splashed water on her face then did her best to finger-comb her short waves, limp from the humid heat, into a small bun at the nape of her neck. The older woman pinned her hat on her head for her.

"Are you all right now?" the younger woman asked.

"I think so." Eloise glanced at her watch, stunned to see how much time had passed. Hopefully, she'd be back in the lobby before Phillip finished his call with Richard. What would he do if he returned to the lobby and found her gone? For the first time, she realized she'd left her handbag behind.

"I need to go." She held out the handkerchief. "I'm sorry I made such a mess of it."

"You keep that," the older woman said. "I have plenty more."

"I'll never forget your kindness. Both of you." She glanced at the newspaper. She should walk away and leave it behind. Forget she'd ever seen it.

But that wasn't possible. Having seen the photo, she had to learn the truth about the man it depicted. With a heavy sigh, she tucked the newspaper beneath her arm and said goodbye to the strangers who'd shown her such kindness.

Strangers or angels?

Either way, they were a gift from God when she needed one most.

CHAPTER SIXTEEN

Phillip ended the call with his uncle then rested his elbows on his knees and hung his head. The executions were over. Six of the eight Germans who participated in Operation Pastorius had been electrocuted and buried in a potter's field. Only Dasch and Berger had been spared.

The men were enemies. Potential saboteurs. So why did their deaths bother him so much?

From the first time he talked to Dasch, a man willing to betray his own countrymen, Phillip had struggled with the ramifications of the investigation. Dasch was praised by some within the FBI for his courage. But that hadn't stopped a military tribunal from finding him guilty and giving him the same sentence as the others—death.

According to Uncle Richard, President Roosevelt commuted Dasch's sentence to thirty years in prison and Berger's sentence to life in prison.

Phillip didn't disagree with the president's decision. Dasch, and Berger too, deserved something for their refusal to go along with Germany's plan. But why had they agreed to be part of the plan in the first place? When had they decided to turn themselves in instead?

He knew the answer for Berger. When he

and Dasch had separated from the other two saboteurs, Dasch had given him an ultimatum—rat on me and I'll kill you. Berger made the wise choice to go along with Dasch, a decision that saved him from the electric chair.

Phillip had never experienced mixed feelings before about a criminal's conviction and sentencing. The line between right and wrong had always been clear in his mind, and he was a strong believer that those he'd brought to justice in previous missions had absolutely reaped what they had sown.

What made this operation different?

Maybe because war blurred the lines.

His thoughts caught a ride on the same merry-go-round they'd been on before—one that wouldn't let him jump off. If he had the chance to sneak into Germany and create havoc, he'd do it in a heartbeat. If he were caught, he would face death secure in the knowledge that he'd done what he could for his country. His life would be a small sacrifice to pay for a US victory.

Unlike Dasch, he'd never have betrayed those on the mission with him. He'd never have turned himself in to the authorities.

The question he couldn't resolve was whether he should respect Dasch for his patriotism to his adopted country or despise him as a traitor to his homeland and to those who trusted in him to carry out their assigned mission. Even though he'd met the man, interrogated him, investigated him—he still wasn't sure of an answer. Or if he had the right to judge.

They were buried in a potter's field, Richard had said. Like Judas Iscariot, the ultimate traitor, who hung himself after betraying the Son of God. An act foretold in the ancient texts of scripture. A betrayal that set other God-ordained events in motion leading to the crucifixion and resurrection. To grace for sinners.

Grace to a wretch like me.

Phillip rubbed his hands across his face as his emotions battled inside him. Maybe he should have stayed in DC. Maybe he should have attended the electrocutions. Or at least he should have visited Dasch one more time. Perhaps the German would have said something—Phillip had no idea what—to provide more insight into his motivations.

Where Phillip shouldn't be was here. In Seattle. Almost as far away from DC as a person could get. An overpaid, glorified chauffeur driving around a woman who in any other year would be teaching a class of giddy teenagers about triangles and theorems. Instead, she'd been elevated to civilian-agent status and sent around the country to talk to bored, silly women who were obsessed with dolls. A trip that so far hadn't gotten them anywhere.

Richard hadn't yet received the package, but

Phillip didn't have much hope that the Clark letters were going to provide any evidence that would be helpful.

As time went on, he found himself doubting that even the original letters meant anything. There was no proof that "Mr. Shaw" referred to a navy destroyer or that the dolls that were mentioned referred to specific kinds of ships. Only Eloise's guesses. And on that basis, Richard had sent the two of them on this giant wild-goose chase when bona fide saboteurs were being executed for their intentions.

Eloise.

He'd seen the confused hurt in her eyes when he'd told her to stay in the lobby. She must have wondered why she couldn't be with him when he called Richard. How could he tell her it was because he knew the call was about Operation Pastorius and that he would need time alone after the call to make sense of the senseless? To gather his thoughts and compose himself before he returned his focus to their current mission?

A fool's errand.

He stood as a niggling thought worked its way into his consciousness. What if his frustration with their current mission had more to do with his own unsettled mood than with the facts? It wasn't like him to be close-minded, an attitude that definitely didn't bode well for any agent.

His uncle had chosen him specifically for this

mission because he had trust in his judgment and because he trusted him to watch over Eloise.

He opened the door as a man with striking red hair and a limp emerged from another office. "Well, if it isn't Agent Clayton," he called out. "What are you doing on this side of the continent?"

"Checking out a rumor," Phillip said with a nonchalant shrug. Agent Bernard "Red" Eckers was the last person he'd expected to see here and somebody he'd rather not see again. "Last I heard, you were working out of Denver."

"You're behind the times then." Red slugged Phillip on the shoulder—hard enough to make a point but not hard enough to appear as anything other than a friendly gesture. Phillip refused to give him the satisfaction of wincing, and he resisted the almost primal urge to punch back. Typical Red. Hiding his hostility behind a not-so-friendly punch just like he hid his cutting remarks behind claims that his victims couldn't take a joke. "I did a stint in Phoenix before transferring here," he continued. "Never could get used to that dry desert air though."

"So, you traded it for rain." Likely story. Knowing Red, he'd been cast out for insubordination or he'd gotten in hot water over a woman. The first had prompted Red's move from DC headquarters to Philadelphia. The second sent him to St. Louis. Maybe it was a combination of the two that had sent him first to Denver then to Phoenix. Phillip didn't care enough to ask for details.

Bouncing troublesome agents from one field office to another wasn't his idea of leadership, but the Bureau didn't like to fire a man after investing time and money in his training. Instead, the higher-ups gave second and sometimes third and fourth chances, then tightened the leash on the unrepentant ones by chaining them to a desk. That allowed them to test the patience of their superiors but limited their interaction with the public.

"You get used to it," Red said with a smirk as he lit a cigarette. "The damp is a good excuse for adding a nip from the flask to a cup of hot coffee. But don't you go telling your uncle I said so."

"My lips are sealed." Phillip started past him, but Red blocked his way.

"You're a long way from home for a rumor. I wouldn't mind stepping away from the paper-work for a while. Perhaps I could give you a hand."

"Sorry, Red. I only stopped here to check in with headquarters."

"Another time then."

"Maybe." Phillip waited for Red to move, but he didn't seem to be in any hurry to get out of the way. "If you'll excuse me . . ."

"Do you know anything about that doll in the lobby?"

"What doll?" With the doll case on his mind, it took Phillip a moment to realize Red meant Eloise. His confusion turned to disgust. "Did you try anything with her?"

Red emitted a harsh laugh. "Don't worry, big guy. I said hello, but she ignored me. Tried to anyway."

Phillip had had enough. He pushed past Red and headed for the lobby. He wouldn't want someone like Red anywhere near one of his sisters, and he didn't want him near Eloise either. His pity party had kept him away from her for too long.

He hurried to the lobby, but Eloise wasn't there. Perhaps she'd gone to powder her nose, as the ladies always said. Where else would she have gone?

"She left," the receptionist said, as if answering Phillip's unspoken question.

"Excuse me?" Phillip walked to the desk.

"That gal who came in with you? She walked out. I think she was crying."

"Crying?" Phillip narrowed his eyes. "About what?"

"My guess is she read something in the newspaper that upset her."

He darted his eyes toward the table where sections of the newspaper were stacked in a neat pile. Her handbag was on the floor beside a nearby chair.

"Don't bother looking. She took the offending section with her."

He grabbed up the stack anyway. The *Seattle Times*. What could possibly have been in it that would upset Eloise? He flipped through the sections. Sports, comics. Entertainment, op-eds.

She took the local section, but why? He shifted his attention to the receptionist. "Did you see which way she went? Did she get a cab?"

"I have no idea. Sorry."

Sure you are.

Phillip rushed out of the building and looked up and down the street. Where would Eloise have gone? And why had she gone at all?

There was nothing for him to do but try to find her. And when he did, he'd give her a reprimand she wouldn't soon forget. The thought caught him short. Eloise wasn't one of his sisters. Even though they'd known each other only a short time, they'd spent much of that time together—on a train, in a car, on a plane. Eloise had a level head on her shoulders. She wouldn't have been recruited by the navy if she didn't. And she definitely wouldn't have been recruited by Uncle Richard. She might be a little naive, but she wasn't given to hysterics.

He looked around the streets and found what he was looking for—a newsstand. He bought a copy of the day's paper and scanned the local section. A story in this paper had upset Eloise—had more than upset her. He was determined to find out which one.

Nothing jumped out at him, so he started again, this time from the last page of the section. "Where is it?" he muttered. The section included stories on local politics, a new construction project, a feel-good story about whale sightings off the Pacific coast. Other stories too, but nothing that could possibly upset a young woman who until recently had never been west of the Mississippi.

His heart racing, he carelessly folded the section and tossed the rest of the paper away. His gut tightened as he scanned the street again. Where had she gone? And more important, why?

Pacing would get him nowhere. He needed to act. For the first time in a long time, he was unsure what to do, and the uncertainty frightened him.

Show me where to go, God. Lead me to her.

CHAPTER SEVENTEEN

Eloise walked out of the department store and gazed at the sky. The dark clouds rolled overhead, threatening a downpour at any second. She doubted she could get to the FBI office before the storm began. She didn't know if she should even try. Her behavior had been horribly unprofessional. But her emotions—in a rare moment—had completely overtaken her reason. Heat reddened her face. What would Phillip think of such ridiculous foolishness? He'd probably send her back to DC on the next eastbound train. Or worse, on a jolting, hot, unbearable bus that stopped at every other junction. She wouldn't be back to the capital for weeks.

She'd been gone too long to have any hope of him finding her in the lobby after his phone call. Even if she managed to get there before he knew she'd been gone, how would she explain her unkempt appearance? Especially if she got drenched on her way back.

Sometimes—not always but sometimes—she felt like he was disinterested in their mission, perhaps even that he felt it was beneath him to have been sent on an investigation like this one. Though she believed she had proven herself to be invaluable in interviewing both Mrs. Clark and Mrs. Walker, Phillip might have been able to elicit the same information from the women without her. And truth be told, they hadn't really learned anything new from Mrs. Walker.

Embarrassed and tense, Eloise trudged toward the FBI field office. She had no idea how many blocks she'd gone when she fled with the newspaper. While in that emotional state, she hadn't been aware of her surroundings. But now her feet ached, and each step in her dressy black pumps was torture. She tried to put the physical pain as well as the emotional pain out of her mind.

If Phillip did send her back to DC, perhaps Commander Jessup could be persuaded to let her return to her code-breaking desk. That's where she belonged. She should never have left the comfort of letters and numbers, patterns and puzzles.

At the crosswalk, she stopped, waiting for the signal to cross the side street.

"Eloise!"

Hearing her name, she looked around. Phillip waved to her from the driver's seat of the car they'd borrowed from the Seattle FBI. He pulled to the opposite curb then stepped out and jogged across the street toward her, her handbag tucked under his arm.

Her mind raced for some explanation she could give him. Anything that sounded plausible. Not even the truth made sense, but she couldn't tell him that anyway. Not yet. Maybe never.

When he reached her, he held her gaze until, unable to decipher what she saw in his eyes, she looked away.

"I brought your purse." His voice was gentle and not at all accusatory as he held out the bag. She clutched it to her chest.

"Thank you."

"Are you ready to be my sister again?"

That wasn't the question she'd expected him to ask. He smiled, and his features softened. In the depth of his eyes, she detected curiosity, but more than that, she found compassion.

"It's been a long day," she said as if the simple words explained everything when she knew—and she knew he knew—they explained nothing.

"For me too." He glanced at the darkening skies. "It's about to be a wet one."

As if to confirm his words, a gust of wind swept scraps of paper and other bits of trash along the street between the buildings. Phillip's suit jacket flapped open, and Eloise clapped her hand on her hat before it blew away.

"We'll get a couple of rooms somewhere," Phillip continued. "Maybe even splurge on a nice steak dinner this evening."

His unexpected kindness added to Eloise's emotional turmoil. It was as if he understood something about her that she didn't understand herself. She lowered her eyes and bit her lip.

"Or we could order room service," he suggested

with a teasing lilt in his voice. "Do you play gin rummy?"

Eloise couldn't help but smile at his attempt to cheer her up, especially when he'd said it had been a long day for him too. Maybe Richard had told him something about the case. Had she been wrong about the jargon code?

She met his gaze. "Bad news from your uncle?"

"I guess that depends on your point of view." He started to say something more, but at that moment, the skies opened with a loud rumble. "Let's go," he shouted over the din of the storm as he grabbed Eloise's hand. She bent her head against the onslaught of slanting raindrops while peering along the street to check for traffic. Together they raced toward the car and clambered inside. A streak of lightning lit up the sky.

Once she was inside Eloise leaned against the seat and looked sideways at Phillip. He removed his hat and water trickled down his face from his hair.

"I feel like a drowned rat," he said.

"You look like one too." Eloise couldn't help grinning, though her insides still felt like mush.

"Have you looked in the mirror lately?" he shot back, his eyes dancing.

She groaned. "Do I dare?"

"No reason not to. You look mighty fine to me."

From anyone else, the compliment might have sounded like a pick-up line. Somehow, Phillip's tone sounded reassuring, like something her brother might have said. If only Allan were with her right now. He'd know what to do about the article she'd seen.

She placed the soggy newspaper on her lap and sensed Phillip's eyes on her. He'd given her a choice: dinner out or room service. Which was the safer option? The one most likely to keep his curiosity at bay. The one least likely to encourage confidences that would later be regretted.

He cranked the ignition and drove around the block, past the field office, and toward the western horizon. About a hundred miles due west of the city, an ocean crashed against the continental shelf. She'd caught a glimpse of the magnificent and powerful Pacific from the plane as it circled the military airport located near the coast. The wide expanse of white-capped waves seemed to extend forever. It was an ocean that hid corpses of ships, of men, within its depths.

Phillip drove, his mood somber again, while quiet tears dampened Eloise's cheeks.

CHAPTER EIGHTEEN

The rain intensified as the day wore on. Phillip reserved a suite in a downtown hotel that busted his expense budget and probably wouldn't slip past the bookkeepers back in Washington. But he didn't care. They'd been staying in small roadside motels since the beginning of the trip. What was the harm in treating themselves a little? He'd deal with any fallout when he returned to headquarters.

The two bedrooms accessed a tiny sitting room with a square dining table and chairs, an upholstered sofa, and a freestanding radio cabinet. After changing into dry clothes, Phillip tried to see beyond the rain that fell in steady sheets in front of the two tall windows. But even the buildings right across the street were difficult to see.

He turned his attention to Eloise when she emerged from her room pressing strands of her damp hair between the folds of a thick towel. She wore a blue cardigan over a scoop-necked top, a shin-length dark skirt, and fuzzy slippers. Her eyes were still red from crying. He resisted the urge to pull her into his arms, a temptation he'd been struggling with since he found her on the street corner. Her vulnerability touched a deep place inside of him, one he hadn't known existed until he met her. One he wasn't ready to acknowledge now.

"I'm starving," Phillip said. "But I'm not sure even Captain Ahab would venture out into weather like this."

"He would if Moby Dick were swimming in the streets." Eloise perched on the arm of the sofa while systematically towel-drying sections of her hair. "He lost his life in pursuit of that whale."

"A foolish obsession."

"Most obsessions are."

Phillip studied her, but she lowered her eyes. Something in her voice caused him to suspect that she was no longer thinking of Ahab's pursuit of the white whale who'd had the temerity to take the sea captain's leg. Perhaps her thoughts were connected to the newspaper section she'd clung to until she disappeared into her room—the unknown reason for her sudden departure from the FBI field office.

His gut told him that asking her a direct question would be a mistake, one he wasn't willing to make. He turned around one of the wooden dining chairs and sat on it, his hands draped over the back.

"Uncle Richard asked about you," he said, keeping his tone casual. "He wanted to be sure I was treating you right."

A smile played on her lips, but she didn't fully commit to it. "What did you tell him?"

"That you haven't complained about sleeping on a lumpy motel bed or eating at a greasy spoon diner. At least not yet."

"What will he think of us staying in a place like this?" She swept her arm to encompass the suite. "It may not be the Ritz, but it's . . . clean. And comfortable."

Phillip swallowed his laugh. She'd been dismayed at the lack of housekeeping at the first motel where they'd stayed. But even then, she hadn't whined or nagged him about it. He'd been put off by the place himself, though he hadn't admitted it.

"Richard won't know we stayed here until it's too late," he said. "Besides, we may be here a couple of days because of the rain. We might as well be comfortable."

"We're not going back to DC?"

"Not until we hear from him again."

"What else did Richard have to say?"

The innocent-sounding question was filled to the brim with unspoken meaning. It assumed that the primary reason for Richard's call wasn't to inquire about their comfort or to give them instructions. If she'd asked if Richard said anything else, he could easily reply, "Not much," and the conversation would be over. The difference was a subtle yet effective questioning technique.

She must have been paying attention in her

interrogation class or she had good instincts. From the way she talked to the doll collectors, it was probably a combination of the two. He knew her well enough by now to know she wouldn't be dissuaded by an offhanded answer. Maybe honesty was the best approach.

"We talked about my last mission. Six of the German saboteurs were executed on Saturday."

Her eyes widened, and her hands, holding the towel, dropped to her lap. "Executed? Like in a firing squad?"

"The electric chair."

"Oh."

Phillip waited for her to ask more questions. They were there, unspoken, in her eyes. In the way her shoulders bent slightly toward him. But they didn't come.

"They were guilty," he said, as if he needed to justify the executions. "They were our enemies."

"But their deaths disturb you." Her gaze was direct, open. "Because you're a good man."

Her unexpected words stunned him. "Is that what you think of me?"

"It's what I *know* of you." She flicked the towel in front of her and stood. "I need to hang this up to dry. Didn't you say you were starving? I'm hungry too."

She disappeared into the bathroom before he could answer.

Her swift change of topic coming on the heels

of her unexpected compliment had him at a loss of what to say, what to do. A rare occurrence for him. He shook away the gloomy thoughts that hung too close for comfort. He wouldn't dwell on them any longer—at least not now. The lady was hungry and so was he.

He lifted the phone and dialed the front desk. "I'd like to order room service. What's the day's special?"

Eloise laid her cards on the table. "Gin."

"Again?" Phillip showed his hand. "Look how close I am."

"Close only counts in horseshoes," she said in a singsong voice as she added the points.

"Have you ever played horseshoes?"

"Can't say that I have. But I'm a champ at playing gin."

Phillip squinted his eyes as he gathered the cards to shuffle them. "The game isn't over yet, sweetheart."

Eloise laughed at his Humphrey Bogart impression. After yesterday's emotional turmoil, she'd tossed and turned throughout the night then slept late this morning. When she'd entered the living area, Phillip was stretched out on the couch, his arm over his eyes. Though she tried to be quiet, he must have heard her because he immediately sat up and greeted her. They braved the rain to eat an early lunch at a nearby diner and purchase a few items, including the playing cards, at a neighborhood grocery store.

Perry Como and other favorites crooned from the radio while they hummed along and pretended all was right in the world. It was a lie that allowed them to enjoy the rainy-day reprieve.

Eloise needed the pretense, and she sensed Phillip did too. The weight that had burdened him yesterday seemed lighter though they hadn't talked any more about the executions. She'd meant what she said—he was a good man. But the words had slipped out, and she'd had to cover her embarrassment by scurrying from the room.

She excused her lapse in professional propriety by admitting, at least to herself, that she'd been touched by how he'd treated her with such kindness. He hadn't poked and prodded for the reason she'd fled the field office. She probably would have fallen apart if he had. Instead, he treated her as her brother would have treated her, giving her the time and space she needed to recover from her emotional fallout.

Perhaps that explained the growing connection she felt for Phillip. It couldn't be a romantic feeling, but maybe it was something more than platonic. She desperately missed Allan, and Phillip was a substitute. That was all.

She wouldn't mind more days like this one. Playing cards with a good man on a rainy day. Though she knew what her mother would have to say about her being in a hotel room with a male companion. The front desk clerk and bellboy knew them as a brother and sister, but her mother wouldn't accept that as an excuse.

"Are you sleeping with your eyes open?" Phillip's voice cut into her thoughts. "It's your turn."

"Sorry." She drew a card and studied her hand. After a moment, she discarded a six of spades.

Phillip picked it up, and she frowned. "So . . . what has you so deep in thought?" He seemed to be choosing his words carefully, going for a casual tone while pretending to care more about the cards he was holding than their conversation. He might have been fishing for an explanation about her behavior yesterday. But she didn't mind. Not that she was ready to talk about that. Not yet.

"My mother."

Phillip raised his eyes to hers. "Your mother? Why?" A gleam appeared in his eyes. "Wait, don't tell me. She doesn't know where you are, does she?" Before Eloise could respond, he answered his own question. "Of course she doesn't. You signed an oath of secrecy. She doesn't know what you do for the navy, and she definitely doesn't know you've been transferred to the FBI."

"Or that I'm now your sister or that I'm on the West Coast instead of in the nation's capital." She drew a card after he discarded a three of diamonds. "She definitely would not approve."

"If it makes you feel any better, neither would mine."

"Does she know you're in the FBI?"

"Are you kidding? It's her biggest bragging right." He raised his voice an octave. " 'My son, the FBI agent, did this. My son, the FBI agent, did that. My son, the FBI agent, is involved in a secret investigation, but I'm not allowed to talk about it.' " His voice turned somber as he took his turn. "Not that she knows anything about our investigations until they're over. Usually not even then."

"She's proud of you." Eloise drew a five of hearts and studied her hand.

"I'm sure your mother would be proud of you too. Despite the sordid details of traveling with a single man," he teased.

"Let's promise never to tell each other's mothers about this trip."

"Good idea."

The phone rang, and Phillip excused himself to answer it. As soon as she realized he was talking to his uncle, Eloise laid her cards face down on the table to focus on the side of the conversation she could hear.

"Three more letters." He raised his eyebrows and mouthed *Wow!* to Eloise. "All addressed to Señora Molinali."

A pause then, "That's fantastic. I wish we could see them."

He finished with the call and returned to the table. "Uncle Richard is arranging for duplicates of the letters to be sent to the Portland field office. We'll pick them up there."

"Why Portland?"

"Two of the letters were supposedly written by the same woman, another doll collector, who lives there. The third came from someone in Colorado Springs."

"Will we be interviewing her too?"

"Sure will." He picked up his cards. "We're leaving for Portland in the morning. That gives me the rest of the day to win this gin rummy championship."

"That's what you think." Eloise turned her cards face up. "Gin."

CHAPTER NINETEEN

The Portland field office was located in a multistoried building that seemed to take up an entire city block. Eloise shook hands with F. A. Watts, the special agent in charge, as Phillip introduced them. After a few pleasantries, he directed them to a bare-bones office that contained a square table and a couple of chairs.

"No one will bother you here." He placed a thin folder on the table, letting his fingertips rest on top of it. "These are the documents from Mr. Whitmer. They make no sense to me, but I expect to be informed if there's something I should know about. I don't want any surprises in my own backyard."

Eloise itched to open the folder and read the letters inside. It wasn't her place to tell the agent that someone may have already given information to their enemies about the ships being repaired at the Puget Sound navy yard. The FBI now had five letters in their possession. But how many had slipped through the censors to the elusive Señora Molinali?

"We're investigating a matter of national security," Phillip said in response to Special Agent Watts's question. "All necessary resources will be utilized to ensure the country's safety."

"A noncommittal answer. I'd expect nothing else from Richard Whitmer's nephew." One corner of his mouth lifted in a reluctant smile as he removed his fingers from the folder. "But I meant what I said."

"I know, sir."

Agent Watts nodded and started to leave when Phillip stopped him. "I have to ask." His tone was apologetic. "Has anyone else seen these letters?"

"Directive from HQ was my eyes only." He directed a polite nod at Eloise before closing the door behind him.

"He didn't answer the question," Eloise said.

"Only because I didn't answer his." Phillip adjusted the chairs so they were sitting at an angle to one another. "But Richard trusts him, so I think we can too. Besides, to anyone who isn't a top-notch breaker of jargon codes, the letters are meaningless."

Eloise dug her steno pad and a pen from her handbag to hide the flush warming her cheeks at Phillip's teasing compliment. He opened the folder and spread out the pages. "Shall we get started?"

Eloise scanned the copies. "Look at this." Someone had written information taken from the envelope—the postmark and the return address—at the bottom of each page.

"That's Uncle Richard's handwriting." Phillip took the letter with the earliest date of the three and placed it between them. "This one was written last February allegedly by a Ruby Lankford who lives here in Portland. But the postmark is for Oakland, California."

Eloise made a grid on a fresh page in her notebook with separate columns for the letter's date, the individual's name, the return address, and the place of the postmark.

"Listen to this," Phillip continued. "She says her grandson will only stay in bed if he can 'play with his father's fishing nets while the little girl demands balloons.'"

"Fishing nets," Eloise repeated as her pulse fluttered with excitement. "Remember the 'old fisherman with a net over his back'?"

"You thought that meant an aircraft carrier."

"I still do. But I don't have any ideas about the balloons." She made a note on her pad.

Fishing net / old fisherman = aircraft carrier

Balloons = ??

Phillip continued reading from the letter.

"You know I have three old China head dolls from England. I do not like these dolls. However, my dear husband bought them for me. It will take this Doll hospital a few months before they will have them completely repaired, then will send. There is so much repair work to do, new parts needed as arms and legs . . . ."

"The doll hospital could refer to a repair facility," Eloise said. "I think she's saying that

159

these three ships won't be ready for warfare for a few more months."

"This letter was written in February," Phillip reminded her. "They're probably repaired by now."

They scanned the rest of the letter then turned to the next.

"May 20, 1942." Eloise wrote the date in her notebook. "Also supposedly written by Ruby Lankford."

"Read this section." Phillip pointed to a paragraph. Eloise read it aloud.

"I just secured a lovely Siamese Temple Dancer, it had been damaged, that is tore in the middle. But it is now repaired, and I like it very much. I could not get a mate for this Siam dancer, so I am redressing just a small ordinary doll into a second Siam doll."

"What do you make of that?" Phillip asked.

"Another ship that's been repaired, I guess. Perhaps there's a second ship just like it?" Eloise's stomach dropped. She wasn't being any help at all. Why couldn't the message have been a substitution code or a transposition code? Given time, she could figure out the patterns and the answer, but a jargon code could mean anything.

"Don't get down on yourself," Phillip said as if he'd read her mind. "Our primary goal is to find out who actually wrote these letters. Solving the jargon code might give us a hint, but we have other avenues too."

"I don't want to be a disappointment," Eloise admitted. She bit her lip, unsure of whether she should have admitted that to him. He was, after all, her superior and not a confidant. Not even after all the time they'd spent together.

"You could never be that."

The awkward moment became even more awkward. Eloise's brain apparently had lost the ability to string two words together. Phillip stared at the table, seeming as ill at ease as she felt.

Finally, he cleared his throat and picked up the final letter. "Dated last February. From a Vera Swaney of Colorado Springs, Colorado. Postmarked from Seattle."

Eloise jotted the information on her pad.

"She says she's going to spend a week with her son," Phillip continued, "who is joining her while he's in Seattle on business."

Eloise pointed to another paragraph. "She's shipping five English dolls home as a Christmas surprise. That's odd since Christmas is already over."

"Agree. Then there's this." Phillip read from the page.

"I purchased seven small dolls which in a short time I hope and expect to make look as if they were real seven Chinese dolls . . . I have almost finished the mother doll. I will then make a Chinese father, grandfather, grandmother and three children . . . the children will be girl, boy, and baby."

"Seven dolls. Seven ships." Eloise grabbed Phillip's arm as a lightbulb seemed to turn on over her head. "A convoy."

"You could be right. In fact, I'm almost one hundred percent sure you are."

"We should ask Richard to find out what ships were brought from Pearl Harbor to the West Coast for repairs," Eloise said. "The type of ship, its name, the amount of damage, the status of the repairs."

"I'll give him a call." As Phillip rose, he placed the letters in the folder. "While I do that, could you ask a secretary to find a number for Ruby Lankford? Try to set up an appointment with her for later this afternoon."

Dismissed. Just like that. Why couldn't she listen in on his call with Richard? After all, she was the one who thought of the convoy. No matter how much she contributed to the mission, he would always be the agent in charge while she would always be the lackey.

She left the office to find someone—another woman, of course—to get Ruby Lankford's phone number. Perhaps she should be thankful for moments like this. They were a reminder that Phillip Clayton was no one special, despite her heart trying to convince her otherwise.

CHAPTER TWENTY

Ruby Lankford perched in a chintz chair as her housekeeper, Claire, rolled a tea trolley into the parlor. Despite the summer heat, a paisley shawl draped her frail shoulders, and a knitted afghan covered her lap and legs. Tiny feet clad in pink slippers poked out beneath the hem of a long mauve dress. Phillip and Eloise sat next to each other on a chintz sofa. The east-facing windows opened onto a view of the broad Willamette River. The clear waters reflected gray clouds and patches of muted blue skies.

Phillip would have liked nothing better than to bolt across the lawn toward the mighty river. Better to stand, small and alone, before the grandeur of water and sky than sit like an awkward giant among an overwhelming onslaught of feminine trappings. Why couldn't they get to the point and then leave?

"Claire has been with me since before Dr. Lankford and I married," Mrs. Lankford explained, though no one had asked about Claire's longevity and Phillip, for one, certainly didn't care.

"Oh, the parties we used to have, and Claire baked the most gorgeous cakes anyone had ever seen." Mrs. Lankford's contented sigh lasted so long Phillip wished he'd counted off the seconds.

"All my friends were incredibly jealous. They often begged me to let her decorate cakes for their parties. I rarely agreed except for the most special occasions. A wedding, say. Or perhaps a very special celebration. Those were the days, weren't they, Claire?"

"Yes, they were, ma'am." The housekeeper, attired in a gray uniform and white apron, lifted the teapot. "Shall I pour?"

"Please. I'm a little tired today." Mrs. Lankford's sharp eyes turned to Phillip and Eloise. He had a sudden urge to pull the lapels on his jacket closer together to prevent her from seeing into his soul. "It's not every day that one has a visit from the Federal Bureau of Investigation. How exciting this is, isn't that right, Claire?"

"Very exciting, ma'am." Claire handed porcelain cups and saucers to Eloise and Phillip.

He'd been to more tea parties than he could count, but he still felt clumsy handling the fragile dishware. He took a sip of the hot tea then set the cup and saucer on the table. He glanced at Eloise, but she didn't seem to be having any trouble balancing the set. Her eyes, bright with interest, focused on their hostess.

Almost as soon as Claire left the room, Mrs. Lankford dispensed with any more pleasantries. "How is it that a young lady such as yourself is involved in espionage?" she said to Eloise.

"It's a temporary assignment," Eloise replied

164

with the same grace and ease as if she'd been asked about the weather. *Espionage?* Phillip mentally shook his head. As if Eloise were a modern-day Mata Hari instead of an ordinary schoolteacher who had traded a classroom for long days of code breaking. Important work, absolutely. But there wasn't anything cloak-and-dagger about this particular mission.

"I'm assisting Agent Clayton with a very important investigation," Eloise continued. "We have a letter to show you. A copy, actually. The original letter is at our office in Washington, DC."

"Ah, Washington, DC." A pleasant smile curved Mrs. Lankford's pale lips. "Dr. Lankford and I dreamed of visiting there someday. But it wasn't to be. My health will not allow it." Her eyes focused on Eloise. Phillip might as well have stayed in the car. He could probably walk out this very moment and no one would notice. If only he dared.

"We are such history buffs," Mrs. Lankford continued. "I do so wish Claire would make the trip on our behalf. She could still do it—her health is so robust—but she won't leave us even when I implore her to do so."

"How fortunate you are to have found such loyalty," Eloise crooned.

"Don't I know it? My friends are very jealous of my good fortune."

"This letter," Eloise said. "It's written to someone named Señora Ines de Molinali who lives in Buenos Aires, Argentina. Is she a friend of yours?"

"I know no one of that name. Nor anyone in Argentina."

"You didn't write the letter then?"

"I did not. And I can't imagine why anyone would think I did."

"May I tell you what the letter says?" Eloise's soothing voice sounded so persuasive that Phillip believed she could get Mrs. Lankford to agree to just about anything. Except perhaps to have the faithful Claire bake a cake for her.

"Please do." Mrs. Lankford rolled her shoulders, reminding Phillip of a banty hen fluffing her feathers. "I'd like to know what that impersonator wrote."

"The letter begins by saying you'll need to send out your husband's monthly statements since it's almost the first of the month."

"Me? Send out the statements?" Mrs. Lankford let out a definitely unladylike guffaw. "There's the proof right there. I know nothing about such statements. Dr. Lankford hires someone to take care of his accounting. You can inquire of Claire if you don't believe me. She'll tell you."

"There's also a second letter," Phillip said, hoping to keep Mrs. Lankford's attention on the letter and away from misperceived indignities or forays into the past. "It says that Karen's room is empty now that she's married. Is Karen your daughter?"

Mrs. Lankford's ruffled feathers rose higher, and to Phillip's chagrin, so did her indignation. "My daughter's name is Carol not Karen. Surely even you can see I wouldn't make a mistake about my own daughter's name."

Even me? Phillip wasn't sure what to make of that. Or how to respond. He opened his mouth, but before he could stick his foot in it—which he was sure was about to happen—Eloise answered in her calm, soothing tone. "We believe you, Mrs. Lankford."

"Though it is true that she married recently." The woman frowned. "And her bedroom is vacant."

"Who would know that?" Eloise asked.

"All our friends. People from church." Mrs. Lankford tilted her head in thought. "I suppose even a few of my husband's patients might be aware of the wedding. And his staff, of course. Actually, I suppose all of Portland. It was announced in the society pages. Carol is the daughter of a renowned physician after all."

"I see." Eloise smiled at the older woman and exchanged a glance with Phillip. Apparently, she didn't know where to go from here, what other questions to ask. Truthfully, neither did he. Two more forged letters had led to a dead end.

167

"Although . . ." Mrs. Lankford said slowly. Both Phillip and Eloise turned toward her. "There's a woman I know, an antique doll dealer . . . but no, she's too well-respected to have anything to do with the FBI."

Phillip's antennae went on high alert, and he graced her with his most charming smile. "An antique doll dealer? From here in Portland?"

"Her shop is in New York City, but she sends me a doll almost every month. I almost always send it back, but over time I have come to consider her a friend. This may surprise you, but I even invited her to stay with Dr. Lankford and me the next time she visited the area."

She laughed, a high-pitched silly sound that grated on Phillip's ears. But he kept his smile in place and stayed silent, certain that Mrs. Lankford would fill in the silence. He wasn't disappointed.

"Velvalee is too dear a friend to forge my name to such a silly letter," she said. "Everyone who is anyone in the sphere of doll collecting knows her. She gives lectures and writes articles. A fount of knowledge, she is. Indeed, she is." Her tone ended on a screech as if she realized she was trying too hard to convince them of her friend's innocence while also beginning to doubt it herself. "She knows we have an empty room," Mrs. Lankford finished lamely. "She knows a great deal about my family." Her eyes widened in fear, and she pulled the shawl tighter around her chest.

"Her name is Velvalee?" Again, Eloise's low voice sounded comforting, gentle even. "What an unusual and lovely name."

"Isn't it, though?" Mrs. Lankford agreed. "It isn't a name I would want for myself or my daughter. Though she signed her name Vee on the postcards she sent me. The space for writing is so small."

"Postcards?" Eloise sounded intrigued. "From New York?"

"No, my goodness, no." Mrs. Lankford's earlier doubts about her friend seemed to disappear as she once again took on the persona of society queen. "Velvalee called it her West Coast tour. I'm not sure how she managed, what with trains being so crowded these days. And the horrid gas rationing. Dr. Lankford is fortunate to get a higher ration because of his profession. But we no longer go on the long Sunday afternoon drives we used to enjoy. I suppose we must all make our own sacrifices, mustn't we? No matter how small."

"Where did Velvalee go on her tour?" Eloise asked in an apparent attempt to steer Mrs. Lankford's attention back to the doll collector.

"Oh, I'd need to look at the postcards again to tell you that." She tilted her head, reminding Phillip of a frail canary. "Seattle for sure. San Francisco. Other places."

169

"I'd love to see those postcards," Eloise said as she primly sipped her tea.

"Then you shall." Mrs. Lankford rang a tinny handbell sitting on the table beside her chair. When Claire arrived, she instructed her to retrieve the postcards from a nearby desk and give them to Eloise. "The pictures are breathtaking, but her messages are brief."

Eloise held the cards, a stack of six or seven, so Phillip could see them too. He sensed her eagerness to turn them over, to read the private messages, even as she oohed and aahed over the photographs. He wanted to do the same.

"I have a tremendous favor to ask," Phillip said. "You'd be doing your country a great service if you said yes."

"That's quite the bowlful of flattery you're serving me," Mrs. Lankford replied. "What favor?"

"Allow me to take these cards to FBI head-quarters. They may be helpful in our investigation."

Mrs. Lankford's eyes opened so wide Phillip feared they would pop out of her head. "I couldn't. Could I?" Before Phillip could answer, she held up a hand. "Do you honestly believe they will help in some way?"

"If I didn't, I wouldn't have asked."

"I don't understand how they could be. Nor can I imagine why Velvalee is causing such a stir. And with the FBI of all things."

"We've already told you as much as we can." Phillip hoped his placating tone and warm smile would convince her to give him the postcards. If not, he'd have to get a warrant. The postcards might not be of any importance, but that wasn't Phillip's call to make.

"I suppose I should agree." Mrs. Lankford sounded doubtful. "Though I do hate giving them up."

"We'll do our best to return them to you," Eloise assured her. "I don't know when but as soon as we can."

"Take them then." Mrs. Lankford gave a dismissive wave of her hand. "I'm growing tired. I'm sure you can find your way out."

"Of course." Phillip rose. "Only one more question. What is Velvalee's last name?"

"Dickinson. Velvalee Dickinson."

"Do you happen to have her address?"

"That's two questions," she said sharply.

"So it is. My apologies."

"Wait for Claire in the foyer." She rang the handbell again. "She'll write out the address for you."

"Thank you for your time and the tea, Mrs. Lankford." Eloise stood beside Phillip. She seemed calm on the outside, but Phillip sensed she was about to explode with excitement. Just like him.

They waited in the foyer, neither one saying a

word, until Claire appeared with a folded sheet of pale pink stationery. "The information you requested."

Phillip unfolded it, noted the Madison Avenue address, then gave the paper to Eloise for safekeeping as they left the Lankford home. Once they were settled in the car, Eloise grabbed Phillip's arm. "Did we just solve the case?"

"Maybe. We can't jump to any conclusions though. Or tip our hand too soon."

"I know it's her," Eloise insisted. "Velvalee Dickinson. What a name."

Phillip wanted to agree with her, but he couldn't. Not without more proof. Though in his gut, he was 99.99 percent sure that Eloise was right.

If so, then this unnamed operation would soon be at an end. No more traveling around the country with Eloise by his side. No more pretending they were siblings in front of their fellow passengers and hotel staff.

While Eloise returned to the navy, he could implement plan B. Flip a coin. Heads, army. Tails, navy. He didn't care which way the coin landed, since joining his cousins in their aerial battles wasn't an option.

As he drove away from the Lankford home, he snuck a glance at Eloise. Her attractive features glowed with excitement and certainty. No doubt she was eager for this mission to end too.

"One more stop," he said.

"Colorado Springs."

"Then home."

To his surprise, a shadow flickered across her face. Though it disappeared so quickly, maybe he'd imagined it.

"Yes. Home."

Her enthusiasm seemed to have dimmed. Or maybe he imagined that too.

Seeing what he wanted to see. Hearing what he wanted to hear. But not allowing himself to admit he didn't want the unnamed operation to end.

CHAPTER TWENTY-ONE

Velvalee Dickinson put the finishing touches on the article she was writing for the Complete Collector. The journal, catering to antique collectors, had published articles written by her before, and hopefully they'd take this one too. But with her mind preoccupied on other matters, she found it difficult to focus on the words.

For the third time in less than two weeks, a man had come into her shop to "look around" then left without buying anything. Not the same man, though that also would have been strange. But three *different* men?

Each one made some offhanded comment about buying a gift for a daughter or a sister yet didn't seem interested in any of the dolls that Velvalee suggested. When she asked questions to help narrow their selections, they mumbled their answers.

Would she prefer a doll from the royal collection or one wearing a folk costume? What about her color preferences? Vibrant shades such as red and purple or pastel shades such as pink and lilac?

She couldn't help noticing, though, that their eyes were sharper than their tongues. While they couldn't come up with sensible answers to her questions, they poked into every corner in the shop. In the end, each man left, empty-handed, with a promise to return at a later date. None of them had.

What if they were criminals planning to rob her blind? She'd read about thieves who posed as customers to learn the location of the cash register and the valuable stock. If she remembered right, they called it "casing the joint" in the movies. Maybe that's what one of the men or perhaps all three of them were doing. Casing her joint.

If they weren't simply hapless men who hadn't a clue what to give their female family members, then she almost hoped they were planning a robbery. As awful as that would be, she preferred that scenario over the other one that kept her awake at night.

What if . . . no, it was too horrible to think about. She'd been too meticulous for the authorities to trace any of those letters she'd written back to her. How could they? With each one, she'd been precise in copying the address to that so-called señora in Argentina who probably didn't even exist. She'd practiced forging the handwriting of the supposed letter writers until her hand cramped, laying a thin sheet of onion skin paper on top of an authentic signature and tracing it again and again and again.

Though perhaps she'd made a mistake in pretending to be Ruby Lankford twice. She'd been in such a hurry to send that information on its way, it had been simpler to forge a signature she'd practiced before instead of learning a new one.

She dismissed the thought, unable to admit that her actions could have raised any suspicions. If authorities were investigating her, then someone else was to blame.

Of course, there was still another option. She was simply paranoid, and the men had been what they appeared—indecisive customers. Except they tried too hard to make that impression. She'd dealt with indecisive men before, but these three had an air of superiority that suggested they weren't nearly as helpless nor as ignorant as they wanted her to believe.

Whoever they were and whatever their reason for being at the shop, Velvalee needed to let her handler know. If they were simply customers, no harm done. If they were potential thieves, her handler could be persuaded to provide security. If they were, heaven forbid, from the government, then her handler needed to protect her.

Yesterday morning, after a second sleepless night, she had entered the bookstore next door by going through a back curtain that separated the store from a stockroom. The same stockroom had a door opening into Velvalee's doll shop, but the lock was broken. The two store owners didn't mind—the access made it easier for them

to cover for each other when the need ar   re
   While chatting with the bookstore   pu
Velvalee had casually played with a N   up
gypsy rag doll, known as Perla Neg   th
her genuine black pearl eyes. Months   m
Velvalee had suggested adding the uniqu   o
to the store's window display. After the   s
small talk, she returned the doll to the wi   c
Only a sharp-eyed observer would notice th
doll's colorful shawl was now over her dark
instead of around her shoulders. This prearra
signal instructed the handler to visit Velvale
soon as possible. Never had it been more th
few hours before his arrival. So why hadn'
come this time?
   Velvalee forced herself to focus on
article's final paragraph instead of allow
her imagination—and her fears—to run w
She rearranged a couple of sentences then p
fresh sheet of paper in the typewriter. In betv
waiting on a few customers, she pounded
keys of the Underwood, mumbling under
breath when she hit the *m* instead of the
some other silly mistake. Each time the bell
the door clanged, she entered the shop expe
to find her handler next to the front display   s
holding the brim of his hat in front of hin   s
both hands. Each time she was disappointe   s
   When she finished the article, she place
an envelope, still fuming that her handler l   i

;ponded to her signal. Was he ignoring her on
rpose? Or . . . surely not . . . had *he* been picked
by the authorities? No. She refused to believe
at. There had to be another explanation. Her
ind searched the possibilities until she landed
1 one. Of course. She should have thought of it
)oner. Obviously, someone had rearranged the
oll's shawl. Only one way to find out.

She put on the red heels that she'd kicked off
vhile typing and stormed through the stockroom,
ast the curtain, and into the bookshop. Her heart
eapt to her throat at the sight of a young girl,
welve or thirteen years old, holding the gypsy
rag doll.

Velvalee rushed to the girl, tore the doll from
her hands, and glared. "That isn't yours. And
you're old enough to know better than to touch
something that doesn't belong to you."

"But she said I could." The girl pointed at the
bookstore owner, who was busy with another
customer and seemed oblivious to Velvalee's
presence.

"Don't touch her again." Velvalee practically
1issed the words. Her heels clattered on the
ardwood floor as she rushed back to her own
hop, dangling the doll by its leg. Once past the
ockroom door, she leaned against it and took
everal deep breaths.

Tomorrow she would return the doll to its place
1 the window. Tomorrow her handler would see

the signal. Tomorrow she would tell him about the three men and their odd behavior.

No matter who they turned out to be, *he* would provide whatever help she needed. Unlike her husband, who had left her with the responsibility of running this business on her own, her Japanese friends never failed her.

Everything would be fine. Tomorrow.

CHAPTER TWENTY-TWO

Once the train from Portland to Colorado got underway, Eloise pulled the postcards that Mrs. Lankford had given them from her handbag. The man-sized handkerchief given to her by the woman in the Seattle department store's ladies room and the newspaper article with her father's photograph almost came out with them, but Eloise managed to shove both back inside before Phillip noticed. During the rainy days at the Seattle hotel, she'd clipped the article from the paper using the only tool she had—her tiny manicure scissors.

The article was an embarrassing reminder of her emotional flight from the Seattle field office. To his credit, Phillip still hadn't asked her any questions about why she'd left in such a hurry or what had her so upset. But sometimes she found him staring at her with a strange look in his eyes. When caught, he pretended to focus on something else or simply smiled and made some off-the-cuff comment.

Each time it happened, her stomach turned to mush. He was obviously observing her fitness as a valuable asset on this mission. She'd managed to handle herself well in the three interviews they'd conducted, but her behavior in Seattle proved that she lacked self-control and discipline.

Agents weren't supposed to get flustered under any circumstances. All her instructors at the academy said so, though in different words. She'd failed that test in the worst possible way, and in doing so, she had failed Phillip, his uncle, and herself.

And for what?

Now she had proof that her father was alive, although she'd never doubted it. Now she knew where he lived. Of course, he had to live somewhere, didn't he? Knowing the details didn't change the fact that he had abandoned his family. It only deepened the hurt.

Now she knew he never intended to return to them. Until she'd read the article, a tiny ember of hope remained. Even though she wasn't sure the adult Eloise wanted him to come home, the little girl inside her sometimes did. The article drenched that hope as relentlessly as the rainstorm that had kept her and Phillip confined to their suite.

"Do you have your steno pad handy?" Phillip moved to sit beside her on the bench seat. The other occupants of their compartment had gone to the train's dining car. "We can go through these postcards in the order they were mailed. Maybe we'll learn something."

Grateful for the distraction from her gloomy thoughts, Eloise shook her head. "It doesn't fit in my handbag."

"Here, take this." He gave her the small pad he carried in his suit's inner pocket then sorted the cards according to their postmarks. On a clean sheet of paper, she drew a grid. In the first column she wrote the dates for each postcard. The second column noted the locations of the postmarks.

The finished table tracked Velvalee's journey from New York City to Chicago to Seattle to Portland to San Francisco to Los Angeles to Phoenix. Presumably, she'd returned to New York City without sending any more postcards to Mrs. Lankford along the way.

"Let's see what we learned," Eloise teased. "Our Miss Velvalee traveled east all the way to the coast, turned left, and headed south. Turned left again. Headed east. Am I missing anything?"

"Don't be a smart aleck," Phillip warned, his tone harsh but with a glint in his eye. He tapped the pad. "Let's check those dates against the dates the letters were sent."

"Good idea. Dorothy Walker's letter was dated January twenty-seventh and had a Seattle postmark." Eloise added a third column for the letters and wrote the initials *DW* in the row for the postcard that had been mailed from Seattle. Though there wasn't a postcard from New York, it was safe to assume that was Velvalee's starting place. Eloise wrote *BC* for Barbara Clark in a new row created above the existing ones.

"Ruby Lankford's first letter was postmarked from Oakland," Eloise said. "Isn't that near San Francisco?"

"Right across the bay."

Eloise wrote *RL – 1* in the San Francisco row. "Vera Swaney's letter was sent in February too. Also postmarked Seattle." She scribbled *VS* beside the *BC* in the Seattle row.

"That leaves Mrs. Lankford's second letter."

"Which wasn't mailed until the end of May," Eloise reminded him. "But the dates for the other four letters show that they were mailed from a city that Velvalee was visiting at the same time. That can't be a coincidence. She has to be the traitor."

"I hate to rain on your parade, but right now all we have is circumstantial evidence. We need more proof."

"What kind of proof?"

"She may not be traveling alone," Phillip said. "Perhaps someone else—a husband, a brother, a cousin, it could be anyone—wrote those letters. Velvalee might not know anything about them."

"I see." Annoyance bit at Eloise's spirit. "You don't think she did it because she's a woman."

Phillip appeared taken aback. "I never said that."

"You didn't have to." She turned away from him and muttered, "Just like all the others."

"All the other what?"

"Other men. Those who can't imagine a woman can do anything besides cook and clean and do the laundry."

"You're wrong about that." Phillip seemed both hurt and amused at her accusation. "Though you're also right. It's hard for me to imagine anyone betraying this country. I don't even understand how those Germans were capable of planning sabotage after having lived here. How could they possibly prefer life in the Third Reich?" He took her hand, his skin warm against hers. "The truth is, until we heard of Velvalee, I assumed the traitor was a man. Richard probably does too."

"So did I," Eloise reluctantly admitted.

Phillip chuckled. "Forgive me?"

He was asking her for forgiveness when she was the one acting like a miffed spinster?

"How about we forgive each other?" she said, not daring to look into his eyes. Though it seemed he was avoiding eye contact with her too.

"Are you still going to beat me at gin rummy?"

"Every chance I get."

"That's my girl."

His girl. Perhaps at a different time, in other circumstances. But when this investigation ended, their paths would separate. Only God knew if they'd ever come together again. Young men who went to war didn't always come home. She wasn't strong enough to endure that heartache again.

Her focus needed to be on their mission. To find the person—man or woman—responsible for giving information about the navy to the enemy. In the scheme of things, that was all that mattered right now.

"What kind of proof do we need?" she asked.

Phillip released her hand, creating an absence colder than ice despite the warmth of the compartment, and tapped the pad she'd been writing on. "Richard needs this information. He can send agents from the nearest field offices to find out where Velvalee stayed during her West Coast tour."

"And who else might have been with her."

"We can send a telegraph at our next stop, that is, if you can encode the message."

"A substitution code? He'll need a key."

"I've got an idea for one."

By the time the other occupants returned, Eloise had written out the coded message for Phillip to send to his uncle. The tension between them had faded away, but something else remained. For a few moments, they'd held hands.

And another thread bound them together.

CHAPTER TWENTY-THREE

At Vera Swaney's request, Eloise and Phillip agreed to meet her at an upscale restaurant in a ski lodge located at the base of Almagre Mountain. "It's also called Old Baldy," Eloise said, reading a brochure she'd picked up at the Colorado Springs train station. "The altitude is close to ninety-five hundred feet."

"I wouldn't mind coming back here in the winter," Phillip said as he pulled into a parking space.

"Do you ski?" Eloise asked.

"Never have," Phillip admitted. "How hard can it be?"

Eloise thought back to the afternoons she'd spent on the obstacle course at the FBI academy. With practice and grit, she'd finally made it over the wall within the time limits. Sliding down a mountain on two long pieces of wood should be a breeze compared to that.

They exited the car and, as if by silent agreement, stared at the surrounding mountain ranges with their snowy caps and forests of pines. "This is such a beautiful place," Eloise said. "I'm grateful God brought us here so we could see it."

"Me too." Phillip's smile suggested his simple words held a deeper meaning, one that caused butterflies to dance inside her. He offered his arm. "We shouldn't keep Mrs. Swaney waiting."

A hostess wearing a simple black dress adorned with gold accessories met them at the entrance to the restaurant. When Phillip gave their names, she smiled warmly. "Mrs. Swaney is expecting you. If you'll follow me, please."

She led the way through a spacious dining hall with huge wintry landscapes hung on paneled walls through open French doors to a secluded patio. Only one of the white-clothed tables was occupied. The woman hid her eyes behind dark-tinted glasses. Neatly coiffed white hair and flawless makeup gave the impression that she'd just stepped out of a beautician's chair.

"Your guests, ma'am." The hostess scanned the contents of the table—bite-size appetizers, a basket of freshly baked breads, exquisite glass jars of various jams, a chilled dish holding pats of butter in the shapes of golden coins, a carafe of orange juice, and a platter of sliced fruits. "Is there anything else you require?"

"Not at this moment." The woman's cultured voice held the hint of an accent that Eloise couldn't place. She turned her attention to her guests. "Please join me. Would you prefer coffee?"

"Not for me, thank you," Phillip said warmly as he pulled out Eloise's chair for her.

Mrs. Swaney seemed to shift her gaze from Phillip to Eloise, though the glasses made it hard to know who or what she was looking at. "I'm fine," Eloise said, though she didn't feel fine at all. A place like this was out of her element, and she didn't understand the reason for the over-the-top hospitality. Sugar was already rationed, and there was talk of other items being rationed too. Meat and dairy. Even clothing and shoes.

After dismissing the hostess with a mere nod, Mrs. Swaney poured juice into three translucent glasses. "This is such a lovely place," she said. "I prefer discussing any unpleasant business in majestic surroundings whenever possible. The mountains calm my nerves by reminding me that I am but a wisp amidst such grandeur."

"Why do you expect our business is unpleasant?" Phillip asked.

"You're from the government." She wrinkled her aristocratic nose. "An investigative branch of the government. How could it be anything but unpleasant?"

"We're here about a letter." Eloise accepted the basket of breads that Mrs. Swaney handed her. "One purported to have been written by you."

"I do write my share of letters, so it is possible. To whom is the letter addressed?"

"To Señora Ines de Molinali," Eloise answered. "She supposedly lives in Buenos Aires, Argentina."

" 'Purported.' 'Supposedly.' Is there anything you know for a fact?"

Eloise felt the comment as a rebuke, though she had to admit the question was a valid one. Everything about these letters so far involved guesswork and supposition. Even her ideas on the possible solutions for the jargon code hadn't yet been verified.

"We know of four other letters written to the same address," Phillip said. "The women whose names and return addresses were used for those letters knew nothing about them."

"May I see the letter purportedly written by me?" She put a slight stress on *purportedly* while giving Eloise what might have been an amused look. It was impossible to know with those opaque lenses hiding her eyes. And impossible to know the reason behind Mrs. Swaney's amusement.

Eloise handed her the letter. "This is a copy. The original is at our FBI headquarters in Washington."

" 'Our'? Are you an agent too, then? I didn't realize young women could hold such positions. How modern of you."

The words might have been a compliment except for the slight edge given to them. Again, as if Mrs. Swaney found the idea of women agents amusing. And beneath her.

"Miss Marshall is a consultant." Phillip's warm tone exhibited pride. "Her expertise is cryptanalysis."

"Oh my. That's a big word one doesn't hear every day." Mrs. Swaney took the paper and scanned it. "Is this a transcript?"

"It's a copy," Phillip said.

"I don't type my correspondence. Such a gauche thing to do for personal letters." Her eyes dropped to the end. "This does resemble my signature; however, I did not sign this." She placed a finger on a paragraph in the letter. "This is odd."

Phillip exchanged a glance with Eloise. He leaned forward. "What is?"

"This line about my son. I did meet him when I was in Seattle." She placed the paper on the table. "And all this about the dolls. I met a woman who was staying at the same hotel. She owns a doll shop in New York City."

Eloise's nerves went on high alert, but she took her cue from Phillip, who remained calm despite this possible confirmation of the true identity of the letter writer.

"Did you mention your son to her?" He asked the question with all the gravitas of one asking about the weather. One of the instructors had told Eloise that agents needed to stay detached. This real-life example solidified the importance of that lesson. She wasn't sure she could have asked the question without her voice trembling with excitement.

"Yes," Mrs. Swaney said. "I believe I did. We

were both in the lobby, you see, and she had this magnificent doll with long dark hair and a satin dress. I thought something similar would be the perfect present for my granddaughter, so we struck up a conversation. One does such things when traveling, of course."

"Do you remember her name?" Phillip asked.

"Velvet something or other." Mrs. Swaney waved her hand as if the name didn't matter. "I thought at first I'd found a suitable companion to tour the local museums and art galleries, but she turned out to be a dreary bore. Dolls seemed to be the only topic of conversation of any interest to her. And, of course, she wanted me to purchase not only one doll for my granddaughter but an entire collection. The child is only six, and while I can be accused of being an indulgent grandmother to the sweet girl, I am not tastelessly extravagant."

"No," Phillip said with a small shake of his head. "My mother always says good taste doesn't come with a price tag, but bad taste is horribly expensive."

Mrs. Swaney emitted a gracious chuckle and patted Phillip's arm. "Your mother and I agree on that. If she ever finds her way to Colorado Springs, please have her give me a call."

"I'll surely do that."

"She must be so proud to have a son serving the government during these difficult times. How fortunate you didn't have to go overseas. Believe me, that's a mother's worst nightmare. My own son is vice president of a small manufacturing firm so it's essential he stay here on the home front. Otherwise, I'd be a nervous wreck."

"You're very fortunate," Phillip said.

Eloise sensed his tension increase when Mrs. Swaney said he was fortunate he wasn't in the fighting. Obviously, he didn't feel that way, but he managed to keep his tone polite, obsequious even.

"Could the woman's name have been Velvalee Dickinson?" he asked.

"Perhaps. In all honesty, I put the entire episode out of my mind." Mrs. Swaney pushed slightly away from the table. "I must run now, but please stay as long as you want. The bill has already been settled."

She stood and Phillip rose too, helping with her chair. "Thank you for your time and for your hospitality. Eloise and I are glad to have met you."

"And I you."

For a moment, Eloise expected the woman to pinch Phillip's cheek.

"If you think of anything else, please notify me." Phillip drew a card from his jacket and handed it to her. "You can leave a message for me at that number."

"I will do that. Ta-ta."

She left, gliding away without a backward glance or even an acknowledgment of Eloise's existence.

Phillip returned to his seat and took a long sip of his orange juice while his eyes danced with amusement.

"Velvet something or other," Eloise said. "She must mean Velvalee."

"I would think so." Phillip glanced toward the French doors as if searching for someone. "Mrs. Swaney wasn't much like our other interviewees, was she?"

"Mrs. Swaney pretended I didn't exist."

"I know." He chuckled then graced Eloise with a teasing smile. "Now you know how I felt. Aren't you glad you had me along?"

"Glad but not tastelessly glad."

Phillip laughed. "They're all alike, these society women. Proud and snobbish."

"Is your mother like that too?" Eloise wished she could have taken the words back as soon as they were out of her mouth, but Phillip simply gave her a strange look then burst out laughing.

"Why would you think that?"

"Because of what you said she said. About bad taste being expensive."

Phillip leaned closer, and for a moment Eloise wondered if he was going to pinch *her* cheek . . . and how she'd respond if he did.

"I made that up, sweetheart."

Ah! The Bogart impression was back again.

"My mother has much more in common with Mrs. Walker than with Mrs. Swaney." He grabbed a muffin then glanced at Eloise's near-empty plate. "You heard what the grand old lady said. 'The bill has been settled.' We aren't going to get another meal like this until we get back to DC. And maybe not even then."

Eloise helped herself to a miniature torte and took a bite. It was mouthwateringly delicious, and she realized she was hungrier than she'd thought. "What is our next step?"

"A phone call to Uncle Richard. And then, unless he says otherwise, we return to head-quarters."

"Ending our trek around the United States." She said the words lightly, but they weighed heavily on her heart. Despite the serious nature of their mission, she'd enjoyed the adventure. Flying on a plane—something she'd never done before. Seeing the Pacific Ocean and the Rocky Mountains—something she'd never dreamed would ever be possible.

Spending time with Phillip—not something she'd wanted when she joined the team. But now she had memories with him that she never wanted to fade away, that she had tucked into a safe place in her heart.

She wanted to find the person responsible for the letters—whether that turned out to be Velvalee

Dickinson or someone else—to discover if she was right that they were written in jargon code. But she didn't want her adventure with Phillip to end—a secret she had to keep from him for the sake of the mission. For the sake of her heart.

CHAPTER TWENTY-FOUR

Phillip and Eloise donned their sibling roles again and boarded a bus for the trip north to Denver's FBI field office. The route skirted the eastern edge of the San Isabel National Forest. Phillip would have much preferred hiking the trails within the forest instead of bouncing around on a bus. Or just about anything else for that matter. Eloise sat by the window, seemingly asleep, though he didn't believe she actually slumbered. She'd been quiet since they left the lodge where they'd met Mrs. Swaney. It seemed as though she had something on her mind; but when he'd asked her about it, she simply smiled her pretty smile and brushed him off. Just like Janie when she thought he was being too nosy about her love life.

But he hadn't asked Eloise about her love life. Only what had her so deep in thought. Though maybe that's why she was so deep in thought. She was thinking of her love life. In all their travels together, she'd never mentioned a boyfriend, but that didn't mean she didn't have one.

From the ski resort, they'd returned the car they'd borrowed from a deputy at the El Paso County Sheriff's Office, and Phillip had called his uncle. Richard's secretary had been glad to hear from him and relayed a message from her boss, who wasn't available to talk at the moment. She instructed Phillip and Eloise to go to the nearest field office so they could make a secure phone call. Richard had important information he needed to give them. After Phillip ended the call, one of the deputies was kind enough to give them a ride to the bus station.

The trip, around two hours by automobile, took at least another hour because of the bus's low speed and the stops it had to make. Phillip paid attention to everyone who got on and off the bus, another tiring activity that made it impossible to relax. He couldn't turn off his inner antennae, so he made his observations into a game. What if the young mother with the clinging toddler and oversized bag was a bank robber who'd stolen money to pay for her own mother's lifesaving operation? What if the old man with the cane, probably a veteran of the last Great War, the one that was supposed to be the end of all wars, what if he was the secret head of a western crime syndicate specializing in counterfeit money?

When that game got old, he changed it for a different version. Instead of *what if,* the question became *what could.* What could he accurately determine about someone from their appearance, their clothes, their posture, their demeanor?

The problem with the game was that he never knew how accurate his observations were. He couldn't very well tell the chosen subject about his deductions and ask for a yes or no. Sherlock Holmes could get away with that kind of assured commentary, but not an FBI agent who was supposed to be undercover when he used public transportation.

When they finally reached the Denver bus station, Phillip hailed a cab. After he and Eloise were inside the vehicle, he gave the driver the address of a hotel about two blocks from the field office. They checked in to their rooms and freshened up then walked in the thin altitude toward the squat building.

Either Richard or his assistant had alerted R. D. Brown, the special agent in charge, that they'd be arriving that afternoon. They were ushered into Brown's office, where Phillip could make the call to his uncle. He hit the speaker button then dialed the number to Richard's private line. The call was answered on the second ring.

"All is well, I trust," Richard said in his jovial tone.

"Better than well," Phillip responded. "Eloise is with me."

"Hello, sir," she said.

"Both of you can hear me?"

"Us and only us," Phillip assured his uncle. "Special Agent Brown has been extremely cooperative."

"I told him enough of your mission to dampen

his curiosity. But we have much to discuss in a short amount of time."

"We're ready."

"Our forensics team had a breakthrough," Richard said. "The Clark letter was typed on a portable Underwood #621465. This same type-writer was used for a letter written *to* Mrs. Clark."

Phillip and Eloise stared at each other. Electricity seemed to spark between them at the news. "Who wrote the letter to Mrs. Clark?" Eloise asked. Her excitement was palpable, and Phillip couldn't help being amused at her eagerness. She reminded him of himself when he was new on the job and the first important clues to an important case had been found. Somewhere along the way, he'd lost that eager excitement. Seemed like it faded away not long after Pearl Harbor.

"Velvalee Dickinson. The woman you mentioned in your telegram."

"That's more proof." Eloise's palpable excitement was catching. She seemed about to jump out of her skin. Phillip stifled a grin.

"The woman we talked to in Colorado," he said to Richard, "told us she met a doll collector in Seattle. She thought her name was Velvet but agreed it could have been Velvalee."

"We have agents watching her doll shop in New York. Plus, we're looking for places where she stayed on her, what did you call it, her West Coast tour."

"I should be there," Phillip said, itching to get a look at this doll collector who wrote strange letters to someone in South America.

"Maybe you will be. But now that we have a name, I need you to retrace your steps. On your way back to DC, stop in Springfield, Ohio. Ask Barbara Clark about Mrs. Dickinson. A copy of the letter Mrs. Dickinson wrote to her will be waiting for you at the Cincinnati field office."

Phillip swallowed a groan. From the look in Eloise's eyes, she wasn't interested in the Ohio stopover either. But when Richard said jump . . .

"Special Agent Brown has your travel arrangements."

"What is it this time?" Phillip asked. "Plane, train, horse-drawn carriage?"

Richard good-naturedly chuckled. "Train. A sleeper-express, if that helps."

"It helps."

After the call ended, Phillip opened the office door. The anteroom was empty, so he opened the door that led to the hallway. Brown stood across from the door, leaning against the wall with ankles crossed and smoking a cigarette. He'd been serious when he said no one would disturb them while they were in his office. Phillip hadn't realized he'd meant to stand guard himself.

"All finished?" R.D. asked. No hint of curiosity was in his eyes, but he had to wonder what was going on. Phillip knew Richard would have been sparse with his information. But Phillip also knew R.D.'s apparent lack of curiosity was feigned. He had developed the important skill of hiding his thoughts, his interest, from even a trained observer like Phillip.

"Thanks again for the use of your office."

"We're here to serve." He stepped toward the open door, and Phillip stood back so he could enter. "Your train leaves in less than an hour." He picked up an envelope from the secretary's desk and handed it to Phillip. "If you don't mind, I'll drive you to the station myself. Just to be sure you get there safe and sound."

"Appreciate that. Thank you."

Phillip's concern that the offer to drive was a ruse to trap them in a confined space for a casual interrogation proved false. Instead, R.D. pointed out buildings of architectural interest and regaled them with historical anecdotes and tall tales. Eloise, whom Phillip had gallantly escorted to the front passenger seat, was wide-eyed with interest. Her curiosity encouraged R.D. to tell even more stories. By the time they reached the train station, Phillip was joining in the conversation too.

Even so, he couldn't escape the questions gnawing on his mind. Was this Velvalee Dickinson their traitor? Why would a doll collector and shop owner betray her own country? The answers could be found in New York City. That's where he needed to be.

CHAPTER TWENTY-FIVE

Eloise stood beside Phillip at the Denver train station ticket window and tried not to think about the logistics of the two of them sharing a sleeper cabin. Swarms of people crowded around them, many of the younger men wearing the uniforms of the various military branches. Besides the need for the military to move their troops efficiently, the rationing of gasoline meant more people traveled by train than automobile these days.

"But I have reservations for two cabins," Phillip said for at least the third time. "Don't you have a duty to honor them?"

"Duty?" The man spat the word as his eyes narrowed, and he gave Phillip the once-over. "Our *duty* is to be sure our fighting men get to where they need to go. As I already told you, one of the reservations was handed over to the army. Now you can take the other one or not. Or I can give it to someone more deserving. It's your choice."

Eloise's stomach lurched at the insult while Phillip's jaw muscle flexed. The unspoken ques-tion behind the words obviously stung: *Why aren't you wearing a uniform?* She longed to shout to everyone in the station that Phillip was one of the FBI agents who had caught the German saboteurs, but that would blow their "we're siblings" cover without solving their immediate problem.

She pasted on a huge smile and slipped between Phillip and the ticket window. "Please forgive my brother. We've been traveling from California, and it's been such a long trip. We're happy to hold on to the reservation we still have. Thank you for all you do for these soldiers and their families. I'm sure you're an angel in disguise for many of them."

Phillip turned away, and Eloise didn't dare glance at him. Was he embarrassed? Angry at her for intervening? Or proud of the way she stepped in? None of it mattered. Only that they got on the train.

The ticket master scowled then handed Eloise their tickets. She tried to thank him, but he was already looking past her to the next person in line. Phillip picked up both their suitcases, and she followed him to a less crowded area near a magazine rack.

"I'm sorry about all this," he said.

The unexpected apology surprised her. "It's not your fault."

"But it is awkward. I don't know what Richard will say."

"We don't have to tell him," she said, keeping her tone light.

Phillip looked at her askance then burst out laughing. "We don't," he agreed. "But he has a way of finding out everything. He'll know."

"Then he should also understand the circumstances. What choice did we have?" Eloise didn't want them sharing a tiny cabin, but she'd rather have Phillip in the other berth than a stranger, even if that stranger was a woman.

"Not much." A corner of Phillip's mouth turned up as he shrugged. "Maybe once we're on the train, we can figure something out."

Before Eloise could object to his plan, he was on the move again, heading for the platform. The situation was awkward, unseemly, and definitely not proper. But she didn't want Phillip in a different train car. They should stay together. Watch each other's backs.

After a short wait, they boarded. Eloise stood in the narrow corridor outside their sleeper cabin, a euphemistic term for a space not much larger than a monk's cell, while Phillip stashed their luggage beneath the lower berth, which was made up as a sofa. A table sat in front of the window and between the berth and a chair.

Phillip shrugged out of his jacket and hung it on a hook behind the door. He rolled his shirt sleeves as he sprawled on the sofa. "You might as well come on in, Sis, and get comfortable." He loosened his tie. "It's hot as the dickens in here."

Eloise removed her hat and patted her hair as she sat across from Phillip. "Maybe it will cool down once we start moving."

"We can hope." He folded his hands on the table. "You handled yourself well back there. Better than I did."

"He didn't need to say what he did," she said. "There could be a thousand reasons why you aren't in uniform."

"Actually, only a handful. And only one that makes sense to most people."

Eloise resisted the urge to cover his hand with hers. During their travels, they'd become more at ease with a casual touch here and there. But in the intimate confines of the small sleeper cabin, the simple gesture might be misconstrued as a romantic one.

The way her pulse sped up at the thought, perhaps there were no more "simple" gestures.

"I wanted to tell him who you are," she said. "What you've done so he would know you're not a coward."

"It doesn't matter."

Eloise wanted to believe him, but his offhanded tone indicated it mattered very much. She placed her hands in her lap and stared out the window. Beyond the platforms, buildings rose into the sky, though not nearly as high as the mountains behind them. Perhaps it was time to change the subject. "Thank you for what you said."

"What did I say?"

Uncomfortable at repeating his earlier compliment, she gave a pointed look. In response, he widened his eyes. He really didn't know?

She released an exasperated sigh. "About how I handled myself."

"I only said what was true." Amusement danced in Phillip's eyes as he held her gaze. "You reminded me of Nancy."

He'd done it again, naming a random woman as if Eloise should know her.

"Is she your girlfriend?"

"Who? Nancy?" His look of disbelief would have been comical if Eloise's heart didn't feel like it was about to be crushed.

"Yes. Nancy."

"Don't you know who Nancy is?"

"How would I?"

"Uncle Richard gave you my dossier. Didn't you read it?"

"As much as I could."

"And you still don't know who Nancy is?" He shook his head in disbelief. "What about Marcy?"

"No."

"Debbie?"

She shook her head.

"Janie?"

Eloise couldn't even muster the energy to answer him. How many women did he have in his life? The edges of her heart crumbled.

Phillip closed the cabin door then returned to his seat. "What did the dossier say about my family?"

"Your family? Nothing." A pinprick of fear traced along her spine. If he thought that his dossier included information about his family, did that mean . . . ?

Her voice rose. "What did my dossier say about mine?"

Phillip hesitated a moment as if choosing his words carefully. When he spoke, his voice was soft. "I've been blessed with four sisters. Marcy and Debbie are older than me. Both married. Nancy and Janie are younger."

"There was nothing about them in the file that Richard gave me."

"He did say he gave you a redacted version, though I don't know why he omitted my family."

"I imagine he had a reason." On one level, Eloise was relieved to learn the women weren't old girlfriends. But her dread of what he might know about her family overshadowed that relief.

"You're trembling." He leaned across the table and clasped both her arms. "Why?"

She hadn't realized she was shaking until his gentle touch steadied her, giving her strength. "I don't know."

He ran his hands along her arms until he held her hands. "I'm sorry about your brother."

Eloise closed her eyes. He knew. Somehow, she'd always known he knew, but now she could no longer pretend that her grief was a secret she hid in her heart. An ache formed in the base of her throat, growing into a lump that threatened to choke her. Phillip ran his thumbs over her knuckles. Again she found strength in his touch. Enough strength to open her eyes and meet his gaze. To face the sympathy and compassion she found there.

"I miss him."

Phillip gently squeezed her fingers. "He would be so proud of you."

A whistle blew and the train lurched. Phillip leaned back in his seat, and Eloise withdrew her hands from his. Once again, she stared out the window, her focus on a distant mountain peak. She sensed Phillip's gaze upon her, but she needed a moment to compose her emotions. To come to terms with the for-sure knowledge that he'd known more about her than she did about him. She'd always suspected it, but the certainty was both reassuring and troubling.

As the train picked up speed and the city was left behind, Eloise's thoughts were as jumbled as a mass of dropped yarn. Phillip didn't break the silence between them with awkward, uncomfortable words or platitudes. She admired that about him—how he allowed silence to breathe, to have its own space. It was one of so many qualities that she admired about him.

"What do you know of my fath—" She stopped herself. "Of my parents?" She asked the question without looking at him, her gaze intent on the passing scenery though her mind processed nothing but swathes of green and blue.

"Your mother returned to her hometown of Camden Falls, Massachusetts in December 1929, taking you and your brother with her. She was valedictorian of her high school class and works part-time in the hospital administration office. She owns the home where you were raised and drives an Oldsmobile that once belonged to her father."

"No wonder you never asked me about her." She turned to him with a joyless smile. "You already know so much."

"I didn't ask because you didn't want me to." His gentle tone almost—not quite but almost—tempted the pent-up tears into falling. "All I know are a few facts. And that she raised an incredible daughter."

"Two compliments in one day?" Though her insides, warmed by his words, were jangled nerves, she managed what she hoped was a coy smile. "Who are you and what have you done with Phillip?"

He had the grace to chuckle at her lame attempt at humor but didn't say anything. She returned her attention to the view outside the window and did her best to sort out her thoughts. She couldn't pinpoint the exact moment the notion, at first a nugget no larger than a mustard seed, occurred to her. Though it must have been after Richard told them to take the train from Denver to Ohio. A route that included a stop in St. Louis. The notion grew into an idea—an impossible, crazy idea.

The *Seattle Times* article and her father's photograph settled into her memory, as crisp and clear as if they were framed by the window instead of tucked inside her handbag. The idea sprouted into a plan but not one she could carry out on her own.

"You didn't mention my father," she said quietly. "But since you know about Mother moving back to Camden Falls, then you must know he didn't go with us."

"I'm aware of that."

Eloise leaned against the back of her seat as if pressed there by a giant hand. Why hadn't she realized before now that Phillip might know more about her father's whereabouts than she did? Her meager information came from a newspaper article. But Phillip had a dossier of facts and details about her life. About her family.

"Do you know where he went? What he's been doing all this time?"

Phillip eyed her a moment, as if weighing his possible responses. But what was there to say except yes or no? Either he did or he didn't.

"It's not that hard of a question," she said. "What do you know?"

"I know he left his wife and two small children

210

shortly after the stock market crashed on Black Tuesday."

October 29, 1929. Events occurred on that infamous day that Eloise had been too young to understand. They were events that she still didn't understand, except that everything in her small world went topsy-turvy and never had been fully righted again.

"What else?" She pushed the question past the blockage in her throat. It sounded harsh. Guttural. Demanding.

"He disappeared." Phillip pressed his lips together and squirmed. "The police investigated. They found nothing conclusive. Unless you know something . . ." His voice rose at the end, turning the statement into a question.

"A couple of weeks after the crash, he didn't come home. Mother pretended nothing was wrong, but Allan and I sensed she was sick with worry. She never speaks of it. I thought she was afraid he'd . . ."

"You don't have to finish that sentence."

Her smile of gratitude lasted a fraction of a second before she was plunged back to those dark days. Despite Mother's efforts to shield her children from the horrific news, they both somehow knew that other men, men of commerce like her father, had taken their own lives rather than face the consequences of financial ruin.

"My birthday was the next day." She hadn't

intended to tell him that, but the words had arisen from her heart as if they were the words she was meant to say and that he was meant to hear. "The party had already been planned, but none of my friends came. Only the police following up on the missing person's report." She gave a harsh laugh. "Mother served them birthday cake while trying to answer their questions. As if it were all a huge mistake and Father would come walking in the door any minute. But he never did."

Phillip seemed about to rise then apparently changed his mind and stayed seated. Somehow his inaction chilled her skin despite the heat of the cabin.

"Didn't he ever write?" Phillip asked. "Surely he sent a message to your mother."

"I used to ask. Every day, the moment I came through the door from school, I asked. The answer was always the same. When he didn't come home for Christmas, I stopped asking."

"I wish there was something I could do to help."

Polite, clichéd words, but Eloise grabbed them like a drowning swimmer clutching a lifeline. She dug the article from her handbag and laid it on the table. The cut edges were as ragged as her emotions.

Phillip scanned the article. "Is this your father?"

" 'Prominent Seattle businessman, Leonard David Mitchell, to attend National Investments

Gala,'" Eloise quoted from memory, "where he will receive the James Madison Award. Mr. Mitchell will be accompanied by his wife and children. The event takes place at the Hotel DeSoto in St. Louis, Missouri."

"This is—"

"Unbelievable? A mistake?" Eloise bit the inside of her lip then grabbed the article and shoved it back into her purse. "He changed his last name, but it's him."

She thought she'd forgiven her father for running away. She'd even been thankful he'd chosen that option of escape instead of a more permanent one. But how could she forgive him for starting a new family when his first one had so desperately needed him?

CHAPTER TWENTY-SIX

Phillip let out a breath of air. Did this mean Eloise's father was a bigamist? Or had her mother kept their divorce a secret? Either way, the man was a first-class scumbag. Did he have any idea of the harm his cowardice had caused? Did he even care?

Phillip longed to take Eloise in his arms, to smooth away the tension around her eyes, and kiss away the tears that she was valiantly holding back. He'd almost stood to go to her side once already but curbed the impulse before he acted on it. A man could offer his sister a shoulder to cry on, but he didn't kiss her. A professional agent didn't kiss a colleague either.

The moment had passed for him to clarify what he'd intended to say before Eloise interrupted him. Not *this is unbelievable,* but *this is why you were so upset in Seattle.* She'd been blindsided by the discovery of her father's betrayal. The best way Phillip could help her was to simply listen. With four sisters, he'd had a lot of practice, but none of them had ever experienced a situation as devastating as this.

Eloise blinked then looked straight at him. "Do you believe in coincidences?"

"Richard says a coincidence is never a coincidence."

She seemed to consider that for a moment while still holding his gaze. "Then you agree it's not a coincidence that I was in Seattle the day my father's photo appeared in the newspaper. That I found it."

He tilted his head in a vain attempt to foresee where she was headed. "What else could it be but a coincidence?"

"Maybe . . ." Her voice faltered, and she took a deep breath to regain her composure. "Maybe God meant for me to find it."

The hopeful expression in her eyes stopped him from expressing his reflexive skepticism. Besides, maybe she was right. He'd first read Oswald Chambers's classic devotional, *My Utmost for His Highest*, when he was sixteen and perhaps four or five more times since then. A notable theme throughout the book was that God engineered circumstances to reveal His will. Had he done so here? If not, the only alternative explanation—that the entire incident was due to happenstance—seemed to take more faith than what Eloise was suggesting.

"Maybe He did," he replied. Eloise's expression didn't change, as if she were expecting something more from him. But what? Phillip floundered with what to say. "Now you know your father is alive. That must be comforting."

Her shoulders drooped.

Or not.

"Aren't you glad—" *Nope, wrong word.* From the disappointed look in her eyes, it was the worst word he could have used. He took a deep breath and tried again. "Aren't you relieved to know the truth? Even if it's not . . . ." The disappointment in her eyes deepened. He wanted to throw up his hands in frustration but managed to maintain his composure. He rarely had trouble consoling his sisters when they were upset. Why was Eloise making this so hard? Didn't she realize he was only trying to help?

The urge to take her in his arms overwhelmed him, and he shrank into the corner of the sofa. Her expectant gaze followed him, silently pleading for . . . what? He didn't know.

"I won't pretend to understand," he said, "how difficult this must be for you." It was the only consolation he dared to give her. The only truth he could offer while keeping as much distance between them as he could manage in the cramped confines of the cabin.

"The train stops in St. Louis." A simple, surprisingly matter-of-fact statement. No pleading. No whining.

He stared at her, then the proverbial light bulb finally turned on over his head. "You want to see him."

"Correction. I want him to see me."

A thousand thoughts clashed in Phillip's mind as he tried sorting through possibilities, scenarios, and ramifications even as he questioned how he could consider going along with such a crazy idea. What did she expect? To confront her father at the gala? Humiliate him in front of the other participants?

Truth be told, he couldn't blame her if that was her plan. He wouldn't mind doing that himself. But he believed that any satisfaction Eloise received from publicly confronting her father would be fleeting.

Eloise broke into his thoughts. "I need to do this."

"Do what, exactly?"

"I'm not sure." Her cheeks flushed. "I understand we have a mission."

"An important mission."

"I can't go to Springfield with you." Her voice caught. "I'm sorry. This is my only chance to get any answers."

His heart dropped to his stomach, not a reaction he expected to have. On the surface, he was miffed—more than miffed—that she would abandon their investigation. But deeper than that, he didn't want her to abandon *him*—a ridiculous notion he couldn't indulge in or should even acknowledge. Richard had chosen him to accompany Eloise because he trusted that Phillip wouldn't become romantically involved with her. And he wouldn't. No matter how much his heart tugged him in that direction. He needed to take control of this situation, to convince her to continue their trip.

"Maybe you should talk to your mother," he suggested. "We can call her from the next station."

"No." Her tone was adamant. "She's not been herself since Allan died. I can't let her know about this until I have more details. It would kill her."

"Unless," Phillip said quietly, "she already knows."

From the shocked expression on Eloise's face, that idea had never occurred to her. "She would have told me."

"Maybe she wanted to protect you."

Her chin trembled as she looked away. Phillip wavered on what he should do. Nancy liked to be alone when she was upset, but Janie didn't. What did Eloise like?

"Forgive me for asking, but if Allan were here, what would he do to console you?"

To his surprise, Eloise emitted a small laugh. "He'd tell me to be brave."

"Then that's what I'm telling you." He swallowed a sigh and hoped his uncle wouldn't disown him. "The next stop is in Topeka. I'll give Richard a call and let him know we'll be a day late getting to Springfield."

"You don't have to go with me."

"We're partners. We stick together."

A weight seemed to lift from her shoulders. "Thank you. I really didn't want to do this alone." *And I didn't want you to.*

Now all he had to do was figure out what to tell Richard. The mission was supposed to come first. Always. But if Eloise was right, if God meant for her to confront her father, then Phillip trusted Him to work out the details.

Eloise lay on her side in the lower berth as the train sped across the Kansas plains toward Topeka. Phillip slept in the upper berth, the soft sounds of his breathing a comforting contrast to the mechanical whir of the train. She wished she could fall asleep so easily.

Despite her weariness, sleep eluded her. How foolish she'd been to show Phillip the article. Instead of telling him about her plan, she should have made an excuse to get off the train in St. Louis or left him a brief note and disappeared into the crowd. She suspected he would have searched for her though. An inexplicable shift had occurred over the past few days as the meager threads that had pulled them together when they first met drew tighter and multiplied.

She'd impulsively given him an injured piece of her heart, and he'd tended it with care. At first, she'd appreciated his offer to postpone their mission. But now? Her restless mind wouldn't quiet down and leave her in peace.

Earlier, after he'd said they were partners, he volunteered to go to the club car so that she could have the cabin to herself. Once he was gone, she splashed cool water from the tiny sink on her stinging eyes. Alone with her thoughts, she pulled out the article and stared at her father's photograph.

He hadn't changed much in the sixteen years he'd been gone. Streaks of gray appeared at his temples, and he had more lines around his eyes than she remembered. But the confidence in his eyes as he stared at the camera suggested a lively personality at odds with the emotionally distant father who resided in her memory.

He'd been a good provider, ensuring his family lived in a comfortable home in a respectable neighborhood in Albany, New York. At her young age, Eloise knew only that her closet was full of pretty dresses, her toy box overflowed, and food was plentiful. Her father joined them for dinner then disappeared into his den until bedtime, when he reemerged.

With Eloise on one side and Allan on the other, he'd read one chapter from a book. Only one. His duty complete, he would send them with a peck on the cheek to find Mother, who made sure they brushed their teeth and said their prayers.

They were in the middle of a Hardy Boys

mystery—she couldn't remember which one—when Father disappeared. Eloise tried to finish the story, reading one chapter a night, and only one chapter, to Allan before bedtime. But it wasn't the same without Father between them. She missed resting her cheek against the worn fabric of his favorite cardigan as his voice adapted to the events of the story. Sometimes it was deep and resonant, other times as soft as an eerie whisper.

She envisioned him reading the same stories to his new family. Could he do so without images of the long-ago bedtime ritual flickering in his mind? In his heart?

Childhood memories drifted around her. A few sad days but mostly happy ones, even after they'd moved to Mother's hometown and rebuilt their lives as a fatherless family of three. If not for this horrid war, the rhythms of their uneventful and peaceful lives would have continued. Each new week began with worship and was followed by days of work and evenings of leisure. The seasons followed one another in a cycle as old as time.

Their renewed peace was brutally interrupted on a day of infamy when bombs dropped from the skies and young men died. The events precipitated tragic grief and unwelcome change.

Though her tangled thoughts still collided with one another, she finally succumbed to a restless, troubled sleep.

Bombs fall. Young men die.

Flames soar. Explosions knock her to the ground.

"Eloise?"

Allan calls her name. He's there, in the distance. She reaches for him, and he grips her hand.

"Eloise, honey, wake up."

"No," she mutters. "No." Deep inside the recesses of her mind, she understands that consciousness will cause her to lose this tenuous connection with her brother. She can't let him go.

"You're having a bad dream." His voice is soft and kind. Familiar. But it interferes with her desperate wish to remain burrowed inside herself.

"A good dream," she says.

"Then sleep." Warm lips touch her forehead as she descends again into welcome darkness.

CHAPTER TWENTY-SEVEN

At the Topeka station, Phillip settled onto the phone booth's wooden bench and closed the door. He didn't want to make this call, but what choice did he have? Eloise had tried to talk him out of it, insisting that, for the sake of the mission, he had to go to Springfield on his own. He tried to persuade her to go with him and even promised to return with her to Seattle once the mission was over.

But she was dead set on seeing her father in St. Louis, and Phillip was just as stubborn. Where she went, he was going to go too, whether she liked it or not. He only hoped Uncle Richard would understand. A day's delay was all he needed. Surely that could do no harm.

Yeah, right.

A lot could change in twenty-four hours, and in his line of work, it often did. But he couldn't very well hog-tie Eloise to the cabin chair during the St. Louis layover. Neither could he allow her to go off on her own. She needed someone beside her when she found her father. Phillip was all she had.

When Richard answered the phone, Phillip launched into his spiel. "Mr. Whitmer, how nice to speak with you. Phillip Carter here." The

223

greeting would put Richard on alert that Phillip was calling from an unsecured line. The entire conversation would be a type of verbal jargon code. Hopefully, Richard could decipher it.

"What can I do for you, Mr. Carter?"

So far, so good. "We've had a hiccup in our travel plans. Turns out good old Dad is in St. Louis. We thought we'd stop in and see him."

The line was silent a moment, but Phillip could imagine Richard's mental wheels whirring as he worked out the message. He was familiar with Eloise's dossier, so it wouldn't take him long.

"How interesting," Richard finally said. "Does he know you're coming?"

"No, it's a surprise."

"Are you sure that's a good idea?"

Nope. Not even a little bit. "Sis has her heart set on seeing him. It's been a long time." Phillip let out a small chuckle. "Quite the coincidence, don't you think, that we'd all be in the same place at the same time?"

"I don't put much stock in coincidences."

"Neither do I. But there are exceptions."

Another silence.

"Take good care of your sister, Mr. Carter," Richard said. "And please stay in touch."

"Thank you for understanding."

"I'm not sure I do, but we can talk about it later."

Phillip wasn't sure whether Richard meant his

224

words to sound ominous, but they made him feel like a boy who'd been sent to the woodshed. The unspoken message was clear. Phillip would be held responsible for any consequences arising from their unscheduled stopover.

Perhaps he shouldn't have mentioned coincidences. But it was his best card, and he had to play it. His unspoken message to his uncle was also clear. If God had engineered these circumstances, then neither Phillip nor Richard had a right to interfere in His plans.

But that was the big unknown. *If.*

"Give your sister my regards," Richard continued.

"I'll do that, sir."

The call ended, but Phillip stayed in the booth. Noise from the crowded station filtered through the cracks in the door, but the booth was still quieter than the rackety train. Despite the nighttime noise, he'd slept well until Eloise awakened him with her tearful moans. At first he'd tried to awaken her, but she resisted his efforts to pull her from sleep. "A good dream," she'd whispered.

He'd given in to the impulse he'd been fighting all day and brushed his lips against her forehead. In the dim light from the shaded night lamp, his gaze had been drawn to her closed eyes, the curve of her cheek, the shape of her mouth. The subtle rise and fall of her chest beneath the thin blanket.

It would have been so easy to slip in the bed beside her, to adjust the contours of his body to hers as she slept. Only to hold her close in case the nightmare returned. But he hadn't dared give in to the temptation no matter its justification. He squeezed her fingers then released her hand. After returning to the upper berth, he lay on his back, his forearm across his eyes, and tried to forget the surge that raced through him when his lips touched her cool, pale skin. He wanted to deny that he was falling in love when the thought of marriage, or even courtship, was impossible. After this operation, he was joining the battle where it mattered. Overseas. He didn't need any potential entanglements to complicate his life or to prevent him from doing his duty.

Though Eloise was already doing exactly that.

His heart lurched as he caught sight of her through the phone booth's glass door when a few soldiers with clipped hair and starched uniforms moved away from the newsstand where she idly flipped through a magazine. He glanced at his watch. About twenty more minutes until they needed to be on board the train.

He picked up the receiver and dialed the operator. When she came on the line, he asked to be connected to the Hotel DeSoto in St. Louis. He inserted the requested coins, his gaze still on Eloise as he waited for someone to answer his call.

"Hotel DeSoto. Switchboard."

"I need the room number for Leonard David Mitchell, please." His hope that she'd say no guest by that name was staying at the hotel was quickly squashed.

"Mr. Mitchell is in room 584, the presidential suite." *That sounded impressive. And expensive.* "Would you like me to connect you?"

"Thank you, yes." *Why am I doing this?* He had nothing to say to the man. Nothing good anyway. And he definitely didn't plan on warning him that his daughter was on her way to see him.

A moment later, a jovial voice came on the line. "Mitchell here." The murmur of voices could be heard over the music that played in the background. "I say, is anyone there?"

Phillip scowled and immediately hung up. His call to the hotel had a purpose, but he should never have agreed to be connected to Mitchell's room. He'd given in to an impulse, something he never did. Trusting your gut, your instincts—that was one thing. But this had been different. A foolish, foolish impulse that gained him nothing except more proof that he was letting his heart rule his head where Eloise was concerned. Good thing Uncle Richard couldn't see him right now. He'd probably send him back to the academy for remedial training and find someone else to accompany Eloise on any more interviews.

The distraction ended now. He'd go to the

Hotel DeSoto with her, and he would stand beside her if she chose to confront her father. But professionalism would rule his conduct. Before long, they'd have the person responsible for the letters, whether Velvalee Dickinson or somebody else, in custody. Eloise would return to her code-breaking duties for the navy, and he'd be on his way to basic training. He doubted their paths would ever cross again.

CHAPTER TWENTY-EIGHT

The train pulled into St. Louis's Union Station late the next afternoon. Eloise, mesmerized by the magnificence of the Grand Hall, wanted to do nothing more than stand in one spot and take it all in. The vaulted ceiling was adorned with frescos and mosaics. Travelers overlooked the midway from a series of third-story balconies outlined by similarly adorned arches. Even the windows were artistically designed.

"Every train station seems more magnificent than the last," she said to Phillip. He carried both their bags while she clung to his arm. She didn't want to risk getting separated from him in this noisy, oversized crowd.

"You should have seen this one before the war." With his hands gripping the suitcases, he pointed his chin toward the ceiling. "There was a chandelier up there with three hundred and fifty light bulbs. I heard it weighed two tons."

Eloise tried to imagine the beauty of such a grand fixture but was certain she failed. "What happened to it?"

"It was made of wrought iron. What do you think happened to it?"

"They turned it to scrap metal?" Even though it was the patriotic thing to do, the loss of the giant

229

chandelier seemed a pity. How could anything like that ever be replaced?

"Along with the platform gates. They sure were a sight to see." Phillip frowned as departing passengers jostled past them. "Let's get out of this crowd."

She had to practically jog to keep up with his long stride, not an easy thing to do in her heels. But she refused to ask him to slow his pace. He'd been a grouch since before they reached Topeka, and it was all her fault.

The day before, once they were back on board the train, he had told her that Richard was aware of their plan. But he refused to share any details of the conversation. He also informed her that he'd used his FBI credentials to secure two rooms at a hotel next to Union Station's Grand Hall. Then he buried his nose in a book, which he didn't seem to be reading. While at supper in the dining car, he asked for her entrée preference before the meal and how had she liked her baked ham as they ate pineapple upside-down cake for dessert. Nothing else.

After escorting her to their cabin, he had retreated to the club car. When he returned, she pretended to be asleep. She didn't hear him leave again, but he was gone when she awoke. Shortly before the train pulled into St. Louis, he sauntered in and reorganized his suitcase.

Once again, she chastised herself for saying

anything to him about her father. If only she'd kept silent until they arrived in St. Louis. He still would be upset at her plan, but he wouldn't have had nearly as much time to brood. Though it was too late now to change what had already happened—Mother once told her the past was set in concrete—Eloise carried the heavy weight of her emotionally wrought foolishness.

They found the entrance to the hotel and crossed the narrow lobby to the front desk. Phillip gave his name and showed the badge while Eloise endured the clerk's curious stare with as much dignity as she could muster. Which wasn't much. She was weary from a restless night's sleep and wanted nothing more than to soak away the dirt and grime of train travel from her hair and her skin.

After Phillip signed the guestbook, the clerk handed him two keys and gestured for a bellboy to take their luggage. He led the way to their rooms, pointing out the communal bathroom along the way. Eloise quietly prayed her room would be nearby then breathed a sigh of relief when the bellboy stopped three doors down.

A corner nightstand held a basin and matching pitcher while a narrow bed took up most of the space in the tiny room.

"Are all the rooms this small?" Phillip asked.

"They're all the same," the teenager said. "People who stay here are usually on their way to somewhere else, so they don't need much in the way of anemities."

Eloise and Phillip glanced at one another, both amused by his mispronunciation. Then Phillip blinked, and the shared moment ended.

He pulled a few coins from his pocket. "We can manage from here. Thank you." Once the bellboy left, he turned to Eloise. "Will you be okay here?"

"It's a palace compared to the sleeper," she said lightly. He merely nodded and picked up his suitcase. Definitely not the response she'd hoped from him. If that's how he wanted to be, fine. Two could play this game. "Why don't you go on to Ohio without me?"

His eyes widened. Because he wasn't used to being confronted? Or because he knew he was acting like a donkey's behind? "I'm not leaving you."

"This is already hard." She folded her arms. "So, either tell me why you're mad or just go."

He refused to look away as he worked his jaw, but Eloise didn't care. She didn't look away either.

"I can do this all day," she said.

He lowered his head but not before she caught the hint of a smile playing on his lips. She was too indignant to care. He met her gaze again. "I'm not mad at you. Far from it."

"You could have fooled me."

He placed his suitcase on the floor and folded

her hands in his. "I can't explain what's been going on with me. I'm not sure I know myself."

"I don't understand."

"It's not important. But I do have something to tell you. Something I should have already told you."

Her stomach clenched at his tone, but she feigned indifference. Despite the warmth of his hands, her skin felt cold. "Oh?"

"After I spoke to Richard, I called the Hotel DeSoto where the gala is being held. Your father is staying there. Room 584."

Her knees turned to water, and she would have fallen if Phillip hadn't been there to support her. "Did you talk to him?"

"No." He eased her to the bed and sat beside her. "The operator connected me to his room, but when he answered, I hung up."

"You heard his voice?"

"I did."

Eloise reached back into her memory, trying to recall the last time she'd heard her father's voice. The last time he'd said *I love you*. But it was impossible to capture a singular moment that could give her that gift.

Phillip patted her hand. "We'll go whenever you're ready. Just say the word."

His change in demeanor along with his lack of an explanation for his earlier behavior confused her, but for now she needed to save her emotional energy. At least he was no longer sullen and was more than willing to accompany her. Though she had meant what she said—she didn't want him along if he couldn't be kind—she needed *someone* to be with her.

"I want to freshen up." And take a bath. Hopefully, the communal bathroom was unoccupied.

"Take as much time as you need." He lifted her suitcase onto the foot of the bed. "My room is right across the hall. Knock on the door when you're ready."

"I will." She followed him to the door and closed it behind him. Now that she was alone, all her nervous energy seemed to need an outlet, but she refused to give in to tears. Not now, when she needed all her strength to face her father.

She took a deep breath, whispered a quick prayer, and unlatched her suitcase. After pawing through her clothes, she placed her hands on her hips. What she needed was a new dress. She'd spotted a few shops as they traversed the Grand Hall. And then she decided on a quick shower instead of a long, soothing bath—an easy sacrifice to ensure she presented herself with confidence. She still had no idea what to say to her father or if she'd say anything at all. Maybe she only needed to see his face and for him to recognize her.

Until they were in the same room, she couldn't know how she would react. All she knew was that she needed every possible advantage. A new dress, confident poise, and Phillip by her side. None of that could hurt.

She ran a comb through her hair, reapplied her lipstick, and grabbed her handbag. Time to find the perfect outfit.

CHAPTER TWENTY-NINE

Phillip opened the door and stared at the vision standing in the hall. Not fair, God. How was he supposed to keep his emotions in check when Eloise stood before him, an intoxicating combination of loveliness and vulnerability? He might not be able to pinpoint the color of her dress, but what did that matter? He'd heard his sisters talk about their fashion choices enough to recognize the heart neckline covered by a dotted swiss lace overlay and the faux asymmetrical wrap of the skirt.

"Hello." His voice cracked, and he cleared his throat. "You . . . you're stunning."

"Are you sure? I'm so nervous."

"I'm sure." He glanced down at his black trousers. Thankfully, he'd had the foresight to have his best suit cleaned and pressed. Otherwise, he'd have looked like a country bumpkin next to a society belle. "Come on in a moment. I couldn't decide on a tie."

He gestured to the two spread on top of his closed suitcase. "What do you think? The blue one or the gray one?" At least he could identify the colors, though the shade of blue was so pale he didn't understand how it could be considered the same as the color he recognized as blue. But

Debbie had assured him it was. Helpful older sister that she was, she'd created a system to help him match his ties to his clothes. She stitched a simple design on the underside of each one. One / for blues, two // for yellows, a # for browns, a + for greens. Those were the colors that gave him the most difficulty. His own personal code, and an especially easy one to break.

"I like the blue one," Eloise said. "It adds a bit of pizzazz to your suit."

"The blue one it is." He slung the tie around his neck and deftly knotted a half Windsor. "Do you have a plan for this rendezvous?"

"There's a reception before the awards ceremony. As one of the guests of honor, he's certain to attend."

"I never would have taken you for a gate-crasher," Phillip teased as he shrugged into his jacket.

"I'm not," she said, obviously offended he'd think her capable of such behavior. Or perhaps prickly because of her unsettled nerves. "I thought we could, oh, I don't know, perhaps meander around the lobby. Just be nearby. Though I'm open to other suggestions."

"It's not a bad plan. I'm assuming you don't want to make a public spectacle."

"Of course I don't."

"Then we need to get to the hotel before the reception starts. Find the best spots to set up

237

surveillance." A task that would have already been completed if this were a real operation. Maybe something he should have done earlier instead of sprawling on his bed and waiting for the time to pass. Though it unsettled him to play a supporting role, he'd accepted that's what he needed to do this evening. This was Eloise's mission, not his. It was up to her to decide how much interaction she had with her father. Whatever her decision, Phillip was determined to stand beside her.

Eloise took a deep breath and tucked her clutch bag beneath her arm. "I'm ready." Her tone was bright, but her adorable red lips were pinched into a tight smile.

"Let's go then." He escorted her from the room, locking the door behind him while he prayed the evening would bring her peace . . . or at least not turn into a disaster.

A taxi whisked them from Union Station to the hotel as the sun appeared to rest above the famous St. Louis arch. A gentle breeze chased away the heat of the August day, creating the perfect early evening weather for a casual stroll. That would have been more to Phillip's liking than the coming storm. Eloise might not want to make a scene, but his gut told him that the situation could quickly escalate into thunder and lightning. He offered Eloise his arm and prayed for nothing more than a quick summer shower.

They entered the lobby, where a few people gathered near the registration desk and bellboys stacked luggage on carts. To the right, widely spaced columns formed an L that allowed easy access to the hotel's bar area. Tables draped with black squares over white floor-length cloths were scattered in front of the bar, which stood before a mirrored wall. Most of the seats were already taken by women in long gowns and their grandly attired escorts.

"I guess I should have packed my tux," Phillip said in a low voice.

"And I should have bought a different dress," Eloise whispered back.

He wanted to tell her that her stunning appearance took his breath away, but the compliment died on his lips. He would hope to say the words in a flirty, noncommittal tone that eased her tension, but that was impossible. He meant the words too much to say them lightly, which meant they couldn't be said at all.

His fingers clasped her elbow, and he steered her toward a vantage spot beside one of the columns. From here, they could see almost all the bar's patrons. "Do you recognize anyone?"

He followed her gaze as she scanned the crowd. A few moments later, the sudden bracing of her shoulders gave him the answer before she could verbalize it.

"There. Standing by the painting of the arch."

Two men were engaged in conversation beside a painting of the famous landmark, but Phillip easily recognized Leonard Mitchell from the newspaper photo that Eloise had shown him. About five ten in height and carrying the typical paunch of a man who ate well and spent most of his time behind a desk, he held a martini in one hand and a cigarette in the other. He laughed at something the other man said, clapping him on the back while squeezing the cigarette between two thick fingers and throwing his head back. He easily—almost too easily—fit the stereotype of "hail fellow well met." Too friendly. Too familiar. Too chummy.

The over-the-top personality no doubt contributed to the accolades he looked forward to receiving later in the evening. But how did that personality reconcile with that of a man who abandoned his family when he should have faced life's harsh realities? He was obviously a successful financier once again. Couldn't he have achieved that same accomplishment without running off to the West Coast?

Eloise may have been asking herself the same questions. Her gaze was directed toward the two men, and her mouth was set in a grim line. Though Phillip couldn't read her mind, he could read *her*. She was intelligent and intuitive—and her mental wheels were in overdrive as she observed her father's bombastic behavior.

Phillip shifted toward her. "What do you want to do now?"

Instead of answering, she slipped away from him, though not in a direct beeline toward Mitchell. Instead, she skirted the edge of the crowd until she reached a column near the wall. Only a few tables separated her from her father. Phillip followed behind, stopping several feet away.

Suddenly, the hairs on the back of his neck stood up. He resisted the amateur move of turning around. Instead, he removed a cigarette holder from his pocket. He wasn't a smoker—primarily because of his mother's sensitivity to strong odors—but the popularity of the habit made the holder an attractive prop.

While pretending his focus was on choosing a cigarette and preparing to light it, he maneuvered behind two matronly women discussing an upcoming wedding. He darted a glance at Eloise, who hadn't moved from her spot opposite her father, then surreptitiously glanced toward the mirror behind the bar. A broad-chested man with wide sideburns perched on a stool nursing a drink. He immediately dropped his eyes to his glass.

Gotcha!

Phillip tagged him at about six feet, a little over two hundred pounds, and in his late twenties to early thirties. While the man pretended nothing interested him more than his liquor, Phillip pivoted away from the matrons and took a position near a column that gave him easy sightline to both Sideburns and Eloise's reflection in the mirror while making it difficult for the man to see him.

Phillip had a choice to make. Confront the man or wait to see what he would do. Given the circumstances, neither option was to his liking. But since his only proof that Sideburns meant any harm was an indefinable yet trusted sensation, he decided to observe a while longer before taking any action. Besides, he needed to stay close to Eloise in case she needed him.

He looked her way again as two women joined her father and his companion. Leonard Mitchell wrapped his arm around the taller woman's waist and pecked her on the cheek. She accepted the gesture with an adoring gaze then laughed at something Phillip couldn't hear. Meanwhile, Eloise stared at the foursome while the man at the bar ran his eyes over the crowd.

Looking for me?

Sideburns turned back to the mirror, again seeming to search the reflected crowd. Then he shifted his eyes to the group by the painting of the arch. And then to Eloise.

Phillip recognized the man's expression. He'd seen it often enough on the faces of his colleagues during various operations as they assessed whether someone was a threat and, if so, how much. He no doubt wore the same expression himself, at least to anyone skilled enough to recognize it.

But why would Sideburns suspect Eloise of being a threat? She was the epitome of girl-next-door wholesomeness. Or was she?

Phillip looked at her again, adjusting his view of her so that she was a stranger instead of his colleague on a weird cross-country FBI operation. How would he appraise her at this moment if he didn't know her?

She appeared stunning in her new dress. More than one red-blooded American male had taken a lingering look or a backward glance since they'd left their rooms at the Union Station hotel. But Eloise paid no attention to her erstwhile admirers. She simply stared at her father and the woman who now stood with him, her eyes intense, her jaw firm, her stance unyielding.

A potential threat. Except she was a woman, thereby more useful as a distraction than the cause of any harm. At least that might be Sideburns's line of reasoning and why he had paid closer attention to her companion—Phillip—assuming he was the one more likely to cause trouble. Though trouble to whom? Leonard Mitchell?

A clock chimed the hour, and as if on cue, several in the bar area prepared to leave. The pre-gala reception was about to begin effectively moving the party to another area of the hotel.

Sideburns slid from his stool, buttoned his jacket, and moved toward the painting of the arch. He seemed to catch Mitchell's eye then darted his gaze to Eloise and back again. Mitchell followed the glance then stared as his jovial smile faded away.

CHAPTER THIRTY

When her father kissed the woman's cheek, Eloise wanted to run from the hotel and board the first train out of St. Louis. But her feet were glued to the floor, and all she could do was stare as the couple laughed with their friends. Everything around her seemed to recede from her senses. She saw only those in the cheerful tableau in front of her. The loud chattering of the crowd was only a distant hum in her ears.

The chime of a clock startled her, but she stayed at her vantage post even as reception-goers vacated their tables and swirled past her. She didn't know what to do, where to go. So, she stayed, still as a statue, and waited.

Laughter bubbled from her father as he turned toward her. When their eyes met, his narrowed as if he were trying to place her, then the smile died on his lips. Her muscles tightened, and she hardened her stare. This was the moment she'd been waiting for, and she still didn't know what to say to him. Or if she should say anything at all.

"Lenny?" The woman shifted her gaze to Eloise then back to her husband. "Aren't you coming? We don't want to be late, darling."

Another man joined the group. He took a position between Eloise and her father, his hands loosely clasped in front of him. Almost simultaneously, she sensed Phillip's presence beside her.

"Everything okay, boss?" the man said.

The question seemed to jolt her father from his stupor. Recognition flashed, and his eyes softened. His hand moved, as if to reach for her, but a cigarette dangled from his fingers and he put it to his lips.

"Lenny?" Annoyance edged the woman's tone. Eloise shifted her gaze toward the person she assumed was the new Mrs. Marshall. No—she was Mrs. Mitchell. Her father had tossed his past aside and taken a new name, a new wife. The venom in the woman's eyes unnerved her. Eloise had never before seen such hatred. To find it directed at her punched her resolve.

If looks could kill, she'd be on the floor taking her last breath.

"I can't believe the nerve," the woman practically hissed. "Thinking you could show up here and embarrass us in front of our friends. You already have your money. Now leave before I have you thrown out."

Eloise opened her mouth then closed it again. She turned to her father, a ten-year-old girl who needed her daddy to navigate a strange world where people said things that didn't make sense. But he'd given up that role when he abandoned his family. His first family.

He gripped his wife's arm. "She's not who you think. . . . This isn't who you think it is."

"You mean there's another one?"

"Honey pie," he said, his voice sickly placating, "you're getting all upset when there's absolutely no reason for it. Why don't you go along to the reception? I'll be along shortly and then I'll explain everything."

"Will you explain everything to *me?*" Surprised by the strength in her voice, especially when her insides were as squishy as warmed gelatin, Eloise couldn't resist striking a match to the dynamite keg. "Father."

His eyes flickered with such a myriad of emotions—betrayal, anger, regret—Eloise couldn't tell what bothered him most. That she stood in front of him demanding answers or that she'd dared to reveal their relationship. Phillip placed his hand on the small of her back, a welcome gesture that comforted her heart and fortified her confidence.

"Father?" Mrs. Mitchell glared at her husband. "You always were one for secrets, but this seems a bit much even for you. What in the world will Daddy say?"

"Go to the reception, Lorraine." His tone was more that of an autocratic boss than a loving husband. All hint of his prior joviality had disappeared, replaced by the countenance that Eloise remembered most from her childhood. He turned to the friend he'd been laughing with earlier and said in a low voice, "If she doesn't control herself, take her to our room and give her a sleeping pill. I won't be long." The friend nodded agreement then escorted both his wife and Mrs. Mitchell away from the bar.

Now they were alone except for the side-burned beast Eloise assumed was her father's right-hand man or perhaps his bodyguard. Either way, he seemed content to observe their interactions while staying near enough to be of assistance if her father needed him. What did he think she was going to do? Slap him?

Though the thought was tempting, any satisfaction she gained would be short-lived. She'd be left with nothing but a stinging palm.

"Shall we go somewhere more private?" Father suggested. "The hotel has a tiny library tucked away in a hidden corner, which I doubt is in use. We can talk there."

Phillip stirred beside her. She could guess why. The words *tucked away* and *hidden* probably raised red flags for him. But she had no reason to fear her father or the hulking goon. "Sounds lovely."

"Who's your companion?" Father asked. "You're not wearing a ring, so I assume he isn't your husband."

"He's a . . . friend." She'd started to say *colleague,* but that might lead to questions about her vocation. Questions she couldn't answer even if she wanted to. And she certainly didn't want to tell her lowlife of a father about either her work with the navy or with the FBI. He could think what he wanted about her traveling with a man who wasn't her husband, even if it sullied her reputation in his eyes. She truly did not care about his opinion. He'd broken Mother's heart, and from what she'd observed, the new wife wasn't faring much better.

"A friend?" He actually smirked. "Does he have a name?"

Phillip extended his hand. "Phillip Carter. Construction."

Father set down his drink, clasped Phillip's hand, and didn't let go.

"That's quite a grip you've got there, sir." Phillip's casual tone showed no indication of rancor.

"A good thing for you to remember." Father dropped Phillip's hand as if he were tossing away a too small fish.

"I will, sir. You can count on that."

"Why don't you take a seat at the bar and get yourself a drink. You can put it on my tab, and Hammer here will keep you company while Eloise and I have a little chat."

"That's not going to happen." The pressure of his hand on Eloise's back intensified. "Sir."

"I'll be fine," she murmured.

"And I'll be right outside the door."

She nodded agreement. She'd been fearful of this meeting, fearful of what she'd find when face-to-face with her father. But now she was more curious than afraid. More angry than hurt. In a few brief moments, she'd witnessed a despicable and selfish person treat his wife with total disregard for her feelings. He might have treated Mother the same way during their marriage. But he had no power to harm her, no matter what he might say or do. Not anymore.

She tucked her hand into the crook of Phillip's arm. "I'm ready."

Father didn't look pleased but neither did he object. They made their way to the library in silence. After the warren of hallways they'd passed through to find it, Eloise was especially glad Phillip had accompanied her. She wasn't sure she could find her way back to the lobby by herself.

True to his word, Phillip took up his post on one side of the door while Father's goon did the same on the other. The rectangular room was lined with shelves. Most held books or magazines. But others displayed memorabilia from the days when the hotel housed a men's academic club and historical items related to St. Louis's beginnings. If Eloise had been here under any other circumstances, she would have enjoyed browsing the displays and reading the placards.

Father offered Eloise a seat at a nearby wooden table. She allowed him to push in her chair then waited for him to speak first. That was one of the interrogation techniques she'd learned at the academy—begin by letting the subject tell his story. He'll probably give you information you wouldn't have gotten by asking premature questions.

"What are you doing here, Eloise? Did your mother send you?"

Somehow, she managed to keep her expression impassive. Phillip would have been proud. But she hadn't expected him to question her or to insinuate that Mother knew where to find him. How could she? Even if she knew he lived in Seattle, she probably wouldn't have known about the gala in St. Louis.

Time to try another interrogation technique. Answer a question with a question.

"Where have you been the past thirteen years" —she remembered how Phillip had paused earlier and how that pause had weighted his next word, *sir,* with an ironic emphasis—"Father?"

"Making my fortune," he said simply, as if the answer should have been obvious. "What choice did I have after my first one was stolen from me?"

"You could have stayed with your family. It's not like you were the only one who suffered."

"Would you have thought better of me if I'd jumped off a building? Drowned myself?" He

251

scoffed. "That was never going to happen. But neither could I stay in Albany and endure the finger pointing and the whisperings. You have no idea what it was like, those days after the crash. The best thing I could do for you and your brother and your mother was to go on my own way. Make a fresh start."

His casual mention of Allan churned a fire within her that she could not control. "Allan is dead."

Father startled. "Allan's dead?" For the first time, he seemed shaken out of the smug complacency he wore like a tailored suit.

"You didn't know?"

"How could I have known?" He stood, paced a circle, then returned to his seat. "When? What happened?"

"Why should I tell you?" It was a cruel question, and she had never believed herself to be a cruel person. But she felt justified in this cruelty. Anything to cause him pain similar to the pain she bore every day.

"He was my son." With the tone of his voice, the expression in his eyes, he pleaded for an answer. But she wanted to twist the knife for a while longer.

"Not once you left. Not after all the birthdays and Christmases you missed. Not after you tossed us away like yesterday's newspaper and found a new family."

He reached for her hand, but she pulled away before he could touch her.

"You were too young to understand." His tone shifted, becoming soft and reconciliatory. "I'm begging you to understand now. Just because I wasn't there didn't mean I wasn't thinking of you. I thought of you every day. And when your birthday came around, I spent the day in tears thinking of my beautiful little girl. I can't count the number of times I started to get on that train and head east. Countless times."

The picture he was painting with his words was so at odds with the father of her memories and the man who sat near her today that she wanted to laugh in his face. How gullible, how stupid, did he think she was? She hadn't made the mistake of placing her absent father on a pedestal, but she realized now that she'd expected more respect from him.

"I don't believe you," she said. "I don't think you once looked back or that you were ever sorry."

His demeanor changed again, and his eyes grew cold. "Do you think I care what you believe or don't believe?" He smacked his palm on the table, and the sound reverberated around the room. "Tell me what happened to Allan. I have a right to know."

The door opened, and Phillip filled the frame. He held a small revolver at his side. Father's goon stood behind him but seemed unsure whether to pull Phillip out the door. "What's going on in here?" Phillip demanded.

"I'm fine." Eloise rose from her seat and joined Phillip. "Goodbye, Father. Congratulations on your award."

As they left, her father's voice boomed after them. "Your mother knows. She knows everything, and she never told you."

Eloise faltered, and Phillip placed his arm around her waist. With his support, she left her father behind.

"He's probably lying," Phillip said.

"It doesn't matter." The words came out glibly. Too glibly. But they were true. "If she kept his whereabouts a secret, it was because she loves us and wanted to protect us. I can't fault her for that."

"How are you feeling now that it's over?"

Unsure of her answer, she considered his question a moment. "He's an unhappy man," she finally said. "And he seems to make everyone around him unhappy too. I guess, more than anything, I feel sorry for him."

Phillip hmphed. "Like the Good Book says, a man reaps what he sows. Mitchell made his decisions. If he's unhappy, he only has himself to blame."

"True," Eloise agreed. Yet it wasn't that simple. His last words had been a cruel attempt to hurt her. To drive a wedge between her and Mother.

But her words to him had been cruel too. She despised the harm he'd done to their family, but that didn't excuse her lack of compassion. The Good Book also said to "be ye kind one to another." To forgive as Christ "hath forgiven you."

Perhaps she should go back and tell him what he wanted to know. But the thought of facing him again churned her stomach. Kindness and forgiveness were all well and good, but neither required her to be in the same room with him ever again.

"I need to stop at the front desk," she said when they finally reached the lobby.

"I understand if you'd rather stay here than at the station," Phillip teased. "But our budget won't stretch that far. And I think I've already used up all of Uncle Richard's goodwill."

"My father asked about Allan. I wouldn't tell him how he died. He deserves to know."

"He deserves a swift kick in the behind."

"That too. But not from me." Her tone strengthened as she recalled Phillip bursting into the library. "Or you. Was it necessary to pull out your revolver?"

"Some men respond best to a show of force."

"Men like my father?"

"I think he fits in that category."

"Then maybe I should have been the one carrying it." At the incredulous look on Phillip's face, Eloise grinned. The teasing banter was the tonic she needed to stop her wallowing in a muddy mixture of resentment and guilt.

"Not until you've had more practice at the firing range. We never did get to go."

His comment took Eloise back to that Sunday afternoon at the Whitmer home. Phillip had suggested they go to the range, but Richard said no. *"It's the Lord's Day. Time for rest and reflection."* What had it been, three or more weeks since then? The days had passed in a blur and yet they were among the most momentous of Eloise's life. God had blessed her with purpose after Allan's death and brought her to this hotel to confront her father. Forgiveness—not that he had asked for it—was difficult. But her spirit prompted her to do one simple, yet very hard thing.

At her request, the front desk clerk handed Eloise a sheet of stationery with the hotel watermark and a matching envelope. Her father wanted to know about his son, and she would honor that request without any recriminations and a minimum of information. The note was brief. If he wanted more details, he no doubt had contacts who could provide them for him.

Allan joined the navy after high school. He was a Petty Officer First Class when he was killed at Pearl Harbor. He's buried next to Grandma and Grandpa.

She sealed the envelope, wrote her father's

256

name on the front, and handed it to the clerk. "Please see that Mr. Mitchell receives this. No one else." The last thing she wanted was for Mrs. Mitchell to read the letter. In the mood she was in, she might tear it up into tiny pieces and burn them.

"He's attending the National Investments Gala," Phillip added as he gave the clerk a few coins. "It's important he receives this as soon as it's over."

The clerk assured them he would see to the delivery personally.

"Feel better?" Phillip asked as they strolled across the lobby.

"Much." She hugged his arm, realized what she was doing, and pulled slightly away. If he'd noticed, he pretended not to. "Thank you for staying with me. And for looking out for me."

"We're partners," he said. "That's what partners do."

"Do they also eat? Because I am suddenly very hungry."

"Good. Because I'm starving." As if to give credence to his words, his stomach emitted a low growl. "Told you."

They hailed a cabbie, who recommended an eatery popular with the locals. As they pulled away from the hotel, Eloise allowed herself to be mesmerized by the city lights. Few of the cities in the country's interior followed the blackout regulations, and she was grateful the Civilian Defense wardens weren't practicing a blackout drill tonight. For a moment she could shut her eyes and pretend that all was right with the world. That there was no war. No need to break codes and analyze letters and interview ordinary women about their ordinary hobbies.

The ordeal she'd been dreading for days was over, and her heart felt lighter than it had in years. She truly could believe that God meant for her to see the Seattle paper for a reason. That He arranged circumstances so that she was in St. Louis the same time as her father. The confrontation had occurred, and she was stronger for it. She still had questions, lots of questions, but none of them truly mattered anymore. The long shadow cast by a disappearing father was gone. She prayed it would never haunt her again.

CHAPTER THIRTY-ONE

At the close of another long and worrisome day, Velvalee Dickinson locked the front doors of her shop and climbed the stairs to her apartment located two floors above. She and Lee had been delighted when the vacancy opened that allowed them to live over their business. But with her husband gone, the apartment lacked the sense of home it once had.

She'd found it difficult to identify that lack. When she finally did, she expected her restlessness would ease. That her familiar belongings would once again bring her comfort. Instead, it seemed that identifying what Lee had taken with him to the grave, all the warm and tender associations of that short and simple word—home—increased her inner angst.

Once inside her apartment, she changed from her prim dress into one of her favorite kimonos. The lovely peacock blue and gold silk garment was a gift from a Japanese naval commander and his wife whom she entertained a few times before his emperor called for his return. That call came a few months before the Japanese attack on Pearl Harbor.

Though Lee no longer sat across from her, Velvalee still dined at the table in front of the window overlooking Madison Avenue. While her simple meal of leftover pot roast and thinly sliced potatoes warmed in the oven, she set the table with fine porcelain china, the silverware she'd inherited from her grandmother, and a linen napkin. These refinements were as necessary to her as breathing and connected her to a lifestyle that was slowly slipping from her grasp.

All the tension she felt, all the worry, was Lee's fault. If only he had held on to life for a little longer, she wouldn't be such a nervous wreck.

She tried reading a novel, *Mildred Pierce* by James Cain, to pass the time while she ate. Though she sympathized with the main character's determination against tough odds—a talented businesswoman not unlike herself—she found it impossible for once to get lost in the story's drama.

Perla Negra, the Mexican gypsy rag doll, had been returned to the bookstore window wearing her colorful shawl over her head. But Velvalee's handler had not appeared. Why not?

After supper, she went over the day's receipts and made the appropriate entries in the ledger. Though she'd once worked as a bookkeeper, she loathed the strictures of mathematics. Lee had always taken care of the doll shop's dreary accounting tasks. Now everything to do with the business was her responsibility. Simply everything.

She totaled a column of numbers, rechecked them, and got a different result. Frustrated, she tried again and broke the lead from her pencil. While muttering an unladylike word, she threw the pencil on the desk. It bounced onto the floor then rolled beneath a bookshelf. As she knelt on the floor to retrieve it, the phone rang.

The unexpected sound startled her, and at first she eyed it with suspicion. Could it finally be *him?* He'd never called before, but neither had he ignored her signal before. She tried to squash the hope rising within her as she answered. "Dickinson residence."

Static came across the line.

"Hello? Is anyone there?"

"Is that you, Vee?"

The sultry voice belonged to a woman but wasn't one she recognized. And though she sometimes signed a note as *Vee,* no one dared to call her by that name.

"This is Velvalee Dickinson." Her tone was sharp and unyielding. "Who's calling, please?"

The person on the other end chuckled. "Be careful, Vee. They're watching you. And they know your secret."

"Who's watching?" she demanded even as her stomach turned to mush. "What secret?"

But the caller didn't say. A second later, the phone line was dead.

A satisfied smile played on the woman's lips as she hung up the phone. None of the men in her life believed her to be clever. But she'd spent her lifetime observing the schemes they concocted to destroy their enemies, both real and imagined, in their thirst for power. The lessons she learned came in handy when navigating her own position in their social circles.

After a few well-timed whispers of salacious gossip and the appropriate backstabs, she was poised to take her rightful place as Queen Bee of her set. The current monarch, a crotchety hag, stubbornly refused to step aside. But soon she wouldn't have a choice, not once the coup de grâce, the innocent dropping of a rumor in the appropriate ear, had been executed.

The most brilliant part? No one suspected her capable of such machinations, a fact that proved her ingenuity. One lesson she'd learned especially well was to destroy her enemies by pitting them against each other. Not that the silly woman she'd telephoned was her enemy. Only the pawn in her current game.

The toppling of the Queen Bee would have to wait. A more formidable enemy demanded her attention.

CHAPTER THIRTY-TWO

Eloise grinned at Phillip when he purposely slowed his steps as they walked toward Barbara Clark's front stoop. "Do I have to go in?" he whined. "You know she doesn't like me."

"Don't mention her husband or moonshine and you should be fine." Eloise playfully grabbed his hand and pulled him along the paved path. "She's expecting both of us."

"That doesn't mean she'll be glad to see me."

"Stop being a baby." Eloise let go of his hand to ring the bell. While they waited, she smoothed her skirt and patted her hair. Beside her, Phillip straightened his shoulders, transforming before her eyes from a sluggish crybaby to the consummate professional agent. His wink awakened the butterflies deep within her. Since the St. Louis stop, they fluttered at the slightest whim. She wished she knew how to make them stop. She prayed they never did.

Mrs. Clark opened the door and ushered them into her spotless kitchen. A chocolate cake perched on a pedestal in the center of the table next to a pitcher of tea.

"Thank you for agreeing to see us again," Eloise said as she removed her gloves.

"I must say I was surprised to get your phone

call." Mrs. Clark gestured for them to take their seats. "I wasn't sure I'd ever hear from you again, and I did wonder what became of my letters."

"We've been visiting other doll collectors," Eloise explained, "who also had their signatures forged on letters addressed to Señora Ines de Molinali."

"There are others?"

"A few," Phillip said.

"Who would do such a thing?" she asked as she served them generous slices of the cake. "I just don't understand why anyone would go to such trouble. Surely no one I know."

"We're still investigating," Eloise said, "but your letters provided an important lead. One of them was written on the same typewriter that was used for the forged letter."

"The same typewriter?" Mrs. Clark came close to overfilling a tea glass but caught herself in time. "How could you possibly know that?"

"Typewriters may look the same," Phillip explained, "but that doesn't mean the keys strike the same or leave the same impressions. We have experts who compared the Buenos Aires letter to the letters you gave us. One of them matched."

"Don't keep me in suspense, young man. Which one?"

"A letter you received from a Mrs. Velvalee Dickinson," Eloise said. "Do you remember it?"

Mrs. Clark clutched at her chest. "You cannot be serious. Velvalee Dickinson?"

"We're very serious," Phillip said.

"You must understand." Mrs. Clark leaned forward as if to give weight to her words. "Velvalee is one of the foremost experts on antique dolls in the entire country. She knows practically everything there is to know. Meeting her was such a tremendous honor. I refuse to believe she forged my signature or anyone else's."

"When did you meet her?" Eloise asked, purposely keeping her tone casual and light, as if they were simply having a conversation instead of a subtle interrogation.

"At one of our Springfield Art Circle meetings. She was the guest speaker." Mrs. Clark's hands fluttered as if she didn't know what to do with them. "All our members were thrilled to have someone of her expertise here in our little town. And all the way from New York City too."

"When was this?" Eloise asked.

"A year ago this past June. I remember because she talked about wedding dolls, and June is the traditional month for weddings. It was a lovely presentation." Mrs. Clark cut into her cake with her fork but didn't take the bite. "I still can't believe it. I won't."

Eloise felt sorry for the woman, but their questions still needed answers. "When we were here before, you mentioned a trip to New York. Did you happen to visit the shop?"

Mrs. Clark nodded. "I went with a friend from

the Art Circle. It was such a delight seeing all those dolls and their fancy costumes."

"When was this?" Phillip asked.

"November. A couple of weeks before Thanksgiving." She placed her fork on the side of the plate, the cake still uneaten. "When we arrived at the shop, we learned her husband had recently died. And yet, she didn't want us to leave. We stayed well over an hour."

"The forged letter mentioned your nephew," Eloise reminded her. "Did you tell Mrs. Dickinson about his brain tumor?"

"I did." Mrs. Clark seemed to deflate with the admission. "Why would she do such a thing? Pretend to be me to some strange woman in Buenos Aires?" She pronounced it *buenas airs,* which Eloise would have found amusing in other circumstances. Not this one, though.

"All we know right now," Phillip said, "is that the same typewriter was used for both letters. That doesn't mean Mrs. Dickinson wrote the forged letter."

"But if she didn't, who did?" Mrs. Clark shook her head, and Eloise feared she might be on the verge of tears. She'd obviously placed the Doll Woman on a pedestal that they had come along and toppled. She exchanged a glance with Phillip.

"Our investigation is ongoing," she said. "And you've been a tremendous help. Is there anything else you can tell us about Mrs. Dickinson?"

"Only that I won't be buying any more dolls from her. Or writing her any more letters."

"I wouldn't either," Eloise replied, "if I were in your shoes."

"In fact, I have half a mind to send back all the dolls I already bought from her. Every single one."

Eloise laid a comforting hand on Mrs. Clark's arm. "Please don't do that. We don't want to raise any unnecessary alarms."

Mrs. Clark eyed her then nodded. "You're right, of course. I just don't appreciate her using my name. Or my nephew. That's unforgivable, that is."

"I agree," Eloise said. "I hope you can find comfort in knowing you did the right thing by turning in your letter and allowing us to read your correspondence."

"Glad to do my part, naturally." Mrs. Clark cleared her throat and lifted her chin, once again the indomitable lady they'd first met. "Someday I'd like to know what this was all about. Especially since those other two agents have been nosing around, asking my friends and families all kinds of questions about me. You would think I was the one under suspicion."

"Other agents?" Eloise shifted her gaze to Phillip.

"No need to worry," he soothed. "They're only

doing their job. In fact, the only suspicion we have about you is how you manage to bake such a delicious chocolate cake. What's your secret?" He took a huge bite as if to prove his point.

She made a locking motion over her lips then smiled when he laughed. Eloise stifled a giggle. *How about that?* Phillip had charmed his way into Mrs. Clark's good graces.

"I can't say I minded the attention all that much," she said, her eyes twinkling. "In fact, it made me a bit of a celebrity around here. Not everyone can say they're helping the FBI with an important investigation. Isn't that so?"

"That's so," Phillip agreed. "Miss Marshall and I appreciate both your cooperation and your hospitality."

"I always was a great one in the kitchen," she said. "Even Mr. Clark said so, and he was never a man to hand out a compliment when it wasn't necessary. Why, there was one time—"

"Excuse me, Mrs. Clark." Eloise had listened to enough stories during their first visit, after Phillip had left the two women alone, to know their hostess's propensity to follow one rabbit trail after another. "It might be helpful for us to hear more about the Springfield Art Circle."

While they finished their cake, Mrs. Clark talked about the group's speakers and events.

As the two women gabbed, Eloise sensed Phillip's restlessness grow. When Mrs. Clark paused to take a break during a lengthy discourse on the horrors of impressionism, Eloise jumped in. "We've taken up too much of your time, I'm afraid." She smiled as she rose and gathered their dishes.

Mrs. Clark protested as Eloise knew she would. "Don't bother with those. I'll take care of them." But Eloise was experienced enough to know that in the world of kitchen visits one sure way to make a speedy departure was to take one's dishes to the sink.

They left soon after with a promise to return the letters after the FBI finished their analysis. Their next stop was Cincinnati, both to return the car they'd borrowed from the field office and then to begin the long train trip to Washington, DC, to meet with Richard. Their round-trip excursion to the West Coast and back in search of the forger of the letters was almost at an end. At least they had a name and perhaps even an itinerary— that is, if Velvalee Dickinson *had* forged the letters and if she had done so on her West Coast tour.

Eloise understood Phillip's reluctance to accept Mrs. Dickinson as the traitor without more information. Her instructors at the academy had also been adamant about jumping to conclusions and relying too heavily on circumstantial evidence. But deep inside, she believed that they had accomplished what they set out to do. More proof may be needed, sure, and yet she couldn't help feeling proud that she'd played a small part in the operation.

As she contemplated their return to the capital, though, her emotions weren't all that neat and tidy but a mass of contradictions. She looked forward to returning to her little room at the back of the Francis Scott Key Bookstore, to no longer living out of a suitcase, to getting a good night's sleep in her own tiny bed.

But she would miss the adventure of being on the road. She doubted she'd ever get the chance to travel again as she had these past few weeks. When she eventually returned to her hometown, would she even be able to tell her mother or her friends about standing on the rocky coast and looking out at the surging waves of the Pacific or about Seattle's incessant rainfall and emerald landscape or the mighty grandeur of the Rockies? Or would she have to pretend she'd never been outside of DC?

Even more important, how would she explain to her mother how she happened to be in St. Louis at the same time as her father? Or how she'd known where to find him?

The coincidence of seeing the Seattle newspaper that carried his photograph still seemed strange. She didn't want to wrongly attribute events to God, but if she believed, truly believed, that He guided her steps, then wasn't it just as wrong to deny that He was the one who'd orchestrated those events?

She had to say yes. Though that led to another question.

Why?

"Why what?" Phillip asked.

Eloise startled. "I said *why* out loud?"

"You did."

Eloise stared out the window, where fluffy white clouds gently floated past the afternoon sun. "Sometimes I wish God would write a message in the sky so I could understand . . . so I could know why."

"Is it okay if I once again ask 'why what'?"

She didn't answer for a moment because she didn't know how to answer. He was another reason her emotions were a mass of contradiction. Even if they still worked together on this case after they reached the capital, everything would be different. When the day's work was done, they'd go their separate ways. No more overnight stays in cheap motel lodgings or sharing a sleeper car on a train. No more drives through the countryside or plane rides among the clouds.

They'd separate. Physically. Emotionally.

Like longtime friends who promise to stay in touch but eventually only send a card at Christmas. She and Phillip probably wouldn't even do that.

When this mission ended, Phillip intended to go

overseas—a place she didn't want to follow, not even in spirit. But as much as she tried to close her heart to him, she couldn't do it. She didn't want to lose him. Neither did she want to love him.

Somewhere along their journey, though, that's exactly what had happened. She loved him. And that admission alone was enough to bruise her heart.

"Do you want me to stop somewhere?" he offered. Perhaps he was mistaking her silence for moodiness. "I think I can scrounge up a couple nickels for two bottles of icy cold Coke."

"That sounds nice." She turned her attention from the passing countryside with its neat farmhouses, painted barns, and tall silos to him. His handsome profile, more handsome to her now than when they first met, caused her heart to race. But it was the man he was inside—the man she'd come to know during their thousands of miles sitting side by side either in a car or a plane, on a bus or a train, who took her breath away. And stood beside her when she needed him most.

"I was thinking about St. Louis," she said. "About why it was so important for me to see my father."

"Isn't that obvious? You needed to know the truth. You deserved to know the truth."

"That's part of it, yes. But I feel like God took me by the hand and said, 'Oh, look. Here's a

272

newspaper article about your dad. And would you look at that? You're both going to be in St. Louis at the same time.' "

Phillip snickered. "Is that what God sounds like? Because that sounded more like my spinster aunt Alice."

"I'd like to meet your spinster aunt Alice."

"She'd probably like to meet you too, though you won't be able to believe half the stories she'll tell you about me."

"Is that so?"

"I'll let you in on a little secret. I'm her favorite nephew. The son she never had, she says. So, when she talks to me in that same tone of voice you were using for God, I know it's her way of saying she loves me."

"Are you saying what happened with my father is because God loves me?"

"I'm not a theologian, sweetheart."

Great! He'd turned into Humphrey Bogart again.

"But you know He does. More than you can fathom." He flashed her a quick smile before returning his gaze to the road. "Do you regret meeting with your father?"

"I'm not sure who it benefitted." *Neither of them? Both of them?* "Except now I have answers. And if he got my note, so does Father. He knows what happened to Allan. Perhaps that was the reason."

Thinking about her brother made the moment

273

more solemn. But she had more she needed to say. "I'm not sure what to tell Mother. Or if I can tell her anything at all, given the circumstances."

"I'd like to give you answers," Phillip said. "But you may never have them. At least not on this side of heaven. What you did for your father, though—writing that note—I don't know that I would have been that generous."

"It wasn't generosity, it was . . ." She wasn't sure how to finish her sentence. What came to mind seemed weird even to her. "It was a prompting. Something I knew I had to do."

"You gave him something he didn't deserve. I think the preachers call that grace."

Is that what she had done? That made the gesture seem more magnanimous than it was. "I did what was right."

"In very difficult circumstances." Phillip's jaw clenched then set in a firm line. "I find that admirable."

Her cheeks flushed at the unexpected compliment. She glanced in his direction, but his gaze was fastened on the highway. A tension existed between them as if those multiple threads of shared experiences binding them together were too taut yet also too strong to break.

She leaned her head against the back of the seat and closed her eyes. What was happening between them? She didn't know, except for this one thing: if his feelings for her were anywhere close to her feelings for him, they were doomed. The future didn't include a path the two of them could walk together. Not in a time of war. He must never discover the hold he had on her heart. That would save her embarrassment if he didn't feel the same. And save her heartbreak if he did.

CHAPTER THIRTY-THREE

Phillip and Eloise were met in the Cincinnati field office's parking lot by Paul Truett, an agent involved in the apprehension of the two Operation Pastorius saboteurs who had hidden in the city. He leaned against the trunk of a black sedan, one foot resting on the bumper as he took a final drag of a cigarette. When Phillip emerged from his vehicle, Truett tossed the butt to the cement and ground it with his foot.

"I wasn't expecting a welcoming committee." Phillip shook Truett's hand.

"Orders from the top," Truett said.

"How did you know when I'd get here?"

"Got word from a deputy sitting on the state highway just inside the Hamilton County line. Said he would have stopped you for going over the limit if he hadn't known you were one of us."

"I always did have a lead foot. Helpful for quick getaways."

"I've got a fiver that says you spotted him, but he swears you didn't."

Phillip gave an embarrassed chuckle as Eloise joined them. After introducing her to Truett, he flashed her a sheepish grin. "Did you see a deputy sheriff's car on the way into town?"

She thought a moment then shook her head. "Should I have?"

"Apparently *I* should have."

"You're going to cover the bet, aren't you, old pal?" Truett asked.

Phillip feigned a frown then pulled out his wallet. "Only because I owe you." Truett could be as brash as a banty rooster, but he'd shown his smarts and professionalism when it counted.

Truett grinned and pocketed the five-dollar bill. "I better get you two inside. You have a special visitor waiting."

"Who?" Phillip lightly touched Eloise's back as Truett opened the building's rear door.

"You'll see." He led the way along a corridor and up a flight of stairs to a broad landing. "They're waiting for us in the chapel."

Phillip knew from a prior visit to the field office that the chapel was a small room located near the reception area. In one corner, an altar stood on a short platform beneath a stained-glass window lit from behind by a floodlight. A set of wooden pews was arranged before the platform. More comfortable seating was located in the opposite corner. Agents came to this room for spiritual reflection, silent contemplation, or simply to be alone. This was also where agents delivered devastating news involving loved ones to family members.

"Who is 'they'?" Eloise whispered. Phillip

shrugged his shoulders. This cloak-and-dagger business seemed over the top even for the FBI. After all, they were in a government building staffed by trained G-men. Why all the secrecy?

Truett opened the thick wooden door and stood back to let Phillip and Eloise enter before him. Phillip quickly scoped the room then held out both arms as his uncle came toward him.

"What a welcome surprise." The two men clasped hands. "What are you doing here?"

"I came to see you, my boy." Richard's gaze slid to Eloise. "And you too, my dear."

"It's nice to see you again, sir."

"What's with all the formality? Come here." As he drew Eloise into a fatherly embrace, an older gentleman stepped forward. "Eloise, this is L. C. Schilder. He's the special agent in charge at this field office. And, of course, L.C., you know Phillip."

With the introductory handshakes out of the way, Richard gestured for them to sit. Phillip sat beside Eloise on a brocade sofa while Richard, Special Agent Schilder, and Truett sat in upholstered chairs.

"I'm sure you're tired after your long day," Richard began. "This little meeting won't take too long, I promise, and then I'll treat you both to dinner." He nodded toward Schilder, who crossed his long legs and cleared his throat.

"Agent Truett has been involved in our local

investigation of Mrs. Barbara Clark." His speech was as formal as his demeanor. "According to those who were interviewed, Mrs. Clark is a law-abiding and respectable citizen who lives a quiet and, one might say, unassuming life. In your personal interviews with her, did you learn anything to suggest otherwise?"

"Not at all," Phillip said. "We are certain Mrs. Clark is the victim here. She has been very cooperative." He glanced at Eloise. "Though she doesn't seem to be too fond of Mr. Clark."

Both Truett and Schilder smiled.

"I heard a few tales about Mr. Clark," Truett said. "Each time the person began with, 'Don't let Barbara know I told you this.'"

They chatted a while longer, then Truett and Schilder returned to their offices. After they left, Richard drew his chair closer to the sofa. "Let's talk about Mrs. Dickinson's West Coast tour. Both the Chicago and Oakland field offices have located the hotels where she stayed. Both those hotels rent out typewriters to their guests. We're waiting for the sample sheets."

"What's a sample sheet?" Eloise asked.

"An agent types a specific document onto a sheet of paper," Richard explained. "The wording provides multiple examples of how each key strikes the paper. Our forensics team will compare each sample sheet to the forged letters. If she typed a forged letter on one of those typewriters, we'll know it."

"Will that be enough proof to question Mrs. Dickinson?" Eloise asked.

"It's still too soon," Richard replied. "We have her under surveillance, and a few of our agents have stopped in at her store. Unfortunately, we still have too many unanswered questions. Though here is interesting news. No one lives at the Buenos Aires address. The neighbors say the house has been empty for months."

Phillip widened his eyes then guffawed. "You mean the señora got out of Dodge and no one told Velvalee? Who needs enemies when you have friends like that?"

"That investigation is still ongoing," Richard said. "We don't know who last lived in the house or even who owns it. The company that manages the property isn't cooperating."

"Probably a shell company," Phillip retorted. "It could take months of tedious record searches to discover the actual owner, who probably lives overseas and is completely untouchable."

"I fear you're right." Richard retrieved a folder from his briefcase. "We've had more success in building a dossier on the Dickinsons. Velvalee was born in October 1893 in Sacramento. Her mother died of tuberculosis in 1919; her father in an accident in 1923. The only other family member is a younger brother who worked for the Labor

Relations War Production Board in DC for a time. Now he lives in New York. Her husband, Lee, suffered from Bright's disease, a kidney disease that apparently led to a heart condition. He died last October."

Richard shared additional biographical information, including the FBI's investigation into Lee in the mid-1930s, when he owned a produce commodity brokerage firm, then handed them a few brochures. Phillip examined the top one. The paper was the same blue paper as the stationery Velvalee used to write Mrs. Clark. The front had scarlet lettering and a border of dolls dressed in international costumes. Along with the name of the shop—Velvalee Dickinson's Doll Store—the front page stated, "We have dolls from nearly every country in the world and state in the United States."

Richard continued the briefing. "We've found advertisements she's placed in a newsletter published by the National Doll and Toy Collectors and in the *Christian Science Monitor*, articles she's written for a journal called the *Complete Collector* and a few similar magazines, and posters advertising her appearance as a guest speaker for various organizations." He pointed to the brochures. "She mails those to her clients—a quite sizable list—both to advertise upcoming speaking engagements and to list the dolls she's offering for sale."

"How much do the dolls sell for?" Eloise asked.

"She caters to both the casual collector and the wealthy. Much of her inventory ranges from twenty-five dollars on up. The rarer dolls cost thousands."

"If she's that successful, I guess we can rule out money as a motive," Phillip said.

"Not so fast," Richard objected. "Since the war started, she can no longer import or export foreign dolls. That has cut into her profits. But even before the war, the Dickinsons were prone to live beyond their means, and Lee's medical bills have been high. Her finances aren't very tidy."

He walked them through various documents, including photographs, financial records, and membership rosters of Japanese organizations located in the United States. "Any more questions?"

"How did you find all this?" Eloise seemed overwhelmed by all the documents. "There's so much."

"Simple," Phillip said. "Good old-fashioned leg-work. Being an agent isn't all guts and glamour."

"Thankfully, very little of what we do at the Bureau involves heroics," Richard said.

"As you should know," Phillip said to Eloise, "after traveling from one end of the country and back again. I only had to draw my gun once." He grinned then realized the temperature in the room had dropped to below freezing. Why was it that when he was with Eloise, he couldn't open his mouth without jamming his foot between his teeth?

"You drew your gun?" Richard asked. "May I inquire about the circumstances?"

"St. Louis," he said, hoping that would put an end to the questioning until he could talk to Richard alone.

"Because of me," Eloise said at the same time.

Richard's stony gaze widened and settled on both of them. "Let's talk about St. Louis."

Phillip glanced at Eloise. The blood appeared to have drained from her face. Her mouth opened, but no words came out. He reached out, placing his hand on her arm. "I'll explain." She responded by giving him a grateful smile, but her worried expression told a different story.

Being seen as competent and dependable was important to her, especially in the eyes of someone like Richard, who had placed such trust in her abilities. She'd put all that at risk because of her father. Phillip had known the moment would come when they'd have to explain the situation to Richard, but he'd expected to have a few more days to figure out exactly how.

"It was my fault—" Eloise began.

"It was no one's *fault*." Phillip shifted his gaze from her to Richard to find his uncle staring at his hand on Eloise's arm. Phillip quickly clasped his hands together. "Eloise wanted to see her

283

father. She needed to see her father. But it was my decision."

"I forced you into it," Eloise insisted then turned to Richard. "Phillip only stayed in St. Louis because I wouldn't leave."

Richard nodded his head, his silent but familiar "I see" gesture. "I have no desire to interfere in your personal business, Eloise. But before I could request your transfer, I needed to acquaint myself with your family. Based on our background check, I believed you weren't aware of your father's whereabouts."

"That's true." The waver in Eloise's voice tempted Phillip to reach for her again. But he didn't dare, not with Richard's sharp eyes on them. When he'd touched her before, the action had seemed so natural—he hadn't even realized what he was doing until it was too late.

"I didn't know," Eloise continued. "I know this will sound strange, but when we were at the Seattle field office, I saw his picture in the local paper."

Phillip released a quiet sigh as she paused to compose herself. This was her story, and she needed to tell it. But he'd give his right arm and left leg to do it for her. Even though Richard's attention was focused on Eloise, Phillip sensed his uncle's awareness of his unease. He might as well be wearing a sign on his forehead that said, "I like Eloise."

He more than liked her. He cared about her. Something he'd rather not admit to anyone, not even himself.

"He resides in Seattle?"

"He works at an investment firm. I was shocked. Beyond shocked." Her cheeks flushed with embarrassment. "The article said he was getting an award in St. Louis. I didn't think much of it at the time, but as the days passed . . . I don't know how to explain it. I knew I had to see him."

"Did you?"

"We talked."

"You'll forgive me for asking, but I must," Richard said. "What reason did you give him for being so far from home?"

"I didn't. And he wasn't curious enough to ask. Or perhaps he didn't care."

"I told him my name was Carter," Phillip put in. "That I was in construction. I think he believed me. Or, like Eloise said, he didn't care."

"It wasn't a pleasant visit," Eloise said. "My father isn't a very nice man."

"I'm sorry to hear that," Richard said. "Sincerely, I am."

"Thank you, sir." Eloise sounded resigned, but to her credit she hadn't burst into tears. Or perhaps she'd already shed all the tears she had in her heart for the man.

"Again, I have no wish to offend." Richard's conciliatory tone eased the difficult words Phillip knew he was about to say. "Since you've been in contact with your father, it's my duty to request that Ray Suran, the special agent in charge of the Seattle office, open a dossier on him."

"Will he know?" Eloise asked.

Richard gave a small smile. "That would not be our intent. Have you been in contact with your mother?"

"I wouldn't know what to say to her." Eloise pressed her lips together then released a heavy sigh. "He has a new family. Either he's a bigamist or my parents divorced and Mother never told us. Perhaps she already knows where he is and kept that a secret too." She seemed to be having a hard time keeping the bitterness from her voice.

"We should be able to find out," Phillip said. "If they divorced, I mean." He'd only wanted to help, but the horrified look on Eloise's face caused him to regret the offer. "If you want us to," he said lamely. "Couldn't we?"

"If a divorce occurred," Richard said, "yes, there would be a public record."

"That's not how I want to find out," Eloise said. "It's not fair to Mother."

"May I make a suggestion?" Richard asked.

"Of course."

"I'm sending the two of you straight to New York City from here," Richard said. "It's past time a woman visited Mrs. Dickinson's doll store."

"You want me to talk to her?" Eloise asked, obviously surprised.

"I want you to be a customer. Establish a relationship with her," Richard said. "She won't be as suspicious of a woman as she seems to be of the agents we've sent in. They did their best, I suppose, but they would have been less conspicuous in a seedy bar than an upscale antique doll shop."

"Okay," Eloise said, her voice gaining in confidence. "I can do that."

"Good. After that, if you're so inclined and we have no other pressing matters, you should visit your mother. You won't be that far from home."

"That's very kind," Eloise replied, her tone uncertain. Didn't she want to see her mother? Or did she suspect this was Richard's way of ending her association with the Bureau? If so, she was wrong. Richard didn't operate like that. If he wanted her out of the FBI, she'd be gone.

Phillip surreptitiously eyed her, but for once her expression gave away nothing. He didn't know what she was thinking.

"Thank you," she continued. "I might do that."

"It's your decision, of course." Richard rose from his chair. "Special Agent Schilder has arranged accommodations for us. I suggest we freshen up a little then enjoy a nice dinner. Any objections?"

"Not from me." As he stood, Phillip started to

extend his hand to Eloise, then grabbed his hat from the coffee table instead. He didn't dare meet his uncle's sharp-eyed gaze. He should also do his best to avoid being alone with Richard. Or he needed to come up with an explanation why his attentions to Eloise seemed to be more than simple gentlemanly gestures before that happened. He wasn't sure what explanation he could give when he refused to acknowledge the reason himself.

CHAPTER THIRTY-FOUR

"I'm not sure I can do this." Eloise played with the pearl necklace she'd been outfitted with for her visit to the doll store. Wearing the expensive jewelry tied her stomach in knots. What if she lost one of the matching earrings or broke the clasp on the necklace? The horrible thought caused her to flatten her hand against the pearls to ensure they were safe.

Phillip turned around from his position behind the steering wheel and rested his arm along the top of the front seat. He wore his chauffeur's hat at a jaunty angle that, along with his reassuring smile, would have her heart pitter-pattering at any other time. Now all she could think about was how many ways this visit could go wrong— and she'd be to blame.

"Tell me who you are." His encouraging tone prompted her to take a deep breath.

"My name is Elena Piperton from Cape Cod." They'd specifically chosen the popular Massachusetts destination because Eloise had vacationed there with a friend's family one summer when the two girls were in high school. "I want to purchase a special gift for a close friend."

"And?"

Eloise stared at him. "And what?"

"Elena Piperton is wealthy. Confident. A woman who knows what she wants." His eyes softened. "That's you."

There went her heart. *Pitter-patter.*

To avoid his gaze, she peered across the street at the spacious storefront housing the doll shop. The blue-lettered sign above the entrance read:

VELVALEE DICKINSON

ANCIENT DOLLS – FOREIGN – REGIONALS

Assorted dolls in a variety of costumes were tastefully arranged in the large window, which was draped with a thick valance.

"It reminds me of a puppet theater," Phillip said.

"Does that make Mrs. Dickinson a puppet master?"

"She's an ordinary woman."

"Who may be a traitor."

"Elena Piperton knows nothing about that. So, *you* know nothing about that."

She scoffed. "Easier said than done."

"Uncle Richard believes in you." He shifted his gaze toward the windshield and lowered his voice. "So do I."

Three simple words, but powerful enough to bolster her confidence. She'd spent the previous two days at the FBI's New York field office working on her cover story, finding enough details in her own life to create someone new. A familiar place. Same educational accomplishments. Same marital status. Same family history—an absent father, a dead brother, a grieving mother.

According to her instructors, such details created authenticity and kept deception to a minimum. "The less lies you tell, the less lies you have to remember," one of them stressed. They helped her dig deep into her childhood to remember the comforts she'd taken for granted before Black Tuesday disrupted her life. To tap into her mother's indifferent attitude toward money before she was compelled to pinch pennies. They were memories that gave her the resources to become a socialite.

She took another deep breath, closed her eyes, and allowed those memories to wash over her. Elena Piperton is a wealthy, confident woman who knows what she wants. *I am Elena Piperton.*

And Phillip believed in her.

She opened her eyes and met Phillip's gentle gaze. "I'm ready," she said in an imperious tone.

"Then I'll get your door, Miss Piperton." Once he was out of the vehicle, he tugged on the hem of his chauffeur's jacket, strolled around the front of the burgundy Cadillac provided by the Bureau, and gallantly opened the passenger door. Eloise took his extended hand and stepped from the car.

"I'll be right outside the shop." He held onto her hand, his back blocking the view of anyone who might be watching from across the street. "If anything goes wrong, scream."

"Isn't the chauffeur supposed to stay with the car?"

"He's supposed to be close enough to carry the lady's purchases back to the car."

"Heaven forbid the lady carry her own purchases," Eloise said in mock horror.

"I suppose that depends on the number of her purchases." His face was set in stone, appropriate for a member of the fictitious Piperton staff. Eloise adjusted her own expression.

I am Elena Piperton. Wealthy. Confident.

He didn't give her any last words of encouragement. The electric warmth of his skin against hers was enough.

She crossed the street, walked past a bookstore, and paused before the doll store's display window. For the benefit of anyone inside who might be watching, she considered the various dolls, feigning special interest in two or three of them. On a raised platform in a corner of the window stood two dolls similar to one she'd seen in Barbara Clark's collection. They wore emerald dresses trimmed in lace and matching hats with black feathers. One doll had blond ringlets while the other had auburn curls.

As if making a decision, she entered the store and smiled at the petite woman coming from behind the counter to meet her. Despite her desire to stay in character, she couldn't help thinking how unlikely it seemed that this person could be a traitor. Even in her red heels, she couldn't be much more than five feet tall.

"May I help you?" she asked as she subtly appraised Eloise's appearance. In an odd way, the appraisal strengthened Eloise's resolve to portray Elena Piperton as perfectly as possible.

"I believe so. Might I speak with the owner of this establishment?"

"I am she."

Eloise's haughty expression turned to all smiles. "How fine! I was passing by and noticed your beautiful display." She gestured toward the window. "Could I have a closer look at the two Irish dolls in the window, please?"

"I'd be honored to show them to you, Miss . . . ?"

"Piperton. Elena Piperton."

"Do you collect dolls?"

"Oh no. Not me. But I have a close friend who has expressed interest in the hobby."

"You wish to make a purchase for her?"

"Perhaps." Eloise gave her an enigmatic smile. "Don't appear too eager," the instructors had warned. "She's courting you, not the other way around."

Mrs. Dickinson returned the smile then walked toward the window. Eloise strolled to a glass display case that served as an additional counter, browsing the shelves as she did so. The assortment of dolls was nothing short of amazing. From plain and drab to elaborate and glamorous, there seemed

293

to be a doll for any taste. When she arrived at the counter, she removed her white gloves.

When Mrs. Dickinson joined her, she set three dolls on the counter, the two Eloise requested and a third dressed in purple satin. "Is your friend by any chance a redhead?"

"She's a brunette," Eloise replied, imagining her schoolgirl chum whose family had taken her with them to Cape Cod. *Stick to the truth as much as possible.*

"I once had a third doll similar to these. She had the most luxurious red hair gathered together into a chic cascade bound with the loveliest tartan plaid."

"Is that so?" *You mean the doll in Barbara Clark's collection?* Eloise shooed the question from her mind. Elena didn't know anything about Barbara Clark, yet she couldn't seem to keep the woman out of her thoughts.

"I may have a photograph of it. I do that sometimes, take pictures of my favorites. If you're interested in the complete set, I'd be more than happy to contact the owner on your behalf. I'm sure we could work out an arrangement beneficial to all."

"That's a kind offer but totally unnecessary." A superior smile lingered on Eloise's lips as she fingered the lace on the auburn doll's jacket collar. "I'm partial to this one. She is what I imagine when I think of an Irish lass."

"An excellent choice."

"Though this one is lovely too." Eloise turned her attention to the blond doll. "The ringlets remind me of Shirley Temple. I loved her movies when I was a girl."

"People say that all the time." Mrs. Dickinson moved the blond doll slightly closer to Eloise. "Since your friend is new to the hobby, you could surprise her with both. They'd make an excellent addition to her budding collection."

"That is a thought." Eloise pretended to consider the idea then smiled again at the tiny woman. She let her gaze roam over the doll-filled shelves behind the counter. "This store is fabulous. How did you get your start?"

"Like everyone, one doll at a time. Though I actually began with two." Velvalee's laugh sounded rehearsed. She'd obviously told the same story a thousand times before. Elena Piperton listened with rapt attention as if fascinated by the anecdote.

"About eight years ago, a friend gave me two dolls from the Philippines. They were beautifully dressed in native costumes. Other friends added to my growing collection. Then one year, over Christmas, I worked as a salesclerk in Bloomingdale's doll department. I'm not too proud to admit that I sold more dolls than anyone else that year."

"How industrious of you." Eloise measured her tone so the words were a compliment while also suggesting a woman of her status would never brag about working in a department store.

"I realized I could do the same on my own." Velvalee failed to keep a reflexive defensiveness from her voice. "I developed a clientele by publishing lists of dolls I had for sale. Eventually, I opened this." She waved her hand in a graceful gesture to encompass the store. "Right here on Madison Avenue."

"That is so admirable," Eloise cooed. "More women should follow your example instead of depending solely on their husbands for their financial security. Not me, of course. All I know about money is how to spend it." She gave a careless laugh. "But women such as yourself, those with intelligence and ambition. Especially with this awful war disrupting all our lives. Do you think it will ever end?"

Velvalee hesitated, as if unsure how to respond to all that Eloise had said. She lowered her gaze to the counter then picked up the third doll she'd brought from the window. "I had the good fortune to acquire a few dolls from the Charles Jopp Collection last year, including this fashionable lady."

"Charles Jopp?" Eloise asked.

"His collection was a doll enthusiast's dream. Filled with rare dolls one couldn't find anywhere else." She eyed the doll with regret. "I never thought to part with this particular one, but she certainly would be a coup for a new collector."

"She is lovely," Eloise replied.

"Her value is more than most are willing to spare, especially during these hard times." Velvalee emitted a long sigh and set the doll to one side.

Following her instincts, Eloise's knowing expression indicated that Velvalee's sales tactics wouldn't work on her. "Value is often in the eye of the beholder," she replied. "But price? There's usually room for negotiation."

Velvalee gave her a begrudging though respectful smile. "My dear Miss Piperton, you have a head for business after all."

"I'm perhaps freer with my money than my banker would like," Eloise replied, "but I'm not flippant with it."

"An interesting distinction."

Eloise gazed at each of the dolls in turn. "I'm afraid I can't make up my mind." She suddenly stared at Velvalee. "I have a fabulous idea. Why don't you join me for tea this afternoon? I'm staying at the Waldorf. Bring all three of the dolls with you and perhaps a couple of others. I'll make a decision then."

Velvalee appeared startled by the unexpected invitation. "I don't know if I can get away."

"Please do. I'm returning home tomorrow, and I don't want to leave empty-handed."

"Naturally not." Velvalee took another moment,

297

obviously wrestling with the possibility of losing an important sale if she didn't make the appointment, then made her decision. "What time should I arrive?"

"Is four thirty convenient?"

"Very convenient. Thank you for inviting me, Miss Piperton."

"I'm the one who should be thanking you, Mrs. Dickinson, for indulging my whims." Eloise slipped on her white gloves. "I really should run along now."

As she turned to leave, the door opened. A bulldog of a man wearing a three-piece suit and carrying a box stormed in followed by a police officer. Phillip stepped in behind them. Eloise glanced at Velvalee, who appeared both shaken and aggrieved by the man's appearance.

"You should have called for an appointment, Mr. Danvers," she snapped. "As you can see, I have a customer."

The man shifted a few dolls arranged on a different display case and set the box beside them. "I can wait."

Unsure what to do, Eloise turned toward Phillip. "May I be of assistance, Miss Piperton?" he asked.

"Would you like us to stay?" Eloise asked Mrs. Dickinson, who seemed befuddled by the question.

"Why would you?"

Eloise didn't know how to answer her. Had she asked so that they could witness the confrontation firsthand? Or because she was genuinely concerned? She hoped the latter, but she couldn't dismiss the former. Right now, the only fact she could hold on to was that Phillip had remained in character and so should she.

"As a new friend," she said simply.

"Thank you, but no. Mr. Danvers and I have dealt with each other before."

"I'll say we have," Danvers blustered. "Cheat you, she will, if you're not careful. That's why I brought along this copper."

Eloise narrowed her eyes, communicating without words what she thought of the man's strong-arm tactics. Then she turned a gracious smile toward Velvalee. "I'll see you at tea. Bring six dolls with you. I'm sure I'll want at least three."

Without waiting for a reply, Eloise exited the store. Phillip followed her close enough to whisper as soon as they were out of earshot. "Don't say anything until we've driven away. She's distracted, but I don't want to give any of them a reason to suspect I'm not your chauffeur."

"Just let me know when I can be Eloise again."

Phillip chuckled. "Soon, Miss Piperton."

Eloise slid into the backseat and rested her head on the fine leather. As they drove away, she speculated on what was happening inside the store. So many questions circled through her thoughts. What was in Mr. Danvers's box? Was the policeman there to arrest Velvalee? On what grounds?

Most important of all was the question that had taken Eloise there in the first place. Was Velvalee a traitor?

After all that preparation and pretense, they still didn't know for sure. Hopefully, the Bureau would be closer to the truth once Velvalee joined Eloise for tea at the Waldorf. During her absence, Phillip and another agent planned to sneak into the doll shop and look for evidence of her guilt.

She hoped they found something, anything, that would bring the investigation to an end, though her hope was bittersweet. Proof of guilt meant an end to her association with the FBI and a new beginning for Phillip as he headed overseas. Proof of guilt meant she no longer had an excuse not to visit her mother. Proof of guilt meant she might never see Phillip again.

Her thoughts too often returned to Phillip these days. He focused on navigating the crowded Manhattan traffic on their way to the Waldorf. Richard would be waiting for their report. And later in the afternoon, Eloise would once again transform into Elena—a wealthy young socialite tasked to engage Mrs. Velvalee Dickinson long enough for her store to be quietly ransacked.

God be with her.

God be with them all.

CHAPTER THIRTY-FIVE

Under the watchful eye of the police officer, Velvalee wrote a check for the amount she owed to Danvers for his collection. He had some nerve coming to the shop during business hours instead of arranging an appointment. And to involve the police was the icing on the cake, not to mention the embarrassment he'd caused her in front of that lovely Miss Piperton.

"That concludes our business." She slid the check across the counter. "You may leave now."

"Don't take that high-and-mighty tone with me." Danvers examined the check before pocketing it as if to ensure each *i* had been dotted and each *t* had been crossed.

"The bank will cover it," she said firmly.

"You better hope they do. I'm going there now, and if they don't, we'll be back." He wagged his thumb between him and the officer. "You're not cheating me again."

"I never cheated you before."

"So you've said, but I know better. And so do my clients."

Velvalee pointed dramatically toward the door. "Be gone with you. Both of you." How she managed to order the officer to leave without her voice trembling, she didn't know. Danvers murmured something under his breath as he left.

Her hand shook as she locked the door after them and flipped the sign to CLOSED. Danvers had lined up the dolls he'd brought with him on top of the display case. Velvalee stared at them, and their eyes stared back, mocking her. If the European markets were still open, she could have sold the entire lot for tens of thousands of dollars. Instead, it might be months before she recouped the money she'd given to Danvers. But she didn't have months, especially not after writing that check.

What choice did she have? Danvers had already caused one scene when he accused her of stealing his clients. Such a stupid allegation to make. Didn't his customers have the right to purchase dolls from anyone they chose? All she'd done was arrange for a copy of his clientele list to find its way to her door. Several collectors wrote to express their gratitude for the brochure she had sent listing her current stock. Danvers was simply jealous of her successful marketing methods.

She might have forgiven him the accusation if not for another one he'd made against her. His claim that she sold fake dolls as authentic antiques made her blood boil. All she had done was create new costumes out of old fabrics a few times. The customers who bought those dolls were pleased with their purchases. Was it her fault they couldn't tell the difference between an old porcelain doll fitted with a "new" costume and a genuine heirloom? The buyers were pleased with their purchases, and she was pleased with the profits. No harm, no foul. Unless Danvers kept opening his big yap.

She returned to the counter near the register where she'd left the two Irish dolls and Charles Jopp's fashionable lady. Miss Piperton seemed to take an immediate dislike to Danvers, which proved she was a good judge of character. She'd requested to see six dolls at their four thirty appointment and promised to buy at least three.

The money would be welcome, but the prospect of the sale didn't relieve the anxiety created by Danvers's unexpected appearance with the police officer. When he'd walked through the door, Velvalee expected to be placed under arrest. The thought had terrified her. It still did.

She made her way up the stairs to her apartment and heated water for tea. After pouring herself a cup, she added a splash of whiskey—a little something to calm her nerves and help her think.

During the past few sleepless nights, a plan had slowly coalesced. Now, spurred on by Danvers's nastiness and the presence of a policeman inside her shop, the plan took on a life of its own. Since her handler still hadn't responded to her Perla Negra signal, she needed to reach out to other contacts. The last time she'd been in Washington State, a former Japanese navy officer had shared his escape plan. He wanted to stay in Seattle, even if it meant hiding from those who'd send him to an internment camp. But if he ever felt threatened, he knew of an escape route to Mexico. From there, he'd return to Japan via submarine.

Velvalee had to find out if her paranoia was justified, and the only way to do that was to travel to Seattle and find her friend. If he was still in hiding, then perhaps she could persuade him to aid her escape. Perhaps her dream of a home in Japan was closer than she realized.

She refused to consider the impracticality or discomfort of traveling across the Pacific Ocean by submarine. For now, she needed to focus on the impracticality and discomfort of traveling across the continent to Seattle. And for that she needed a plan.

The ringing of the phone startled her already fragile nerves. She decided not to answer it, but the jangling didn't end. Finally, she snatched it up. "Yes. May I help you?"

"Did I catch you at a bad time?"

Velvalee's blood ran cold as she recognized the woman's sultry voice.

"Who are you?"

The woman's throaty laugh crackled through the phone line. "That's not the question you should be asking."

"Why not?"

"Because my identity isn't important. However,

I can tell you the names of a young couple who are asking questions about you. Even better, I can give you a photograph."

"Why would you do that?"

"My reasons are my own. Are you interested?"

"Yes. Of course I am."

"Good. The information is within the pages of *Bleak House* at the bookstore next to your shop. Go find it, Vee." The call ended.

Velvalee clutched the handset against her chest then slammed it onto the cradle. Whoever called her was dangling the photo in front of her like a carrot in front of a donkey. What if this was all an elaborate plot by the government to trap her? She supposed that was possible, but if the government wanted to question her, wouldn't they simply do so? Why all the cloak and dagger? A question she'd asked herself before and still one without an answer.

There was nothing to do but retrieve the photo. She smoothed her skirt and returned to her shop then wound her way into the bookstore. The owner was nowhere to be seen, but Velvalee could hear her humming from the front stacks. *Bleak House* should be in the classic literature section located near the rear of the store.

Velvalee took off her shoes and padded toward the section. Within a few moments, she'd found three copies of the Dickens novel. She pulled out the first and flipped through the pages. Nothing.

She pulled out the second and repeated the process. A high-quality ivory envelope fluttered to the floor. She hurriedly grabbed it, listened to be sure the store's owner was still busy at the front, and scurried back to her apartment.

Once inside, she tossed the envelope onto her writing desk and took a moment to catch her breath. She stared at the offensive envelope, knowing she had no choice but to open it; however, she was inexplicably afraid of doing so.

It's only a photo. It can't hurt me.

She slit open the flap with an Oriental letter opener and tilted the envelope so the photo fell out, facedown, on the desktop. A feminine hand had written two names on the back:

Phillip Clayton

Eloise Marshall

Not names she recognized. As if fearful the photo would burn her fingertips, she gingerly lifted it by a corner and flipped it over.

She stared at the two people standing next to each other at a train station, unable to believe her eyes. The young couple smiled at one another, seemingly oblivious to the crowd milling around them, as they waited their turn to board.

Anger mingled with fear and bubbled up in Velvalee's throat as she picked up the photo for a closer look. "If it isn't my dear Miss Piperton."

Velvalee leaned back in her chair and tapped her chin with the photo. She carefully replayed

Miss Piperton's visit to the shop, like a movie theater's newsreel, reliving their conversation. Nothing in her words or behavior set off any alarm bells at the time, but what had the woman hoped to gain from her little visit?

"Why don't you join me for tea this afternoon?" The eager invitation echoed once again in Velvalee's mind. *"I'm staying at the Waldorf."*

So that was the reason. Eloise Marshall and Phillip Clayton—whoever he was, she didn't recognize him—wanted Velvalee out of her store, away from her home, at a time of their choosing. If they were working for the government, then a noose was gathering around her neck, one so quiet she'd had no idea how close it was to choking her.

She no longer had time to plan an itinerary. Without a moment's hesitation, she stuffed the photo back into the envelope. Her first priority was to leave Manhattan without being followed. Her second was to travel west without getting caught. For that she needed more money than she had in her cash register. That meant a stop at the bank to raid her safety deposit box.

Just as important, she needed to send a message to her friend in Seattle. Taking a seat at her desk, she thought for a few moments then rolled a sheet of paper into her trusty portable Underwood. Though the note would seem innocent to anyone who didn't understand the code, she planned to take no chances of it being seen by the post office censors. She tucked the completed note into a doll costume created especially for hidden messages, packaged the doll in a box wrapped with brown paper, and wrote out the mailing address.

A few minutes later, while tossing clothes, shoes, and other items in her suitcase, she muttered a thank-you to her mysterious benefactress. At least someone still cared about her safety. Someday she hoped to learn the woman's name and the reason for her help. If she made it to *someday*.

Every woman needed a knight in shining armor to slay her dragons in the romantic traditions of the medieval courts. The trick was finding a man willing to do one's bidding in exchange for favors to come without ever bestowing such favors. Thankfully, Lorraine Mitchell had such a knight.

Years ago, during a brief period of adolescent rebellion and long before she became a wife and mother, they dreamed of eloping. But even then, the dream was more his than hers. She liked him, even cared for him, but marriage to someone with such few prospects was out of the question. Even if her parents had given their permission—which never would have happened—he was too much of a dreamer to give her the status she deemed to be her birthright.

After all these years, he still believed she loved

him, that they would be together if not for her parents' antiquated notions. He pitied her for being tied to a man more than ten years her senior and had raged against the engagement when it was announced. She indulged his emotional outburst, crying crocodile tears while privately understanding what he did not. When the time came, she happily married the man whose wealth allowed her family to avoid financial scandal.

But her new husband had deceived her. And her father, who knew all about Leonard's first family, had deceived her too. Only her knight stayed loyal. Without asking why—he never asked why when she asked him to snoop around—he'd done everything she requested and more.

As a longtime journalist for the *Seattle Times*, he'd developed contacts at other newspapers throughout the country. A colleague at the *St. Louis Post-Dispatch* put him in touch with a freelance photojournalist who took the photo of Leonard's despicable daughter with her own trusty knight. A former police detective nosed around and learned that the man who introduced himself as Phillip Carter was actually named Phillip Clayton and had used his FBI credentials to rent two rooms at the hotel located next to Union Station.

Finally, Lorraine's knight invited his confidential contact at the FBI, Agent Bernard "Red" Eckers, out for drinks. Plied with liquor and a monetary inducement, Red told all he knew about Phillip and Eloise's investigation into a New York City doll collector named Velvalee Dickinson, who was suspected of passing treasonous information to the country's enemies. Red even showed him a copy of a postcard that "Vee" had mailed from Seattle, and he complained that he'd been given the mundane task of finding the hotel where she'd stayed. The photograph of Eloise and Phillip was soon on its way to a friend in New York who visited the bookstore next to the infamous doll shop.

Lorraine's phone calls had frightened the doll collector, and the photograph identified the adversary. What would happen next was anyone's guess, but at least Eloise and her knight were compromised, their quarry warned to beware of them.

A satisfied smile played on Lorraine's lips as she contemplated the potential outcomes of the game she'd set in motion. Neither her father nor her husband believed her to be clever. But she'd spent her lifetime observing the schemes they concocted to destroy their enemies, both real and imagined, in their thirst for power. She'd learned those lessons well.

CHAPTER THIRTY-SIX

Eloise checked her watch for the third time in less than five minutes. Velvalee Dickinson, much to Eloise's surprise, was more than ten minutes late. She'd have thought the promise of a large sale would have motivated the Doll Woman to be prompt if not early. The inclination to glance at Richard, who read the latest edition of the *New York Times* at a nearby table, was strong. But she managed to resist the temptation by people-watching.

At least the delay gave her an opportunity to play one of Phillip's favorite travel games. What could she deduce about the three matronly women in the corner booth? Or the couple with two young children sitting by the window?

The elderly waiter, who wore a black apron over black pants, a starched white shirt, and black bow tie, stopped by her table. He'd brought her a pot of tea shortly after she was seated by the maître d', but she'd told him that she would wait for her guest to arrive to place their order.

"Excuse me, miss. Are you Elena Piperton?"

The question sounded odd, especially coming from a stranger. Only a handful of people knew of that name, and he wasn't one of them. "I am," she said, perhaps with too much enthusiasm for a snooty socialite.

"The front desk requested I give you this message." He handed her a folded slip of paper then took a step back.

"Thank you."

The message read:

Mrs. Velvalee Dickinson expresses her regret that she is unable to join you. A family emergency has called her to Florida.

Eloise read the message twice then stared at her teacup to avoid looking toward Richard. She couldn't recall anything in the Doll Woman's dossier about family in Florida. It had to be an excuse. A lie. Did that mean she had seen through their cover stories? Had they scared her off?

The waiter stepped closer. "Would you like to order now, miss?"

"Thank you, no." She needed to leave the dining room. To tell Richard about Velvalee's strange note. To warn Phillip in case she was still at the doll shop. "My friend isn't coming, so I'll be leaving now."

"Very good, miss."

She left enough money on the table to cover the check and a generous tip then strolled into the lobby as if she didn't have a care in the world. Fortunately, Richard joined her a moment later. "What happened?"

Eloise gave him the note. "What do you think it means?"

"Anything I say would be mere speculation."

"We have to warn Phillip."

"He won't enter the store without ensuring it's safe to do so. You mustn't worry about him."

"This is my fault."

"How so?"

"It must be. Something I did, something I said made her suspicious. And now she's gone to Florida of all places."

"I'm positive it's safe to say that the one place she hasn't gone is Florida."

"But the note says—" Eloise stopped as the realization hit her. "She wouldn't have mentioned Florida if that's where she was going."

"Most people's instincts when they're in trouble is to seek the familiar. My hunch is she'll head west again. She has friends there, even acquaintances such as Dr. and Mrs. Lankford, who may provide accommodations."

"Without even realizing what they're allowing under their own roofs." Frustration tugged at Eloise's spirit. "What do we do now?"

"Return to our rooms and wait for Phillip." Richard peered at his pocket watch. "At least, that's what you should do. I have another engagement. However, we can share a taxi."

The doorman flagged a cab for them, and Eloise settled in for a quiet ride to their accommodations. She'd observed that, except for the niceties of etiquette, Richard rarely spoke in the presence of strangers. Though what was there to say?

Between the visit to the doll shop and the tea appointment, she and Phillip had reviewed every moment of her encounter with Velvalee. During the debriefing, Richard asked several questions about the man, Danvers, who had interrupted their conversation. Eloise answered each one to the best of her ability. When the debriefing ended, Richard complimented her on achieving her objective to get Velvalee out of the store. Then he excused himself to make a phone call. Phillip had been astute enough—experienced enough—to note both Danvers's license plate number and the policeman's badge number. He believed Richard meant to find out more about Danvers.

The compliment now rang hollow. She had failed in her task, but she didn't know how. Velvalee had seemed eager to meet with her at the hotel. She also had seemed grateful for Eloise's haughty attitude toward Danvers. What had changed?

Unless it was Danvers who had scared her away. Or maybe the police had returned and arrested her after all. Undoubtedly, that was a possibility Richard had also considered. Eloise wouldn't be surprised to learn that his sudden engagement included a visit to the local police precinct.

Her thoughts shifted from her own possible culpability in Velvalee's sudden departure to Phillip. Was he still waiting to enter the doll shop? Or

314

had he seen Velvalee leave and followed her? Or maybe he was searching the shop and apartment for more evidence. Any of those scenarios was plausible, but she'd have to wait for his return to learn any more.

Or she could return to the shop herself.

The thought seemed daring. And exciting.

Would it be all that implausible that Elena Piperton, whose heart was set on purchasing a doll for her friend, decided to return to the shop? Elena didn't know that Velvalee might be forging letters in an effort to give information about naval ships to the enemy. She didn't know Velvalee was lying about having family in Florida.

Elena could do this.

When they arrived at their destination, Richard asked the cabbie to wait while he escorted Eloise to the door. She waited inside, peeking through the window, until he'd returned to the cab and was out of sight.

Pressing the pearl necklace against her skin, she breathed a quick prayer then hailed a cab of her own.

"The Velvalee Dickinson Doll Shop," she said to the cabbie. "The address is 718 Madison Avenue."

CHAPTER THIRTY-SEVEN

Before returning to the doll shop, Phillip changed from his chauffeur's uniform into dungarees and a T-shirt. Two other agents had been observing the shop since before Elena Piperton and her chauffeur had arrived. They'd seen Phillip drive off in the luxury Cadillac and were still there when he returned in his casual disguise. Both assured him that Velvalee had closed the shop, but she hadn't left the building.

He sat in a parked car, a forgettable black sedan, a few stores down from the doll shop. The basic plan remained the same with one notable revision: when Velvalee left the premises, Phillip would tail her while the other two agents searched her shop and her apartment.

He didn't have long to wait. Velvalee exited the building through the door that led directly to the upstairs apartments. She wore what to him looked like a beige jacket over a beige dress, a beige hat, and low-heeled shoes. A package wrapped in brown paper was tucked under one arm, and she gripped a plain suitcase. A drab little bird unlikely to catch anyone's attention.

She walked at a quick pace southwest along Madison Avenue. Her head never stopped moving, turning this way and that, as if she didn't want to miss seeing anything along her path, especially anyone who happened to be following her. Phillip needed to make a quick decision. He could either stay in the car and risk being noticed for driving too slowly or he could tail her on foot. He didn't like leaving his vehicle, but if she hailed a cab, then he would too.

He stepped from the car and walked at a similar pace several yards behind her and on the opposite side of the street. She turned right on West Fifty-Ninth Street.

First stop, a bank located near Fifth Avenue. Phillip pretended to fill out a deposit slip while she waited for someone to escort her into the vault of safety deposit boxes. *What do you have hidden away in there? A rare doll? Cash?*

Most likely the latter.

Unable to loiter in the bank lobby without arousing suspicion, Phillip waited across the street. When Velvalee finally emerged, she continued along West Fifty-Ninth, hurrying along beside the southern border of Central Park. She crossed Broadway and scurried along West Sixtieth. Second stop, the post office.

Again, Phillip kept his distance even though he desperately wanted to hear Velvalee's conversation with the postal clerk. But he couldn't take the risk she'd realize he was following her or that she would recognize him as the chauffeur who'd been in her shop earlier in the afternoon.

If only he knew where she was sending the package. That might give them a clue to where she was going. He waited for her to leave the post office, noting her direction toward Columbus Avenue, then hurried to the counter.

"I'm sorry to cut in," he said to the woman purchasing a book of stamps. He held out his FBI badge. "Official business."

"That's no excuse for being rude, young man." She huffed then gave him an appraising look. "You don't look like you're with the FBI."

"Again, I'm sorry." He switched his gaze to the area behind the postal clerk and pointed to the package. "What's the address on that package?"

"I'm not sure I'm allowed to tell you that, sir."

Phillip tamped down his impatience. He didn't have time to argue, but he couldn't let that package go anywhere either. He pulled out a business card and scribbled the number to Richard's direct line on the back. "Call this number. Tell whoever answers about the package. And say these words: 'Hen on the move. Fox on her trail.' "

The wide-eyed clerk took the card. "Hen on the move. Fox on her trail."

"That's right. Good man." Phillip tipped his hat at the woman and raced from the post office. All he could do now was hope that the clerk followed his instructions. What happened to the package was no longer under his control.

As soon as he exited the post office, he jogged

toward Columbus Avenue. Despite Velvalee's hurried pace, it didn't take long for him to spot her. She hugged the storefronts, her head still swiveling from one side to the next. A couple of times she stopped to stare at the window displays.

Window-shopping? Or checking the reflection in the glass for anyone suspicious?

An easy question to answer.

Before them rose the imposing Gothic Revival architecture of the stately Church of St. Paul the Apostle with its arched stained-glass windows set within the gray granite stones. Could the church be her next destination? Surely she didn't intend to walk much farther, especially lugging that suitcase.

As if to answer his question, Velvalee stopped at the corner of Sixtieth and Columbus. She looked around then raised an arm to hail a cab. Phillip wasted no time in doing the same. A cab stopped for him first, and he hurriedly slid into the backseat. "I need to follow that woman. The one dressed in beige on the corner."

"You mean that gal up there?" The cabbie retorted around the unlit cigar hanging out of his mouth. "That's not beige. More like a sickly green if you ask me. I'm not sure I want a fare who doesn't know his colors."

Phillip tamped down his burst of frustration and leaned over the front seat to show the cabbie his credentials. "I'm with the FBI."

"You can't be with the FBI. Those fellas wear suits."

"Sometimes we do, sometimes we don't." A cab stopped for Velvalee. Before she could get in, the driver rounded the vehicle to stow her bag. He opened the boot and placed it inside. *Good.* That gave Phillip a little additional time to convince his cabbie to help him out. He checked the registration card hanging from the visor. The guy's name was Nick McDonald.

"You going to pay me for the fare? I can't afford to get stiffed."

"That and a nice tip as long as you stick with that cab. And Nick?"

"Yeah, Mr. FBI man?"

"Don't let her see you."

"Won't ever happen." As if to prove his resolve, he revved his motor. "What are you after that dame for, iffen you don't mind me asking?"

"I don't mind, but that's a question I can't answer."

"It's crazy times, isn't it? You must have heard all about those Germans coming all the way here in one of those U-boats to blow up our factories."

Of all the times to be reminded of Operation Pastorius. "Yeah, I heard a little something about that."

"They got what they deserved in this life, and it's up to God to judge them in the next. That's what I said when it happened and that's what I'm saying now."

Nick's mouth didn't stop, an amazing feat since his lips never lost hold of the cigar. Thankfully, the conversation required little from Phillip except an occasional grunt. But true to his word, Nick stayed behind Velvalee, sometimes allowing another vehicle or two to separate them but never losing sight of her cab. Phillip hung over the front seat, intent on keeping the cab in sight while wishing he had an inkling of where Velvalee was going.

They headed south, eventually turning left on West Thirty-Fourth Street. Velvalee's cab parked beneath the shadow of the Empire State Building. Nick pulled to the curb a few car lengths back.

"Hold tight, pal," Phillip said. "Let's see what she's up to."

"You don't suppose she's going to blow up the Empire State Building, do you?"

"What? No!" Phillip shook his head as if to rid himself of such nonsense. While keeping an eye on Velvalee's cab, he counted out the coins needed to pay the meter plus, as he promised, a generous tip.

"She's getting out," Nick said. "What are you going to do now?"

"Follow her on foot."

"What if she gets into another taxi?"

"Then I'll get another one too." The other cabbie opened his boot and lifted out Velvalee's suitcase. Phillip reached over the seat to hand Nick the fare. "Thanks for the ride."

He started to open the door, but Nick stopped him. "How about if I follow along too? In case you need help."

Phillip's initial reaction was to scoff at the idea, but instead he grinned. "It's kind of you to offer. But I've got to do this on my own. You understand?"

"Sure I do."

Velvalee was out of the cab now. She picked up her suitcase.

Phillip grabbed Nick's hand and shook it. "I've got to go." Without waiting for a response, he exited the cab. Velvalee headed toward Fifth Avenue then entered Saks department store. She often stopped to glance around, but Phillip avoided making eye contact with her while staying on her tail. He followed her across the high pedestrian bridge that crossed Thirty-Second Street to connect Saks with Gimbels.

The skywalk's three-story windows, separated by an ornate metal facade, provided a unique view of New York City's bustling vibrancy even during war. But Phillip couldn't take time for sightseeing when his priority was not to be seen.

Taking the bridge was a clever move on her part. Instead of entering Gimbels directly, her roundabout trip might reveal a tail. At least a tail with less experience than Phillip. But why go to Gimbels at all? Had she planned a rendezvous here?

As he followed her past the ground floor and into the basement, the answer became clear. A maze of underground tunnels accessed Penn Station. Velvalee hesitated near the ticket station then hurried through the gate without buying a ticket.

Where in the world was she going?

Phillip's only choice was to follow her. He started toward the gate when a hefty hand grabbed him by the arm. "Hey, Mr. FBI man," a rough voice whispered. "Remember me?"

Phillip glanced from Velvalee to Nick and back again. "What are you doing here?" He couldn't lose sight of her. Not now.

"You're not from New York, are you?"

"Speed it up, Nick. I don't have much time."

"I didn't suppose you were." Nick took a deep breath. "After you left, I got to thinking that if I was running from the law, I wouldn't take no time for shopping at Saks. But here's Gimbels right across the street, and what's under Gimbels?" He waved his hands in an expansive manner. "A train station. So, I locked up my cab and came over here to wait on you in case I could be of help."

Phillip stared at him in amazement. "You came straight here?" It wasn't really a question, and the cabbie didn't bother answering it. "That was smart thinking."

"It did seem to work out, didn't it?"

That was an understatement. "Great. Now listen

323

to me. Whatever train that woman boards, I'm boarding too. Can you stick around, see where that train is headed, and then make a phone call for me?"

"Sure, sure. I can do that."

Once again, Phillip found himself writing Richard's number on the back of one of his business cards. "Tell whoever answers where I'm going and that I'll be in contact as soon as I can."

Nick took the card, read both sides, then stuffed it in his pocket for safekeeping. "Looks like she's found her train." He gestured toward Velvalee.

Phillip clasped Nick's hand again and then sprinted through the gate. He waited for Velvalee to board then entered the car behind hers. From there, he maneuvered among the other passengers to the rear of her car and found a seat. From his vantage point, he watched her purchase a ticket from the conductor. While he waited to do the same, Phillip peered through the window. Nick stood on the other side of the gate. When their eyes met, he tipped his hat and Phillip responded with a two-finger salute.

Seemed like God had sent him an angel in the disguise of a cab driver. He didn't yet know where he was going, but at least someone did.

CHAPTER THIRTY-EIGHT

Eloise stepped out of the cab in front of Velvalee Dickinson's Doll Shop. The sign on the door said CLOSED. She shaded her eyes as she looked through the display window. The Irish dolls and the Charles Jopp fashionable lady were still on the counter. And the counter where Danvers had placed his box now held a willy-nilly row of dolls. The box lay on the floor.

What had happened here? Had Eloise frightened Velvalee away? Or had Danvers?

She straightened, touched the pearls, and took a deep breath. Eloise Marshall had no business being here. But what would Elena Piperton, a woman who knew what she wanted—a doll to take home to a dear friend—what would Elena do?

Elena would want to know why Velvalee stood her up. Why she'd shown such disrespect to a customer with the means of purchasing several of her rare dolls without a thought of the total purchase price. Elena would want answers.

Eloise shifted her gaze to the bookstore next door. Perhaps someone there would know.

When she entered the store, a middle-aged woman with a pleasant face greeted her with a smile. "I'll be with you in a moment. This young lady has an important purchase to make."

The young lady, who couldn't be more than twelve or thirteen, also smiled at Eloise. She pointed to a stack of coins beside a small canvas bag on the counter. "I've been saving my allowance for the longest time."

"What are buying with your savings?" Eloise asked, charmed by the girl's enthusiasm. She remembered her own youthful days of squirreling away every penny, every nickel she could find or earn for a coveted object. Once she'd seen a lovely golden hair clasp in the local five-and-dime. She'd worked at a variety of odd jobs for an entire month to save enough money to buy it. The following Sunday, she'd worn it in her hair with such proud delight it was only through God's grace that she hadn't suffered the fall that often accompanied such pride.

"This doll." The girl pointed to a rag doll with a Mexican shawl around her shoulders and black beads for eyes. "That is, if I have enough money. I need to count it."

Eloise took a closer look. "Are those pearls?"

"Her name is Perla Negra, but I don't have any idea if those eyes are pearls or beads," the bookstore owner said. "Velvalee, the woman who owns the shop next door, would know. But I don't think the doll is worth much. She put it in my display window months ago."

The girl paused in her counting. "She didn't like it when she saw me playing with her, though. I thought she was going to tear her arm off."

"That seems odd," Eloise replied. Certainly, a respected expert like Velvalee would be careful with her inventory. "Do you know why she did that?"

"She said I shouldn't touch things that don't belong to me. But all I did was pick her up to fix her shawl. I often see her in the window and usually her shawl is around her shoulders. But someone had put it over her head. It's too hot to wear a shawl on your head."

"I agree," Eloise said with a smile. "Did Mrs. Dickinson return the doll to the window?"

"I guess she was too angry. She took it to her store. But I saw it again a few days later."

"With the shawl on her head?"

The girl nodded. "But I left her alone until Papa gave me this week's allowance. I'm sure I have enough money now."

As she resumed her counting, Eloise motioned for the owner to join her as she stepped away from the counter. "I had an important appointment this afternoon with Mrs. Dickinson, but her store is closed. Do you know if anything happened or where she might be?"

"She stopped in earlier. Apparently, there's some kind of family emergency, though come to think of it, she never said exactly what. She was in such a rush to be on her way."

"I don't suppose she left a message for me."

"I'm sorry, no. She didn't leave messages for anyone."

"Has she done anything like this before?"

"Not as long as I've known her. She moved to this location sometime last year. September or October, I think it was. I know it was before Halloween because she decorated the front windows with pumpkins and gourds. All the dolls wore orange and gold costumes. Autumn colors. She has quite a talent for creating beautiful displays."

"I suppose it's a mystery then," Eloise said. A mystery she wished she could solve.

"I suppose." The woman turned back to the girl, who had finished counting. "How much money do you have?"

"A total of ten dollars and seven cents."

"Then this is your lucky day. The price is exactly ten dollars. You still have seven cents to spend on penny candy."

The girl squealed in delight and clapped her hands.

"May I see the doll before you take her?" Eloise asked.

"If you'd like."

She counted seven pennies to return to her canvas bag while Eloise turned away to examine the doll, looking for any signs that messages could be hidden inside. But none of the seams appeared to have been opened and stitched closed again. She handed the doll to the girl who soon left with her treasure and her seven pennies.

"Will Mrs. Dickinson be upset with you for selling the doll?" Eloise asked.

"Perhaps, but I don't care. She treated the child horribly and for no good reason. It's a rag doll, not one of her precious porcelain creations. Besides, I tried to get her to take it with her this afternoon and she refused. Maybe she was in too much of a hurry, but as far as I'm concerned, she left it behind. If she makes a fuss, I'll pay her for what it's worth."

The woman released an exasperated sigh. "I know people spend a lot of money for those antique dolls. And I don't mean to offend. But to my mind, dolls should be loved by little girls, not kept out of reach on high shelves."

"I'm not at all offended," Eloise said. "I think it was very kind of you to let the girl have Perla Negra. I do wonder about those eyes, though."

"Yes," the woman agreed. "That doll may be worth far more than any of us know."

Which only deepened the mystery of why Velvalee had left it behind.

CHAPTER THIRTY-NINE

"Phillip is where?" Eloise stared at Richard as if seeing his mouth form the syllables could make it easier for her to understand the words.

"As I said," Richard repeated, obviously amused by her reaction, "my nephew is on his way to Philadelphia."

"Why?"

"Because our indomitable Mrs. Dickinson is on her way to Philadelphia."

"We frightened her." Eloise's stomach fell to her feet. "I must have done something, said something, that made her suspicious." But what? She'd been over and over their conversation a gazillion times. "Or Danvers did."

"I don't think so. He isn't so much a doll collector as a doll merchant. He buys and sells— that's all."

"How is that different than what Mrs. Dickinson does?"

"I'm not sure, but he certainly wanted to make a distinction. When we talked, he admitted that bringing a policeman to the store wasn't necessary. But he believes she cheated him before. He wanted to intimidate her, yes, but he made no threats. He claims he took his check and left. The policeman says the same."

"Then the blame comes back to me."

"You're being too hard on yourself. I'm sure there's another explanation. We simply need to find it. Now that we know she's left the city, two of our agents are searching the store and her apartment. Hopefully, they'll find something that will either prove her innocence or her guilt."

"Phillip is already on a train with her. Why doesn't he just ask her?" Then they could put an end to all this cloak-and-dagger business. "Perhaps she's frightened enough now to tell the truth."

"Perhaps. But what about those who are working with her? If she is guilty of treason, we need to know who else is involved. The timing is important. And so is having enough evidence to convict anyone and everyone who'd assist our enemies."

Eloise nodded agreement then rose and wandered to the window. A restlessness had been building within her ever since she learned that Phillip was on that train. Would the trip end in Philadelphia? Or would Velvalee lead him west? Perhaps all the way to Portland or Seattle or San Francisco.

Wherever she went, Phillip would follow while Eloise stayed behind. She couldn't bear the thought of not being there—wherever *there* might be—when the timing was right to arrest Velvalee and her accomplices. She'd been part of this case from the beginning, but now she'd been cast aside as if her contributions didn't matter.

In the deep places of her heart, she knew that wasn't true. Phillip hadn't left her on purpose. He had a job to do, and he did it. He was still doing it. Yet, she couldn't shake the painful notion that he'd abandoned her. Just like her father. Just like her brother.

Except . . . no.

They had left her alone to pick up the fractured pieces of her broken heart. Phillip, whether he knew it or not, had taken her heart with him. He would return, but the case might be solved before he did. And then what? Possibly a trial where each of them would be expected to testify. But there would be no reason for them to see each other outside the courtroom.

Even before that, her association with the FBI would be over. She'd return to the navy cryptology unit, and Phillip would join one of the military branches. Her heart would travel with him wherever he went. But there would be no last-minute romance.

If she couldn't bear a separation of a hundred miles, how could she bear a separation of three or four thousand? A separation that might never end? She didn't have the courage.

A knock at the door interrupted her self-absorbed thoughts. There were too many other things going on in the world for her to be wallowing in pity.

Richard answered the door and returned with a package wrapped in brown paper. "Our good men at the postal service have done it again. Mrs. Dickinson considered this package important enough to mail before making her escape. Shall we see what's inside?"

"I'm guessing a doll."

"I imagine you're correct."

Eloise joined him at the table. The package was addressed to Isaac Hirano in Seattle.

"We must unwrap it with the utmost care," Richard cautioned. "That way we can wrap it up again after we take a peek inside."

When they finally opened the box, they found a wooden doll nestled in tissue paper. Richard gave Eloise the task of undressing the doll and examining her clothing.

The lining of the jacket was constructed in such a way that the silk fabric overlapped at the back. Eloise slipped her fingers between the flaps and drew out a piece of paper. Her heart skipped a beat as she scanned the words.

"It's written in jargon code." She felt herself beaming at the discovery.

Richard returned her smile. "Shall we attempt to decode it?"

"We shall."

Eloise retrieved her steno pad and pencil then placed the letter between them.

"Read it aloud," he prompted.

"It says:

'I hope this finds you well as I am not. I return this doll to you with a wish that I may visit quite soon. Travel arrangements must be made, but I am impatient. Home is where the heart is so they say, and you know where my Heart belongs. Please take care of this little Doll. I feel her heart breaks. All she needs is a friend.'"

"What do you think it means?" Richard asked.

"She knows we're after her or that someone is after her, and she's afraid."

Richard steepled his fingers beneath his chin. Eloise waited, giving him time to think, but her own thoughts were whirling like a dervish.

"Would you please copy the message word for word?" he asked.

"Sure. Are we sending it to Phillip?"

"Not yet."

"I could take it to him. Then we could tail her together."

"That simply won't work, Eloise. She's seen you. She knows you."

"She saw Phillip too."

"Yes." Richard slowly nodded. "But she may not recognize him. At least we can hope she doesn't. I'll do my best to arrange help for him."

"There has to be something I can do. Something besides copy messages."

"I have an assignment in mind for you." He fingered the brown wrapping paper. "Once we

334

have a copy of the message, place the original in the doll jacket exactly as it was before. Then we'll wrap the package so no one can tell it's been opened. This may be a way for us to find Mrs. Dickinson's accomplices."

"That's exactly what I was thinking."

"Patience, Eloise. I can't let you join Phillip. But how would you like to deliver this package to the Seattle post office?"

"You want me to travel to Seattle? By myself?"

"You won't be alone, though it may seem like you are. We'll figure out the fastest train routes so you'll arrive before Velvalee. Yes, I think this will work. This will work just fine."

Eloise wasn't as confident, but she made no objections. She'd been handed an assignment as if she were an agent instead of a civilian colleague. The mission was simple and not even dangerous. As far as Velvalee knew, the post office was transporting her package across the country. No one knew that Eloise had it except for Richard.

Still, it was a mission and a chance for her to prove herself.

CHAPTER FORTY

Phillip couldn't allow Velvalee to give him the slip at Philadelphia's Thirtieth Street Station; neither did he feel comfortable standing behind her in the ticket line. He also did not want to draw undue attention by flashing his badge. He studied the departure board and made a gut-level guess. The train to Chicago was scheduled to leave in less than thirty minutes. Other west-bound trains had later departure times. On a hunch, he purchased a ticket to the Windy City. If he was wrong, he'd rely on the same maneuver he used in New York—board the same train as Velvalee and buy his ticket from the conductor.

In the waiting area, he perused the magazines and papers at the newsstand while keeping an eye on the Doll Woman. She perched on a bench, her suitcase at her feet, and clutched her handbag to her stomach. No doubt she was protecting the cash she'd retrieved from her safe deposit box. All the while, her eyes darted among the crowds as if she expected danger at any turn.

"Pardon me, sir." An army captain gestured toward the section of the rack half-hidden behind Phillip. "Mind if I take a look there?"

Phillip shifted his position. "Not at all."

The captain clasped his hands behind his back

336

as he scanned the selections. "My uncle Richard says one should never ride the rails without something to read."

Phillip's ears perked up, but he feigned indifference. "What else does your uncle Richard have to say?"

"That the fox needs a friend." The captain lowered his voice but never once made eye contact. "Especially when the hen is on the move."

An amused grin stretched Phillip's lips. He should have known Richard would send reinforcements. "The fox is on her trail."

"Destination?"

"Chicago, I think."

"I'll purchase a ticket and pass that thought along." The captain selected a magazine then turned away to pay for his purchase. Without any further acknowledgment, he disappeared into the crowd.

Phillip didn't try to speculate on how his uncle had arranged the rendezvous. In his years with the FBI, Richard had made numerous invaluable contacts. It probably had taken only a phone call or two to find someone who could pass the message to Phillip that he wasn't alone in his quest. Funny. He usually preferred working alone. The G-man who went where he was needed, worked with other agents as necessary, then moved on to the next assignment. He'd never minded that role before.

But now, truth be told, something—or perhaps someone—important seemed to be missing as he sat a few rows behind Velvalee during the trip from New York. Knowing that Richard had sent the captain to work alongside him filled that lack. From a practical and tactical standpoint, Richard's motivation was his belief that four eyes were better than two. But Phillip's gut told him that his uncle also meant to reassure him. Nick the Cabbie had done as he promised, and Phillip wasn't working alone.

Unfortunately, Richard hadn't been able to send Eloise. A few weeks ago, Phillip had been miffed that Richard wanted her to play such an important role in the operation. Figure out the jargon code? Sure. That was her area of expertise. But to travel with him to interview the supposed letter writers? Never in a million years. Of course, he only agreed to the mission as a favor to his uncle. But then for Richard to add a woman who wasn't even a trained agent into the deal had seemed an undeserved punishment.

Now that they had traversed the continent and back again, however, Phillip missed having Eloise beside him. But Elena Piperton from Cape Cod had no reason to be on the same train as Velvalee Dickinson. Neither did her chauffeur, but Mrs. Dickinson had paid him no mind when he entered the shop. He was hired help and of no consequence, especially not with Danvers bellowing out his accusations in front of a police-man. Though Phillip still intended to keep as much distance between them as possible, he doubted she would recognize him without the chauffeur's uniform. Thankfully, Richard hadn't insisted Phillip return to New York and leave the trailing to others.

The minutes ticked by, and the loudspeaker announced the boarding call for Chicago and points west. Phillip lowered his head as Velvalee Dickinson's sharp eyes scanned her fellow travelers. He sensed her movement as she stood, gripped her suitcase, and walked toward the plat-form. He waited a few seconds before following. On the way, he spotted the army captain talking to a lieutenant. Phillip guessed the subordinate would soon send a one-word telegram to Richard: Chicago.

On board the train, neither Phillip nor the captain acknowledged one another. The officer, his anonymity a benefit that Phillip didn't have, managed to secure a backward-facing seat across the aisle from Velvalee while Phillip once again sat a few rows back. At least his weren't the only eyes on the drab little hen whose admiration for the Japanese culture had turned her into a modern-day Mata Hari, though one lacking the femme fatale sultriness of the legendary spy.

Oh well. It took all kinds.

Phillip turned to the *Saturday Evening Post*

he'd purchased and settled in for the long ride to Chicago. The drawing on the cover was of a freckled-faced boy, eyes wide and tongue sticking out of his mouth, wearing a ball cap and holding a giant watermelon that in real life would have weighed as much as he did. The image invoked memories of lazy Sunday afternoons, picnics on hot summer days, and swinging on the tire overhanging Deer Creek to fall into the sun-dappled water. It was an image Americans needed to hold on to as they faced a devastating enemy none expected to have experienced once—let alone twice—in their lifetimes. Especially not after their victorious stint in the War to End All Wars. The uneasy peace had lasted less than twenty-five years. Less time than he'd been alive.

He eyed the back of Velvalee Dickinson's dreary hat, momentarily caught the captain's eye, then turned back to the magazine.

In the deepest recesses of his heart, he wished Eloise were by his side.

Eloise set out the next morning, several hours behind Phillip and Velvalee, on the same route through Philadelphia and Chicago. At both stops, she sent prearranged telegrams to Richard and received one-word messages from him in return that revealed Phillip's next destination. After Chicago, Velvalee chose to take the Union Pacific Railroad to Des Moines and Omaha. Richard sent

Eloise along the northern, less populated route, through Minnesota, North Dakota, and Montana. With fewer stops to make, Eloise should arrive in Seattle before Phillip and Velvalee.

Before she embarked on her trip, Eloise and Richard met with the postmaster in charge of all of New York City's post offices. Ever since Velvalee had been identified as a possible traitor, he ensured that all packages she placed in the mail were turned over to the Bureau. So far, the searches hadn't uncovered any hidden messages, and the packages were sent on their way to the intended recipients.

Thanks to Phillip's quick thinking, Velvalee's latest package had been delivered straight to Richard instead of the FBI's field office. He met with the postmaster, who stamped the proper postmark with yesterday's date on the wrapping. If Velvalee saw the package before it was unwrapped, she wouldn't suspect it hadn't been shipped across the country by the postal service.

Eloise passed the time on the train by reading the local papers she picked up at each station, smiling at the comics, working the crossword puzzle, and sometimes fending off the flirtatious remarks of soldiers either traveling to or from home on leave or heading to the coast, where they'd eventually ship out for a life-changing— and in too many tragic instances, a life-ending— experience.

While traversing the seemingly non-ending plains, where the land and the sky met on a far-away horizon, she chatted with a newly minted private who'd signed up within an hour of receiving his high school diploma. His parents persuaded him to wait until after graduation, though it had been hard to see his friends going off without him earlier in the school year. He'd managed a short leave after basic training, and now he was on his way to Cut Bank Army Airfield.

Eloise oohed and aahed over the photo of his sweetheart, a cute blond with an engaging smile and sparkling eyes. When she returned the photo, she caught the gaze of a shabbily dressed man across the aisle. He immediately turned his head away.

A shiver of alarm raced up Eloise's spine. She had noticed the man when he boarded but only because she was heeding her instructors' warning about paying attention to her surroundings. Until now, he'd seemed harmless. Judging by his threadbare jacket and battered hat, he was just a down-on-his-luck passenger traveling alone. Not exactly the wardrobe she'd envision for someone who was in league with a traitor. Or for an FBI agent.

Richard had assured her that one or two agents were accompanying her on each leg of her journey. If they did their job right, he said, they'd blend in so well with the other passengers that she'd never notice them. She'd accepted that as a challenge. Could she pinpoint the agents without making it obvious she was trying to find them?

In all the hundreds of miles she'd traveled so far, she hadn't been confident she'd identified a single one. But this wasn't the first time she'd sensed someone watching her. It happened in Chicago after she exited the 20th Century Limited, then again at Minneapolis's Great Northern Depot.

While the young man chatted about his plans for the future once Hitler's soldiers had either surrendered or been killed—almost as though, with the bravado of youth, he could single-handedly bring about either of those possibilities—Eloise took surreptitious glances at Mr. Shabby Man. In his turn, he seemed content to watch the passing landscape. Perhaps he was as harmless as he appeared, the shared gaze nothing more than what sometimes occurs among strangers in cramped surroundings. But his amiable demeanor didn't alleviate the alert tension in her muscles. She planned to keep a quiet eye on him until their paths separated and to keep a lookout for him after that.

Her young companion said goodbye to her in Shelby, just east of the Montana-Idaho state line. Mr. Shabby Man didn't acknowledge her presence when he got off at the next stop, the small Sandpoint, Idaho, station. Perhaps she'd been mistaken after all.

When she finally arrived in Seattle, she sent a one-word telegram to Richard: *Arrived.* His response: *Next: Spokane.* That's where she'd been about eight hours ago. Since only one daily express traveled from Spokane to Seattle, Phillip would arrive at about this same time tomorrow.

Her pesky butterflies flittered with anticipation. But as Eloise left the station, she did her best to focus her thoughts on her mission instead of daydreaming about a reunion with Phillip. The reality—two colleagues greeting one another without so much as a handshake—would be nothing like the romantic scenes that popped unbidden into her head.

Juggling her suitcase and the package, she took a taxi to the central post office, where Richard had arranged an appointment with the postmaster. After reading the letters from Richard and the New York City postmaster requesting his assistance, he assured her the package would be delivered the following day. She'd successfully completed her mission.

With nothing else to do, she checked into a hotel not far from the FBI field office. All she could do now was wait.

Wait for the package to be delivered.

Wait for Phillip to arrive.

CHAPTER FORTY-ONE

As the train pulled into Spokane, Velvalee considered her two best options. She could take the express to Seattle, the quicker route, or she could go on to Portland then north to her destination. The second option might be the safer one. If she lost her shadow in Portland, he'd never know she had a rendezvous in Seattle.

Phillip Clayton was a clever young man but not clever enough. She first spotted him during a stop at Omaha's Union Station when he pretended to be reading a newspaper while leaning against one of the marble columns in the terminal. She wouldn't have given him a second look if not for the mysterious photograph. But she'd studied it, off and on, through all the long hours of travel from New York. By the time she crossed into Nebraska, she'd memorized the laugh lines around his eyes, the wrinkles in his forehead, the slant of his jaw.

Velvalee made the decision then to exit the westward train to Cheyenne. Instead, she took a commuter train to Lincoln, Nebraska, which connected to a route that curved northward to Billings. For a brief time, she thought she'd lost him. But after they entered Wyoming, she spotted him in the dining car playing cards with three soldiers. So unrefined, the heathens. He didn't so much as give her a glance, and it took all her willpower not to confront him. But she knew he'd only deny any accusations she made.

Knowing his name wasn't enough. She needed to know why he was following her now. His motives couldn't be good, but he was obviously resourceful. If she were going to get away from him, she needed help from someone she could trust, and that person wasn't in Portland.

Her mind made up, she switched trains in Spokane for the express to Seattle. During the long journey, she stared out the window at the passing landscape, napped, and read an Agatha Christie mystery she'd picked up in Chicago, which was much more to her taste than that sordid *Mildred Pierce*. Even when napping, though, Velvalee was somehow aware of her pursuer.

She jerked awake as the memory wavered in front of her. He wore a chauffeur's hat low over his eyes. He followed the policeman into her store then left with the fraudulent Elena Piperton. She pulled the photo from her purse, staring at the young couple who, oblivious of the photographer, only had eyes for each other.

Velvalee had barely noticed him in New York. But now she had no doubt that her pursuer was the fake socialite's fake chauffeur. Eloise Marshall and Phillip Clayton. *Who are you really?*

The obvious answer terrified her.

Most of the German saboteurs were executed even though they'd been caught by the FBI before they caused any harm. It was a brutal punishment, being strapped to an electric chair while a current zapped through one's body. They died because they *planned* to blow up a couple of factories.

She'd written letters, secret messages, to her Japanese friends. A little information in return for money she desperately needed after Lee's death. To her, it was a simple business transaction. But others might misconstrue the situation, even accuse her of traitorous actions, which definitely was not her intent.

So what if her friends wanted to know which ships were damaged at Pearl Harbor? Which ones had been repaired and were ready again for battle? They'd have found the information another way, which would have done nothing to improve her dwindling financial situation. Her rationalizations didn't ease the tightening knot in her stomach. Only ridding herself of her pursuer would do that.

That realization ignited a new line of thought. One that calmed her terror and made it possible for her to breathe again. If Phillip Clayton wanted to follow her, then so be it. He could follow her straight into a trap from which he'd never escape. At least not alive.

In the Spokane terminal, both Phillip and the undercover agent joining him for this final leg of the trip boarded the express train. By silent agreement, they took turns napping and observing Velvalee on the long trip. When the train pulled into Seattle, the agent preceded Velvalee off the train. Phillip held back, waiting to be sure she got off at the stop then keeping an eye on her through the windows until it was his turn to exit.

He and the agent trailed her from different angles as she exited the station. Phillip expected her to hail a taxi, which could make things tricky. But to his surprise, Velvalee wandered to a bank of phone booths, maneuvered her suitcase into an empty one, and shut the door. Phillip slid into a booth five doors away from the one she occupied. While holding the receiver to his ear as if he were having a conversation, he scanned the crowd. The agent from Spokane had taken a seat on a bench that allowed him to observe both Phillip and Velvalee.

The minutes ticked slowly by. Phillip tried to curb his impatience by speculating on Velvalee's conversation. Was she calling a hotel or a friend who could offer her a place to stay? Or was she calling the recipient of the package to let him know of her arrival? Despite Phillip's best efforts and the revolving door of agents who'd helped with his surveillance, did she know she was being followed?

The loudspeaker crackled, but Phillip couldn't clearly hear the announcement through the booth's glass door. Passengers were either being called to board an outbound train or an inbound train had just arrived. A moment later, he suspected it was the former as a swarm of people swept past the booths toward a platform. Phillip lost sight of Spokane, his nickname for the agent. He tried opening the booth's door, but it wouldn't budge against the crush of the crowd.

He tried again, and the door opened a crack. He still couldn't squeeze through. One more try, and he escaped from the booth only to be pressed between it and the swarm. Sidling next to the booths, he squeezed his way to the one before Velvalee's. It was occupied by a heavyset man who frowned when Phillip stopped in front of his door.

He didn't care. All he needed was a quick peek to ensure Velvalee was still on the phone. Since the booth's wooden seat faced the phone, her back would be to him. As long as she was focused on the phone and not the crowd outside the booth's door, he'd be able to get a glimpse of her shoulder without her seeing him. Before making his move, he scanned the crowd in search of Spokane. Too many travelers blocked his view.

It was now or never. He took a half step toward the booth, but Velvalee's shoulder wasn't against the door. The woman admittedly had a tiny frame, but the booths weren't that big. He took another half step forward, and his stomach dropped to the floor. The door to the booth was closed, but Velvalee was gone.

He smacked the door in frustration then noticed something on the seat. A recent Agatha Christie novel called *N or M?*. He took another quick and futile look around for Velvalee and for Spokane, then he retrieved the book. Why had she left it behind? As he flipped through the pages, he found a photograph that made his blood run cold.

He and Eloise stood beside each other at the St. Louis train station, eyes only for each other. She'd been crying, and it had taken every ounce of his willpower not to pull her into his arms and kiss away her pain. And while he was caught up in that moment, he'd let down his guard. Someone had snapped their photo, and he hadn't even been aware that they were being watched.

Now he held the evidence of his negligence. A chilling photograph with a black X drawn across Eloise's body.

A thousand questions raced through his mind. Who had taken the photo? How had it ended up with Velvalee? Why hadn't he realized someone was watching them? More important than any of them—where was Eloise? He needed to call Richard. He needed to know she was safe in New York.

As he entered the booth to make the call, the photo fluttered to the floor, landing upside down. He picked it up and read the writing on the back.

Someone had written their names near the top. Below their names, someone else had scribbled a frightening message.

Taxi stand. Five minutes. Or Eloise pays with her life.

CHAPTER FORTY-TWO

If only Eloise hadn't been so eager to play the part of Elena Piperton. Because of that decision, she couldn't join the agents staking out the Chinese restaurant or at Isaac Hirano's house.

She had promised to stay inside the car and out of the way, but her pleas had fallen on deaf ears. Velvalee knew Eloise as a wealthy young woman she'd met in New York City. There could be no plausible explanation for her presence in Seattle should the two women accidentally meet.

But how could they expect her to stay at the hotel and twiddle her thumbs? At the very least, she could wait for their return to the field office. If she was there, then she'd hear a firsthand account of what happened at the rendezvous when they returned. Besides, Phillip would be trailing Velvalee from the train station. Eventually, he'd come to the field office. When he did, she wanted to be there.

She walked the few blocks to the Vance Building but hesitated outside the entry. Her cheeks burned with the memory of her last visit—how she'd run away like a tormented child. She thought she'd put the past behind her, but in that moment—seeing her father's face, reading about his new life—the past had crashed down around her once again.

Most of those feelings had been reconciled after the confrontation with her dad. Perhaps those that lingered would be put to rest after she talked to her mother. She dreaded the visit and was relieved when it had to be postponed so she could deliver Velvalee's package to the Seattle post office.

For now, though, her embarrassment needed to be set aside for more urgent matters. She took a deep breath and entered the lobby. She approached the receptionist's desk with a forced smile. "Do you remember me?" she asked, mustering as much confidence as she could gather. *"Act like you belong,"* an instructor had said, *"and others will believe you do."* She hoped that little gem of wisdom worked on FBI staff who had probably heard it for themselves. "I'm Eloise Marshall. I was here not too long ago with Phillip Clayton."

"I remember you." The woman's tone seemed both amused and dismissive at the same time. A nice trick if you could achieve it. Eloise wasn't sure she ever had or ever could. "It's not often I see one of the Bureau's finest carrying a ladies' handbag."

Eloise didn't allow her smile to falter but instead infused it with warmth. "I imagine not." Her unspoken but clear message was that not every man was as considerate as Phillip, and his masculinity was enhanced not threatened by his action.

The receptionist released a breath, as if she

353

didn't have time for small talk. "What can I do for you, Miss Marshall?"

"I came to see Special Agent Suran's secretary. Is she in?"

"Have a seat. I'll let Rebecca know you're here." She picked up the phone's receiver. "While you wait, you can read the paper if you'd like. But, please, don't run away with it this time."

"I wouldn't dream of it." Eloise settled on the couch but didn't have long to wait before Rebecca entered the lobby. She perched on the edge of the couch, her body angled toward Eloise.

"Welcome back to Seattle." Despite the pleasant expression on her face, her eyes seemed guarded. "I didn't expect to see you today."

"I couldn't stay away." Eloise glanced at the receptionist, who pretended to be busy at her typewriter even though the keys were silent. She lowered her voice. "Please don't make me leave. Perhaps I could help with the filing or type correspondence."

Rebecca tilted her head, considering the request, then stood. "Why not? Let's go to my office."

Eloise summoned all her willpower not to throw a triumphant look at the receptionist. But she felt the glaring daggers in her back as she passed through the door into the field office's inner sanctum. When the door closed behind them, she let out a breath she didn't even know she'd been holding.

Rebecca chuckled as they walked the corridor to her office. "Don't let her highness get to you. She's jealous of any woman who has done better for herself than she has."

"Why would she think that about me?"

"You're not sitting at the front desk, are you? Unfortunately, she lacks a few attributes that are necessary to move out of reception to a secretarial position."

"Such as?"

Rebecca counted off each attribute on her fingers. "Diplomacy. Tact. Her tendency to take an instant dislike to someone for reasons known only to her."

"If that's true, I'm surprised they keep her here at all."

"They're men. And she has other attributes that make up for her failings." Rebecca's eyes danced with amusement. "I'm no expert, but apparently her legs rival Betty Grable's."

"Lucky her," Eloise replied, her tone lighter than her heart. Now that she was here, the burden of waiting seemed even heavier. Though the typewriter keys from the secretarial pool pounded out an irregular clatter, the offices were silent. Were all the agents involved in the stakeout?

"Please give me something to do," she said. "Anything to take my mind off this operation."

"It might be hours before they return." Rebecca's soothing tone was meant to ease Eloise's jitters.

But nothing could do that except for Phillip's arrival. Suddenly unable to trust her voice, she merely nodded.

"All right then. I understand you have a math degree."

"I do," Eloise managed to squeak out. She exhaled a short breath and straightened her shoulders. "What can I do to help?"

"It's a thankless job." Rebecca retrieved a thick folder from her desk. "But it would be a big help if you could review the agents' expense reports. They're not great at keeping records, so someone must match the receipts with the entries and check the totals. Are you sure you don't mind?"

"Not at all." Getting lost in a world of numbers would distract her from mindless speculation on the operation.

Rebecca pointed to a desk she could use that came equipped with paper, pencils, and a calculator. With a glance at the wall clock, Eloise opened the folder and sifted through the stacks of forms and receipts.

How much longer before the agents return, Lord? Before Phillip arrives?

CHAPTER FORTY-THREE

Velvalee sat upright on a bench near the taxicab stand, her suitcase at her feet and her handbag, stuffed with a few thousand dollars she'd removed from her safety deposit box, resting in her lap. The purse hid the revolver she held in her right hand. Desperate times call for desperate measures. And bold moves.

The plan she'd concocted during her last hours on the express was based on one giant assumption. If she was wrong, then her world threatened to crash down upon her. But she would not be taken without a fight.

While in the phone booth, she'd broken the no-call rule. When Isaac answered, she said she needed to cancel her reservation to attend an emergency garden club meeting.

"Understood," he replied.

"The rats are causing me a great deal of trouble. I have a solution but will need your assistance."

"Anything else?"

"I wish to hire a boat. Perhaps you can recommend someone."

The pause lasted too long for comfort, but Velvalee hadn't broken it. After all the information she'd provided, she refused to be abandoned in her time of need.

"It may not be possible."

"Make it possible." She took a deep breath and softened her tone. "I bring a gift."

She'd hung up before he could say any more. Her next step had been to bait the trap for Phillip Clayton.

Now she waited for him to join her. When he did, she would test her assumption. She only needed enough leverage to persuade him to cooperate. As long as he was unsure of that Marshall woman's whereabouts, she'd have it.

Phillip left the book and the message in the phone booth then hustled through the crowd to the taxi stand. If the Spokane agent checked the booth soon enough, he'd know where to find Phillip and Velvalee and he'd see the message Phillip had added: *Confirm Eloise in NYC. Find her.*

Outside the station, he spotted Velvalee sitting on a bench with her back to him. A gutsy move on her part. Though perhaps that was because, at least for now, she held all the cards. Given her ticking clock, he hadn't called his uncle to check on Eloise. Was she still in New York or had she returned to DC? Perhaps she'd finally gone home to visit her mother. Phillip prayed for any one of those to be true.

He rounded the bench, stood in front of the Doll Woman, and tipped his hat. "Mrs. Dickinson."

"Please have a seat, Mr. Clayton." She gestured

to the space beside her. "Or should I say, Agent Clayton."

"I prefer to stand."

"I prefer you don't." She spat the words with the ferocity of a substitute teacher corralling a bunch of rowdy boys.

After a moment of deliberate hesitation, he took the seat. Let her believe she had the upper hand. They both knew he could physically overpower her anytime he wanted. They both also knew he wouldn't.

"So, you are with the FBI. Interfering . . ." She mumbled the rest under her breath.

"And proud to be."

"What about the delightful Miss Piperton? Or should I say the deceitful Miss Eloise Marshall? Do you know her whereabouts?" She glared at him as if she had the power to make him melt into a puddle of water. Did she honestly believe she could intimidate him with a look?

He held his gaze steady. "She's under the watchful care of the FBI."

"Is she?" One eyebrow arched, forming a sharp, penciled angle. "I'm sure you're an excellent poker player, but this is not a game. We know exactly where Miss Marshall is." A sinister smile twisted her lips. "And she's not where you think."

His blood turned to ice, and his jaw involuntarily flexed, a bluffing tell he was usually skilled

359

at concealing. If they'd been talking about anyone but Eloise . . .

"If you harm her in any way—"

She interrupted him with a harsh laugh. "We don't want to harm her. Though she deserves a slap or two for pretending to care about my dolls the way she did. I am not a fool, Mr. Clayton. I don't appreciate being treated like one."

"What you are is a traitor."

"You're wrong. My husband was the traitor. I had no idea what he was up to."

Phillip couldn't believe what he was hearing. True, the evidence was still mostly circumstantial, but he never expected an excuse like this. "Your husband is dead."

"Miss Marshall will be too if you don't cooperate." She shifted her handbag. The black muzzle of a snub-nosed revolver was pointed right at him. At this close range, she wouldn't miss.

"I also have one of those, Mrs. Dickinson."

"Let me make myself clear." The hatred in her eyes deepened. "If you do not cooperate, Miss Marshall *will* pay the price. Perhaps not today or tomorrow but soon. And *you* will not be here to save her."

Her threats couldn't be possible. Whoever she was feeding information to had left her high and dry. Isaac Hirano's house was surely being watched. He couldn't do anything to help her or to harm Eloise. But what if they had missed

360

something? What if she had other contacts, other resources they hadn't uncovered? He couldn't take the chance that she was bluffing. Not when Eloise's life was at stake.

"What do you want me to do?"

"Take a cab ride with me."

"Where to?"

"One of my favorite places in this city."

"Shall I hail a cab or will you?"

She feigned a laugh and pulled a scarf from her handbag with her free hand. "First things first, Mr. Clayton. Please wrap your weapon in this and return it to me."

Despite his misgivings, Phillip did as she requested. He'd go along with her little game, at least for a while. It'd give him a chance to learn more about her operation—whether she did have partners who could go after Eloise or if she was on her own. When the time came, he'd take control. And Mrs. Velvalee Dickinson, the infamous Doll Woman, would face the consequences of her actions.

Outside the deserted Kubota Garden, Velvalee instructed Phillip, now responsible for carrying her suitcase, to precede her along the path. His scarf-wrapped revolver nestled next to the cash in her handbag while her snub-nosed version pointed at his back.

She'd never shot a person before, only silly

361

targets Lee had set up in the woods behind their spacious home outside San Francisco. Those had been their short-lived glory days, when Lee's produce commodity brokerage company flourished. Their cherished relationships with his Japanese clients granted Velvalee's dearest wish to immerse herself in their culture.

Her life had been perfect until the FBI appeared at the brokerage company with their suspicions of financial improprieties and a warrant. By the time the ordeal ended, their business was in ruins. And for what purpose? Lee was never accused of anything except being too chummy with his clients. They couldn't put him behind bars for that, but the damage had been done. Now the FBI wanted to destroy her again. Not this time.

Her brooding anger sharpened with heartache as she and Phillip walked beneath the wooden entrance, which had been stripped of its iron gates. Though many of the gorgeous flowering shrubs and ornamental trees that had brought Velvalee such delight on past visits were thriving, vining weeds overran the border plants and rock gardens. Such a travesty and for no purpose.

She directed Phillip to sit on a grassy bank close to a footbridge. Once he'd complied, she perched behind him on her upright suitcase and stared at the vista before her. The water lilies in the narrow stream gathered against the bridge's column, and thick algae bordered the bank. The odor of dead fish and rotting decay assaulted her nostrils.

"What do you know of this place?" she asked.

"I've never been here before," Phillip replied.

"It was a labor of love for a most distinguished gentleman named Fujitaro Kubota. He and his family lived here, worked here, entertained here." Velvalee momentarily closed her eyes, letting herself return to happier days when she visited this garden refuge. "One could imagine herself in Japan while strolling these paths."

"Why did you bring me here?" The impatience in his tone caused her anger to flare.

"Do you know where Fujitaro Kubota is now?"

"How would I?"

"He's in an internment camp. The man that created all this beauty, who gave us this generous gift, is now a prisoner. His only crime is his Japanese heritage." She poked Phillip in the shoulder with the revolver. "That's the government you work for."

As he twisted his neck to look at her, he rubbed his shoulder. She pointed the gun at him. "Don't turn around. Don't move."

"Okay, okay." He raised both hands chest high as if in surrender. "Why don't you tell me what we're doing here? What can I do to help you?"

Velvalee gazed beyond him to the unmown grass and the untrimmed hedges. The garden's neglect pierced her heart as if it symbolized all that was wrong in the world. If only she could have protected this place and prevented her friends from being taken to the camps. If only the FBI hadn't once again interfered with her private business.

"Tell me, Velvalee. What is it you want?"

She glared at the back of his arrogant head, eyed the revolver in her hand, and with all her strength and might, smacked him behind his ear.

He fell sideways but caught himself. Before he could rise, she struck him again. He sprawled on the bank, his fingertips floating in the stream as his blood soaked the ground.

She squatted beside him, listening to his shallow breath, watching the slow rise and fall of his chest.

"What I want is to leave this place." Her voice was low and harsh. "I want to live with people who understand culture and refinement. And I want to take you, a United States federal agent, with me as a gift to my friends."

CHAPTER FORTY-FOUR

Eloise smiled with satisfaction as the dollar amount on the calculator roll equaled the dollar amount on the expense report. A small victory but one that had taken several minutes to resolve, thanks to Agent Red Eckers's sloppy book-keeping. Concentrating on the numbers took the edge from her worry but hadn't obliterated it completely. On the surface, the other women in the office seemed content to type their reports and answer the phone calls. But Eloise sensed a tension in the atmosphere as if all of them were holding their breath while waiting for news.

A commotion sounded in the hallway followed by the receptionist's voice screeching, "You can't go in there."

Eloise glanced around the secretarial pool in alarm. All the women seemed frozen at their desks. Rebecca emerged from her office and faced the door to the corridor. She held a gun behind her back.

The door flung open revealing a broad-chested man in a rumpled suit, the receptionist close behind him. "Where's Suran?" he shouted to no one in particular while waving the book he carried. "I need to see him now."

"I told him he couldn't barge in here," the receptionist insisted.

"It's fine. This is Agent Thomas Bolman from our Spokane field office." Rebecca's shoulders relaxed, and she smiled as she looked around the room. "Everyone, return to your duties."

"I need to see Suran." The man's voice was calmer now. "I lost them. Both of them."

Eloise's heart leapt to her throat. Whom did he mean? Whom had he lost?

"Come with me." Rebecca gestured toward her office. "Eloise, please join us."

Eloise's knees shook as she rose from her desk and entered the office. Rebecca closed the door and folded her arms. "Special Agent Suran is out with a surveillance team. What's so important that you stormed in here and upset my girls?"

Bolman took a deep breath then stared at Eloise. "You're her," he exclaimed. "The one in the picture. I'll show you." He opened the book, removed a photograph, and gave it to Rebecca. Her expression didn't change, but something in her eyes snapped.

"Let me see it." Eloise held out her hand.

Rebecca held the photo close to her chest. The writing on the back was too small for Eloise to decipher. "It's a photograph of you and Agent Clayton," Rebecca said.

"We've never had our picture taken together."

"Nevertheless, one exists. Someone has drawn

an *X* over you." Rebecca put the photo in Eloise's hand and turned to Agent Bolman. "Please stop pacing and tell me exactly what happened."

"When we arrived in Seattle, the subject entered a phone booth. Clayton got in a different one, and I positioned myself to see both."

As he talked, Eloise stared at the photograph. The initial shock took her breath away, but then she looked beyond the horrid black mark and was transported back to the unguarded moment when the picture had been taken. This was the morning after the confrontation with her father, shortly before they boarded the train east for their appointment in Springfield.

She remembered her eyes were puffy from too many tears and too little sleep. Phillip's gentle compassion, as he navigated the blurry line between saying too much or too little, had almost done her in. But the warmth in his gaze had bolstered her spirit. She couldn't look away from him, not even when his gaze dropped to her lips. In the moment captured by the camera, her heart ached for him to kiss her, to hold her in his arms. Instead, he'd turned away, and she'd renewed her vow to guard against her deepening feelings for him.

"When I couldn't find either of them, I went back to the phone booths," Agent Bolman continued, and Eloise realized she'd missed part of his story. "The book and photo were just lying on the seat. But you can see Clayton's message there on the back. He said to find you, and I guess I did but not where he thought you'd be."

Eloise turned the photo over, as Rebecca stepped closer to read over her shoulder. Three different people had written on the back. Below her and Phillip's names was a message threatening Eloise with harm. Scribbled across the bottom was Phillip's message to Agent Bolman.

"I ran out to the taxi stand, but they weren't there. So, I came straight here to give this to Suran. Figured he'd know best what to do."

Eloise pointed to the threatening message. "This is Velvalee Dickinson's handwriting. I've read several postcards she sent to a friend." She hadn't realized until she read Phillip's note that he didn't know about her trip to Seattle. Richard must not have thought it important to tell him. Was that because her role in this investigation ended when she delivered the package? Because Richard, like her father before him, was done with her?

A loud and resounding *no* echoed inside her. Richard was not her father, and Phillip cared about her as she cared about him. She held the photographic evidence of that in her hands.

"Do you have any idea who wrote your names on here?" Rebecca asked Eloise. "Who took the photograph?"

"No, only that it was taken when we were in St. Louis. Whoever did must have known we were investigating Mrs. Dickinson. But I don't know how or why anyone would have given this to her."

"Now that I know you're safe," Agent Bolman said, "I need to find Clayton. Since he isn't here, we can assume he went with that doll lady."

Eloise emitted a sharp laugh and her cheeks flushed as Agent Bolman and Rebecca stared at her. "It's just that Phillip warned me about making assumptions and then you said, 'We can assume,' and I . . ." Could a hole open in the floor and swallow her up now?

"He's right about that," Agent Bolman's mushy features contorted into an amused smile. "Let's say she's the best lead we have right now."

"Then we need to find her." With her no-nonsense tone, Rebecca took charge of the situation. "Thomas, you go back to the taxi stand. Talk to the dispatcher and the other cabbies. Find out if Velvalee and Phillip took a taxi and, if so, where they went. I'll get a message to Special Agent Suran."

"I'm on it." Agent Bolman bounded out with as much energy as when he'd arrived.

"Wait for me." Eloise started after him, but Rebecca grabbed her by the arm.

"You're not going anywhere. At least not until Special Agent Suran gets back."

"I have to go," Eloise insisted. "Phillip needs me." *And I need him.*

"Phillip needs you to do your job."

"I can't find Phillip sitting behind a desk."

"You and Phillip know more about this case than anyone," Rebecca said. "Review everything you've done, everything you've learned. Find out who took that photograph."

Eloise shifted her gaze from Rebecca to the photograph and back again. "How do I do that?"

"It's simple. Start with who knew you were in St. Louis."

"Nobody knew. Except Richard Whitmer, but he wouldn't . . ."

"He wasn't the only one." Rebecca tapped the photograph. "The person who took this did too."

"But—"

"Think of it as a puzzle, Eloise. A code." Rebecca returned to her desk and picked up the phone. "Solve it."

Eloise walked slowly back to the secretarial pool, gingerly carrying the photograph as if it were made of china. She moved aside the piles she'd made reviewing the expense accounts and found a clean sheet of paper.

Who knew that she and Phillip were in St. Louis?

Richard knew. Though Eloise couldn't imagine he had anything to do with the photograph—he certainly wouldn't have given it to Velvalee—she wrote his name at the top of her list. She retraced their steps from the moment they'd arrived at Union Station until they left, writing down everyone she could think of:

1. *Richard Whitmer*
2. *The front desk clerk who checked us in (Note: we used our real names.)*
3. *The bellboy who carried our luggage*
4. *The salesclerk at the dress shop*
5. *Father, his new wife, his bodyguard*
6. *Father's friends at the bar*
7. *The clerk at Hotel DeSoto who gave me stationery*
8. *Taxi drivers—to and from the Hotel DeSoto*

Perhaps there were other hotel staff but no one significant enough to include in the list. She drew a line through numbers 3, 4, 6, 7, and 8— none of them knew her name—as she postponed admitting the inevitable answer.

Number 5. *Father, his new wife, his bodyguard.* Of those three, only one made sense. She drew a circle around *Father* then tapped the eraser end of the pencil against her chin. *Now what?*

She bowed her head in a quiet plea for wisdom to choose her words carefully and strength to stay calm and composed. No accusations. No recriminations. Simply present the facts as she knew them and ask one critical question: *Did you hire the photographer?*

After taking a deep breath, she returned to Rebecca's office.

"I haven't heard back from Special Agent Suran," she said. "I promise I'll let you know as soon as I do."

"Thank you." Eloise held up the sheet of paper. "I made a list."

"And?"

"Is there someplace I can make a private call?"

Rebecca thought a moment then rose from her desk. "I'll be in the secretarial pool if you need me."

Once the door was closed, Eloise reached for the phone. An operator connected her with her father's investment firm, but his secretary said he was out for the day. Gathering her courage, she asked the operator to connect her to her father's home and prayed he'd answer. When his familiar voice came through the line, she blurted, "It's me. Eloise."

"Eloise?" His voice sounded relieved but also wary. "I hoped you'd get in touch again. I wanted to contact you, but I wasn't sure how to do that. Or if I should."

"This isn't a social call." She tried as hard as she could to keep her voice steady, but still it wavered.

"No, of course not." A beat of silence then, "Are you all right?"

Eloise bit her lip and stared at the ceiling,

praying once again for wisdom and strength. An inexplicable calmness descended around her. She could do this. *With Your help, Lord, I can do this.*

"I can't give you all the details," she began then took a deep breath and started over. "When my friend and I were at the train station the morning after . . . after we talked . . . someone took our picture. Only a few people knew we were in St. Louis. I need to know if you had anything to do with the photograph. Anything at all?"

"No." He gave a short laugh as if suddenly embarrassed. "Though I did do a little snooping."

Eloise tensed, her nerves on high alert. "What does that mean?"

"I know that your friend isn't in the construction business. That his name isn't Phillip Carter but Phillip Clayton."

"What else?"

"That he's with the FBI." His voice lowered. "So are you."

"If that's true," she said, choosing her words carefully, "it's only temporary."

"Are you in trouble, Emmie?" His use of her unusual nickname took her immediately back to those bedtime stories. No one else called her that, only him, a name taken from her initials. Eloise May Marshall. *EMM.*

He finished the chapter—always only one—and closed the book. Then he tousled Allan's hair and kissed Eloise's temple. "Night, my boy. Sleep tight, my Emmie. I love you two to the moon and back again." The same routine every time. How could she have forgotten?

"Eloise?"

"I'm here."

He cleared his throat, and his voice wrapped her in a protective cocoon just as it did all those years ago before he disappeared. "Tell me about the photograph. Why it's important. Maybe I can find out something for you."

She didn't have the authority to tell him anything—not about the forged letters or the message hidden in a doll's jacket or the suspected treason. But Phillip was missing, and she'd break any rule to find him. "The photograph and our names were given to a woman we're investigating. She wrote a message on the photograph threatening me and made sure Phillip saw it. Now they're both gone. We don't know where."

"In St. Louis?"

"No, here. In Seattle." She took a quick breath. "I'm in Seattle."

"Where? I'll come get you and take you somewhere safe. I'll hire a security detail."

Surprisingly, his exuberant concern made her smile. "I'm safe where I am."

"Where's that?"

"At the FBI office."

"Of course."

"If you can't help me, then I need to go."

"Wait a minute." The silence seemed to last forever but was probably only a second or two. "I want to thank you for telling me about Allan. I should have behaved better that evening, and I'm sorry I didn't. Seeing you again brought up . . . I'm sorry, Emmie. Truly sorry."

"Me too."

Before she could hang up, he made her promise to call anytime, day or night. She agreed, but her stomach and her heart were in turmoil. She wanted to believe he had nothing to do with the photograph. But it was difficult to reconcile the man on the phone with the man she'd met at the Hotel DeSoto.

Despite how he'd made her feel during their conversation—that he cared deeply about her— she had to face the fact that he was the most likely suspect on her list. If not him then who? And why?

CHAPTER FORTY-FIVE

At the first sign of Phillip regaining consciousness, Velvalee picked up her revolver and aimed it at him. Not that he was in any position to cause trouble. Once Isaac arrived at the Garden, he'd unceremoniously dumped the agent into a wheelbarrow and wheeled him to the greenhouse as if he were a bag of fertilizer. Now Phillip lay on a wooden pallet, his hands and feet tied with twine.

He groaned, attempted to lift his hand, then groaned again. He blinked his eyes a few times then slowly moved his head until he caught sight of Velvalee and her gun. "You don't need that." His voice sounded drowsy and out of sorts. He took a deep breath, exhaled, and closed his eyes again.

Velvalee wasn't fooled. He was fully conscious and no doubt scheming a way to overpower her. She'd take every precaution short of killing him to ensure that didn't happen.

"You won't get away with this, you know." His eyes were still closed, as if dragging himself out of the foggy depths he'd been in had taken all his strength. "The Bureau will be looking for us."

"I suggest you pray they don't find us unless you want Miss Marshall to experience a fatal accident."

She expected him to threaten her in return—something especially inane such as *Don't you dare touch her*—but his only response was to tense his jaw and clench his fist. Even those small gestures gratified her. His feelings for the duplicitous woman would be his undoing and Velvalee's salvation. As long as he believed Eloise was in danger, he'd behave himself.

"Does Miss Marshall know you're in love with her?"

"I'm not."

Velvalee emitted a harsh laugh. "Perhaps that's for the best. Especially since you'll never see her again."

"Why not?" He still seemed to struggle with his words, pausing between each one as if to catch his breath.

"Because you and I are going on a long trip." Her pulse quickened when she said the words out loud, as if that made them even more true. The desire of her heart was almost within her grasp. Only one more hurdle, and they'd be on their way. "When we arrive at our destination, your head will be delivered to the emperor on a silver platter. I speak figuratively, of course. You will be interrogated, and if you don't reveal the national secrets that you're privy to, you'll be tortured."

"I don't know," he paused and took a deep breath, "national secrets."

"Then your time would be well spent in making up a few. Though perhaps they'll be content with learning the FBI's investigative techniques. Its weaknesses."

He clumsily rolled over to his side, so he faced away from her. It didn't matter. She'd have many opportunities to goad him and torment him once they were on the boat to San Francisco. From there, they'd wait for the arrival of the submarine that would take them to a ship far out in the Pacific. Finally, they'd reach Japan, where Agent Phillip Clayton would be taken away, never to be seen or heard from again, while she took her rightful place in society. Perhaps she'd even marry again. Husband #4.

Could her future be any brighter?

Phillip seemed to be sleeping, and Velvalee rested the revolver in her lap. She too must have dozed off. Alerted by a sound outside the greenhouse, she startled awake and immediately glanced at her prisoner. He hadn't changed his position on the pallet. She rose from the damp floor, stretching the kinks from her neck and back, then stood over him. His hands were still bound in front of him, his ankles still tied together. Dried blood caked above and behind his ear.

Footsteps shuffled along the pavestones leading to the greenhouse. Velvalee quietly made her way to the door, the gun by her side, and peered through the glass. Finally, Isaac had returned. "Tell me you have good news."

"Arrangements have been made. I bring you a message." He bowed as he handed her a slip of paper.

She grasped it from him and stared at the nonsensical letters. They were grouped in four blocks with each block consisting of nine letters in total. A three-square code.

"What does it say?"

"I cannot read it. I am only a messenger. More than that, I do not know."

"Why didn't whoever sent this just tell you so you could tell me?"

"I do not want to know."

"Of all the . . ." Nothing for her to do now except decode the message. Fortunately, she had packed her guidebook. She flipped past the pages that had suggestions for the jargon code she used in her forged letters until she found the three-square key. Decoding the message required substituting one letter for another, but it wasn't as simple as *A=C, B=D, C=E* or some similar pattern. These were random and took more time to work out. At least the message was short.

She wrote the decoded message on an empty page in the code book. *Misty Blue at Bell Harbor Marina by four*.

Velvalee returned to Phillip and poked his side with her foot. He groaned but didn't move. She poked him harder. "Time to go, sleepyhead. Get up."

"All right, all right." His voice sounded stronger than it had earlier. Still, it seemed he took his sweet time sitting up. Isaac cut the twine around his ankles and helped him to his feet.

"You follow Itsuki," she ordered, using Isaac's true name, then waved her gun. "I'll follow behind. No tricks."

"No tricks," Phillip repeated.

She nodded, and Isaac, carrying Velvalee's suitcase, led the way to the door. When Phillip reached the threshold, he lost his balance and stumbled backward into Velvalee. She dropped both the gun and her handbag, which popped open. Loose bills fluttered to the floor as she grabbed at a table holding an assortment of ceramic and clay pots to steady herself. Phillip, cradling his head in his bound hands as if in agony, fell against the table and knocked it over. The pots clattered to the floor, and shards of ceramic and clay flew in all directions.

Cursing under her breath, Velvalee immediately fell to her knees to retrieve the gun and her money while Isaac stared at the cash. "Don't move," Velvalee ordered. "Nobody move." Once the money was safely tucked away, she retrieved the gun from beneath a broken ceramic planter. She shoved it into Phillip's side. "Get up. And don't do anything like that again."

He moaned as he struggled to stand. "It was an accident."

"I don't care. Not all bullet wounds are fatal, but all are unpleasant."

"I'll take your word for it."

Phillip followed Isaac through the door, his gait still unsteady. Velvalee didn't know if he was faking, but it didn't matter. Isaac had come into the gardens through a rear entrance and parked his sedan in a small lot near the greenhouse. He hurried ahead of them and put Velvalee's suitcase in the car's backseat. "Later I will report the car as stolen," he said. "I leave you now."

Before Velvalee could protest, he made a quick bow then jogged away. *The coward.* Thankfully, she knew how to get to the marina.

Velvalee waved the gun at Phillip. "You drive."

"With my hands tied?"

"I'm sure you can manage."

As they headed for the marina, Velvalee took comfort in overcoming another hurdle. Despite a few setbacks—such as Isaac running away like a frightened mouse—her bold plan was working. In a few days, all the unpleasantness she'd had to suffer would be behind her. Yes, the future was very bright indeed.

CHAPTER FORTY-SIX

A clatter of voices and footsteps filled the back hallway as the agents returned to the field office through the rear door. Eloise stood beside Rebecca as they filed into the conference room. Among them were Special Agent in Charge Ray Suran, Red Eckers, and Thomas Bolman from the Spokane office.

Suran stopped beside her. "I'm glad you're still here. Come into my office. You too, Bolman. Rebecca, bring your pad."

As soon as everyone was seated, Special Agent Suran closed the door. "I'll make this as brief as possible. Turns out the restaurant where the rendezvous was to take place was closed. Had been for quite a while. No one showed up. As you know, we also had a team watching Isaac—his real name is Itsuki—Hirano's house. The postman delivered the package, but Mr. Hirano never checked his mail. Turns out he managed to give us the slip. The house was empty."

He gestured for Agent Bolman to pick up the story. "It took some time, but I finally tracked down our cabbie. He remembered Clayton and this doll lady because they looked so odd together. Her being so short and all. Said they didn't say a word to each other the entire trip. He dropped them off near the corner of Renton and Fifty-Fifth Avenue South. I contacted the boss here, and we all met up there."

"As soon as he told me the address," Special Agent Suran said, "I knew where we needed to look."

"You found Phillip?" Eloise asked, unable to hide her excitement. Or her anxiety. "Where is he?"

"We found where they'd taken him. To Kubota Garden. But they'd left before we got there."

"Where is he now?"

"I'm hoping you can tell us." Special Agent Suran pushed a slip of paper to her. "There'd been some kind of melee in the greenhouse. A knocked-over table and broken pottery. We found this beneath an overturned pot. Can you solve it?"

Eloise smoothed out the wrinkled paper. "It's a three-square code. Four blocks. Not a very long message. Of course I can solve it."

"We'll leave you to it then."

Rebecca handed Eloise her steno pad and followed the men from the room. Eloise created an alphabet key, then tapped her pencil on the desk as she whispered the order of frequency for single letters, "E T O A N." A moment or two later, she switched to doubled letters and digraphs, tapping the beat with her pencil. "S S, E E, T T . . . T H, E R, O N, A N, R E . . ."

The combinations didn't help, so she returned to order frequency. *I R S H D L*

That was enough for her to decipher the code:

X Misty Blue at Bell Harbor Marina by four. YZ.

The first letter and last two letters were fillers, but the *Misty Blue* must be the name of a boat. Eloise glanced at the clock. It was past three thirty now. If Phillip was on that boat and it left the marina, how hard would it be to find him again? She started to take the message to Special Agent Suran then hesitated. What if he didn't let her go with them? She couldn't give him the chance to say no. All she needed was a little head start.

She quietly opened the office door and approached one of the typists in the secretarial pool. "I need to go to the ladies room." She gave an awkward grin. "A little emergency if you know what I mean. Could you please take this to Special Agent Suran? It's very important."

"I'd be happy to."

Eloise thanked her and hurried toward the front door. Once outside, she headed in the direction of the hotel where she was staying in hopes of finding a taxi along the route. A Chrysler Imperial passed her then pulled to the curb. Eloise slowed her pace. She hadn't seen Shabby Man since he got off the train in Idaho, but what if he had somehow followed her here?

In a Chrysler?

That seemed unlikely, but a couple of months ago, she would have been skeptical that an unassuming antique doll collector was using jargon code to pass along information to the Japanese.

When the driver's door opened, Eloise braced herself to run back to the field office. A man emerged and lifted his hand in greeting. *Father.*

"Can I give you a lift?" he asked as she neared the vehicle.

"I know where Phillip is."

"Get in."

She hurried to the passenger side and gave him the name of the marina. As he drove, she told him how an agent had found the message she'd decoded and her fear she'd be forced to stay behind at the field office. "I have to be there when they find Phillip."

"I know." He maneuvered a left turn and then a quick right. "You never were one to let life pass you by."

The Bell Harbor Marina turned out to be only a few blocks from the FBI field office. Father parked the car then placed his hand on Eloise's arm. "This woman who took Phillip knows who you are."

"I'm not staying in the car."

"I'm not asking you to. Let's just do this smart." He reached into his pocket and pulled out a silver derringer. "Do you know how to use one of these?"

"Yes. But I'm not very good."

"No one's asking you to be a sharpshooter. Only to protect yourself."

She took the shiny gun from him, surprised that something resembling a toy had such heft.

"Here's the plan. I'll locate the boat and you wait for my signal."

"It's almost four. They may be leaving soon."

"We're going to find him. I promise."

She wanted to believe him. But how did one believe the promises of a father who promised to read the next chapter in a Hardy Boys mystery and then never came home? He must have seen the doubt in her eyes.

"I promise to do my best. Will you believe that?"

She nodded.

"Watch for me." He got out of the car and strolled along the pier, admiring the boats as if he belonged there. *"Act like you belong and everyone will think you do."* Her father seemed to be a natural at this spy game.

She stepped out of the car but stayed by the front fender until he returned, a broad smile on his face. "I found her. Beautiful lines but in need of repair."

"Did you see Phillip?"

"I didn't see anyone." His eyes were drawn to

the streets behind them. "Your friends are coming."

She turned around in time to see two black Fords waiting for the light to turn. They'd be at the marina in less than a minute.

"What do you want to do?" he asked.

"Save Phillip."

"Then let's go."

The wooden cabin cruiser was white with faded blue trim and gave the appearance of an elegant lady past her prime. No one seemed to be on board.

"What now?" Eloise asked.

"We flush them out."

"How?"

"By getting on board. Just don't let anyone see you. And keep your ears open."

They quietly slipped onto the bow and knelt below the cabin window. Father motioned for Eloise to stay put, then he stood and rounded the cabin to the stern while singing a rousing rendition of "O Danny Boy" at the top of his lungs. It seemed an odd song choice. Definitely unpredictable . . . just like her father.

A few seconds later, someone joined him on the deck, and the singing stopped. Eloise couldn't make out all the words, but it seemed her father wanted to buy the boat at top dollar.

She crept toward the stern in the narrow space between the rail and the cabin. From her vantage point, she watched in awe as Father put one arm around the shorter man's shoulders and waved the other in a wide arc as if to encompass the entire bay. The man struggled to get out of Father's grip, a tussle ensued, and seconds later the man went headfirst over the back of the boat. Father's shouted apology was nearly drowned out by the huge splash.

"What's going on here?" Velvalee Dickinson's voice shrieked.

"My dear lady, was that your husband?" Father said. "We were haggling on a price for this boat when he must have had a sudden whim for a swim. Over he went."

"This boat is not for sale. Go away." She appeared in Eloise's line of sight on her way to the stern. "Get back on this boat," she shouted to the man. "We need to be on our way."

While her attention was on the man, Father motioned for Eloise to slip into the cabin. As soon as she was down the stairs, he closed the door after her. She held the derringer at the ready, but no one was in the galley. Two doors opened off a tiny passageway. The room on the left, containing only a narrow bed and a square nightstand, was empty. She peeked in the other room then covered her mouth to stop from squealing with joy.

Phillip sat upright on the bed with his hands bound and a white bandage wrapped around his head. "Hello, sweetheart."

"Humphrey Bogart at a time like this?"

"It's always a good time for Bogey."

She placed the derringer on the nightstand and tried to undo the knots on the rope around his hands. "What happened to your head?"

"A little misunderstanding." He stared at her, his eyes soft and questioning. "How did you get here?"

"We need to hurry." The knots came undone, and she unwrapped the ropes to free his hands. "My father is on deck with Velvalee. Special Agent Suran is here too. That is, he's on his way."

Phillip slid his hand down her arm to entangle her fingers with his. "Hold on a minute."

"What is it?"

"I thought I'd never see you again. But here we are, together. The future . . . who knows what will happen. I only know I want to be with you for whatever time we have." He caressed her cheek and tears welled behind her eyes. When he disappeared, she had stopped denying the truth that was in her heart.

"If you ask me," she said, "I will wait for you. However long this war lasts."

"I'm asking." His fingers slipped behind her neck as his lips covered hers with a fervency and desire unlike anything she'd ever experienced before. This moment, this very moment when love declared itself and two hearts beat as one, held enough joy to surround any sorrows.

CHAPTER FORTY-SEVEN

A shot rang out on the deck above, interrupting the sanctity of love's first kiss. Eloise scrambled to her feet, fear for her father pushing against her need to hold on to the thrill of being in Phillip's arms before the sensation faded. She grabbed the derringer and headed for the stairs.

Phillip followed close behind her. At the foot of the stairs, he caught her. "I'll go up first." He tried to take the derringer, but she didn't let go.

"My dad's up there." Her concern nearly choked the words, and a tiny corner of her brain registered that this was the first time she hadn't referred to him as *Father* since she'd been a small girl. What had changed? She didn't know, and now wasn't the time for self-analysis.

"Eloise." Phillip held her wrist. "Please."

Common sense told her to give him the gun. He was the trained agent, the better marksman, the skilled fighter. But instinct propelled her to slip from his grasp, to scurry up the steps and slam open the door.

Time slowed as she stood on the deck and took in the scene. Velvalee pointed a revolver at the man Eloise had loathed for years. He clutched at his bicep as blood flowed among his fingers.

Velvalee turned, her face twisted with hatred and a strange satisfaction as she aimed the pistol at Eloise.

Someone shouted *no* and a gunshot reverberated in Eloise's ear as Phillip collided into her. As she fell, she lifted the derringer, closed her eyes, and pulled the trigger. Her head hit the deck, sending her into a tailspin that echoed with a woman's screams.

The fog lifted to too many voices. Too many people. Eloise cared only about the two who helped her sit up then knelt beside her, love and pride shining in their eyes.

Her dad had appeared like the cavalry in a dime Western when she needed him most. He wore the bandage covering his grazed arm like a badge of honor. Phillip had pushed her to the deck, covering her with his body when Velvalee fired her gun. The bullet struck the boat's woodwork instead of Eloise.

Velvalee huddled on the deck, screaming unladylike obscenities at the FBI agents who tried to administer first aid to her shattered kneecap.

"Did I do that?" Eloise asked.

Phillip twirled the derringer on his forefinger. "Couldn't have aimed better myself."

"I didn't actually aim."

"Shh," her dad said. "That crazy woman dropped her gun when you hit her, thereby saving us all. Nothing else matters." With a groan, he rose to his feet. "Enjoy the accolades, Emmie. They don't come around that often."

Before she could respond, he joined the agents surrounding Velvalee.

"He's right, you know." Phillip put his arm around her, and she rested her head against his shoulder. "You saved us. You caught the Doll Woman. You're a heroine."

"You saved me." She slipped her hand between his collar and his neck to bring his face closer to hers. The shift in position caused her head to throb, but she ignored the pain. "You're my hero."

Without caring who might be watching, she pulled him into a lingering kiss that pulsed with the promises and possibilities of a future that was meant to be theirs.

CHAPTER FORTY-EIGHT

The following days passed in a blur with debriefings and interrogations and even more debriefings. Even though he'd participated in meeting after meeting after meeting, Phillip still wasn't sure he knew how all the puzzle pieces of the mission fit together to make a complete picture. Maybe they didn't.

The owner of the *Misty Blue*, the man Eloise's father had thrown overboard, proclaimed total ignorance of Phillip's kidnapping. He still maintained he'd been paid to take two passengers south to San Francisco, no questions asked. So, he'd asked no questions.

A warrant had been issued for Itsuki "Isaac" Hirano, but he had disappeared. Phillip doubted they'd ever see him again.

The biggest surprise was Lorraine Mitchell's role in the entire ordeal. She blamed her journalist pal, who managed to drag Red Eckers, of all people, into the fray. Leonard was considering a divorce though, in a weird and twisted way, he also enjoyed the notoriety.

Best of all, the Doll Woman was in jail. She still blamed her deceased husband for the forged letters—an impossibility since he died before they were written—but she couldn't blame him for the kidnapping or the threats she'd made against Eloise. Phillip suspected she'd be spending the rest of her life, however long that might be, behind bars.

He winced as Eloise changed the bandage behind his ear. The wound from the second blow was even more tender than the wound from the first.

"I wish I could kiss the hurt away," she said.

"I like that idea," he teased as he grabbed her around the waist and nuzzled her neck.

She giggled and made a halfhearted attempt to escape his grasp. "Behave yourself and let me finish this. Your uncle is waiting."

Phillip let her go while she affixed the new bandage. "You should probably know he chose me for this mission because he knew I wouldn't fall in love with you."

"If he says anything about that, just tell him that God had other plans." She gathered the medical supplies back into their box.

"Yes, I suppose He did." He slid his arms around her in a gentle embrace. "Are you sure you want to go through with this?"

"I'm positive. You?"

"Absolutely."

He offered her his arm and escorted her to the car waiting to drive them to the courthouse for plan C: *marry Eloise.*

AUTHOR'S NOTE

Dear World War II Fan,

This story is based on the FBI's investigation of Velvalee Dickinson, also known as the Doll Woman, who received money from the Japanese government during World War II in exchange for information about American ships damaged at Pearl Harbor and our shipyards on the West Coast.

Since this is a work of fiction, I did take a few liberties with the facts. Though the FBI had the five forged letters in August 1942, it seems that Velvalee wasn't identified as the letter writer until sometime in 1943. She wasn't arrested until January 1944. That was too many months for Eloise and Phillip to be on her trail!

Lee Dickinson died in March 1943 not in October 1941, as indicated in the story. It's true, though, that Velvalee tried to blame him for her treachery.

I also changed the names of the women who were victims of Velvalee's forgeries. This allowed me the freedom to create these characters "from scratch," so to speak. However, I kept the names of the Special Agents in Charge of the various FBI field offices—Cincinnati, Denver, Indianapolis, Portland, and Seattle—as a small gesture to honor these men.

My primary sources of information for this novel were a book titled *Velvalee Dickinson: The "Doll Woman" Spy* by Barbara Casey and the FBI's archival and historical pages found on their website. When I found conflicting information, I put the needs of the story first.

The Code Girls: The Untold Story of the American Women Code Breakers of World War II by Liza Mundy was an incredible help in creating Eloise's character and backstory.

For more information about my research and sources, please visit *The Cryptographer's Dilemma ~ Behind the Scenes* at www.johnnie -alexander.com.

I hope that you enjoyed your travels from one end of the country and back again with Eloise and Phillip as they sought the identity of an unlikely spy—and the first American woman to face the death penalty for her wartime betrayal. (Velvalee served seven years of a ten-year sentence, changed her name to Catherine Dickinson, and, with the help of Eunice Kennedy Shriver, obtained a position at a New York hospital.)

May God's blessings be upon you!

Johnnie

ACKNOWLEDGMENTS

Writing a novel is rarely a solitary endeavor, and I am grateful to those who walked this journey with me. Special thanks to:

- Tamela Hancock Murray, my amazing agent to whom this story is dedicated, for her guidance and encouragement;
- JoAnne Simmons, whose editing skill and suggestions were invaluable to this story;
- Hebe Alexander, my sister, brainstorming buddy, and keeper of my angst;
- Patricia Bradley, a superb novelist I'm honored to call friend, who provided valuable feedback after reading the first draft;
- Cathy Gambill, an Ohio friend with a green thumb who never tires of my questions;
- Jill Lancour, my daughter, who surprised me with an egg sandwich and hot chocolate after I stayed up all night writing;
- Presley Lancour, my nine-year-old granddaughter, who retrieved Manhattan maps and cross-country train routes from the printer and delivered them to my desk time and time again.
- The Barbour team for their support, encouragement, and advice. It's always a pleasure to work with each of you.

- As always, all my love and gratitude to my family: Bethany and Justin Jett; Jeremy, Jedidiah, and Josiah Jett; Jill and Jacob Lancour; Kaydi and Presley Lancour; and Nate and Bre Donley. You are bits of my heart walking around without me.

Johnnie Alexander creates characters you want to meet and imagines stories you won't forget in a variety of genres. An award-winning, bestselling novelist, she serves on the executive boards of Serious Writer, Inc. and the Mid-South Christian Writers Conference, and cohosts Writers Chat. Johnnie lives in Oklahoma with Griff, her happy-go-lucky collie, and Rugby, her raccoon-treeing papillon. Connect with her at www.johnnie-alexander.com and other social media sites via https://linktr.ee/johnniealexndr.

Books are produced in the United States using U.S.-based materials

Books are printed using a revolutionary new process called THINKtech™ that lowers energy usage by 70% and increases overall quality

Books are durable and flexible because of Smyth-sewing

Paper is sourced using environmentally responsible foresting methods and the paper is acid-free

Center Point Large Print
600 Brooks Road / PO Box 1
Thorndike, ME 04986-0001 USA

(207) 568-3717

US & Canada:
1 800 929-9108
www.centerpointlargeprint.com